L·O·D·E·S·T·O·N·E

L·O·D·E·S·T·O·N·E

RUSSELL JACK SMITH

Bartleby Press
Silver Spring, Maryland

The characters in this novel are fictional, sired and nurtured by imagination. They are not to be identified with any actual persons.

Printed in the United States of America

Published and Distributed by:

Bartleby Press
11141 Georgia Avenue
Silver Spring, Maryland 20902

Library of Congress Cataloging-in-Publication Data

Smith, Russell Jack.
Lodestone / Russell Jack Smith.
p. cm.
ISBN 0-910155-26-7
I. Title.
PS3569.M537974L64 1993
813'.54—dc20 92-43035
CIP

To my mentors at Miami University
in Oxford, Ohio

Joseph Bachelor
Read Bain
Walter Havighurst
Robert Hefner
Harold Hoffman

...buried deep,
The lodestone summons through mists of sleep.
—Sir Andrew Gilchrist

One

I looked up from the Underwood typewriter, my eyes searching the air for the right word, when suddenly and incredibly a vision of Sally O'Shaugnessy floated across the busy newsroom of the *The Denton Daily News*. Time froze and the universe held its breath. As my unbelieving eyes followed the slender figure joy mixed with apprehension took over my mind. But then as quickly as it appeared the vision transformed itself into a stranger, an unknown girl in a maroon sweater and plaid skirt. Time resumed its steady pulse and the sounds of tapping typewriters and conversational buzz resumed in the newsroom.

It had been a trick of the eye, something about the way the girl carried her head, like Sally, with that air of childlike confidence, a kind of fragile certainty. I looked again as she walked across the room. She was nothing like Sally. But then, no one on the planet was much like Sally.

I turned back to the incomplete sentence, the one for which I had been seeking the right word, but for a moment I could not pick up the thread. For longer than I care to admit, my professional newsman's mind had reverted to young lover, snared by memories of a long lost time. I had not thought about Sally O'Shaugnessy for several months. I had not wanted to think about her for several years. I wondered whether she was still involved—I could think of no more neutral word—with Judson Graver.

Finally the dangling sentence about political divisions within the Free French movement under General Charles de Gaulle came into focus. "Divided at present, the Free French movement is—paralyzed, becalmed, immobilized?" I chose "immobilized" though I preferred "becalmed." Becalmed was a metaphor, and my editor, Walt Murphy, had a scunner against metaphors. "Last thing we need around here is a frigging poet!" I typed one more concluding sentence, tore the sheet out of the typewriter and walked it into Murphy's office.

I was never quite sure whether Walt Murphy, with his green eyeshade and his raspy bark and cynical scowl, was patterning himself after the hardboiled editor in the stage play, "The Front Page," or was simply being the man that God and life had made him.

"Izzat the French think piece, Brown?"

"Yes, it is."

"Any goddamned good?"

"Best I could do. I've written this piece three times this past month."

"Prolly write it another three times before that mucked-up outfit gets itself straightened out." He scanned the page. "Looks about the right length for op-ed. Okay." He looked up at me. "Got any more stories to write?"

"No, that's it."

"Well, stand by for a while, case something else turns up."

I strolled back across the newsroom to my desk. The girl in the maroon sweater and plaid skirt was walking toward the door. Nothing like Sally O'Shaugnessy. I picked up the day's edition of *The Cincinnati Enquirer,* looking to see how our nearest competition was handling the European situation. But my mind showed a decided preference for fondling memories of Sally instead of engaging *The Enquirer's* long columns of print. I rattled the newspaper sharply to break up this foolishness, and about half my mind responded while the other half went on sniffing a long cold trail of memories.

It was then that I realized that with a solitary evening ahead of me I had a mind-management problem. I had planned on a quick supper at a White Tower, a walk home to my apartment on Grand Avenue, and an hour of listening to Fred Allen's radio program with a bottle of Carling's Black Label beside me. But clearly this would not do.

I picked up the telephone and called Saul Zollerman who worked at the Cosmopolitan men's clothing store across Fourth Street from the *Denton Daily News* building. "Saul? Dana Brown. Do you have any plans for dinner tonight?"

"Nothing special."

"How about joining me? I thought we might try the Van Steed Hotel dining room. I hear the food is pretty good and not too steep."

"Fine by me. Okay, Dana, I'll come by your office after we close."

A little after 5:30 Saul and I were walking up Lillow Street toward the Van Steed. As we stopped for the traffic light at Third and Lillow, Saul turned to me, his face a question mark. Like my other Jewish friends, Saul was taking the news from Europe very hard. All of us were appalled by the naked violence of Hitler's anti-semitism, but for Jews, especially sensitive, gentle Jews like Saul, it was far worse. "What's going to happen in Europe, Dana? Is anybody going to be able to stop that mad son of a bitch or is he going to sweep over all Europe and end western civilization?"

"God, I don't know, Saul. Someone's got to stop him

but it doesn't look as though the British and Russians can do it." Saul nodded, his eyes speaking of ancient sorrow.

At the Van Steed the head waiter led us to a table for two at the far end of the dining room. The Van Steed was Denton's newest hotel, built in 1936, and it had that modern finish like the Netherlands Plaza in Cincinnati with lots of glass and chrome. The room was nearly full and rippling with conversation. Near us was a table with four young people, college kids I would guess, the girls brightly pretty and slender, and the boys with faces that, compared with the fulfilled beauty of the girls, looked immature and half-formed. Saul and I ordered draught beers. On the far side of the room a fair to middling pianist was making pretty sounds that floated over the chattering voices. He was playing "Sweet and Lovely" and suddenly came sweeping over me, like the fragrance of a well-remembered perfume, memories of Sally O'Shaugnessy, piquant and haunting.

I looked across the table at Saul who was gazing vacantly across the room. "Do you remember Sally O'Shaugnessy?"

He turned his sorrowfully wise Jewish eyes toward me. "Remember her? Certainly. She was in our class at Stowell High School. You and she went together."

"Four years."

"What about her?"

"Nothing. I just happened to think about her." But "nothing" was not a truthful answer. What I wanted in defiance of painful experience and good judgment was to talk about Sally or hear Saul talk about her. But Saul did not respond as I wished.

He took a sip of his beer. "I don't suppose you've played much golf lately, this late in the season."

We ate a reasonably good dinner of fried oysters, talking about such odds and ends as the Cincinnati Reds' prospects next season. Later we walked home through the gathering night which was now sharp with cold.

Back in my apartment I took a quick shower and settled down in my pajamas in my easy chair with the book I was reading, Andre Malraux's *Man's Fate*. I had picked it up at the bookstore in the hope it might give me some insight into the French mentality. God knows that I and the rest of the western world could damn well use such insight in 1941. I had just got to the part where the Chinese revolutionaries were waiting in ambush for the detested Chiang Kai-shek when the telephone rang. A quick glance at my wristwatch told me it was 10:20, and I hoped to hell it was not the office calling.

It was not. An eager feminine voice said, "Dana? It's me!"

Victorian novelists used to say that the hero's heart skipped a beat in surprise or joy. It would be more accurate here to say that mine did three forward somersaults and a barrel roll. The "me" was undeniably Sally O'Shaughnessy.

"Sally! Where are you?"

"Home."

"Home to stay or visiting?"

"Just for the weekend and I would love to see you."

I paused. "Yes, when?"

"Is it too late tonight?"

I paused again. Long pause.

"Dana?"

"Well, Sally, yes, I think so. I'm pretty beat." Like my answer to Saul at the Van Steed about "just happening" to think about Sally, this was less than truth. Beat I was not. I was more than wide awake and my pulse had quickened considerably beyond the state of rest. But I needed time before meeting Sally, time to marshal my forces and prepare to defend against the full-bore assault on my carefully wrought stability that seeing Sally again would surely bring. "What about sometime tomorrow?"

"In the morning?"

"No, I have to go into the *News* office for a couple of hours."

"On Sunday?"

"Yes. Suppose I pick you up around noon and take you to lunch."

"Wonderful! See you then. Goodnight, Dana dear."

"G'night." I put the telephone down, that "Dana dear" still tingling in my ear like a silver bell.

It was just after 12 when I stopped my 1937 Plymouth coupe in front of the O'Shaugnessy house. Before I could get halfway up the walk Sally came bounding down the steps and threw herself into my arms, her cheek warm against mine and the fur collar of her gray coat tickling my nose and teasing it with the faint fragrance of her familiar perfume. "Oh, Dana, I'm so glad to see you!"

Just for the record, my reply bore more relationship with emotional truth than factual reality.

At the Van Steed, Sally ordered a Manhattan so I followed suit. I took a sip from the amber brown drink with the scarlet cherry inside and asked. "How is life in New York?"

She wrinkled her nose in that way I first found adorable when we were both seventeen. "Some days I love it. Other days I hate it."

I gazed at Sally across the table. An objective observer, I suppose, would not have found her remarkable to look at. Attractive, maybe; pretty, doubtful. She had a small soft face with merry gray-green eyes. Her hair had settled on a color midway between blonde and light brown and she wore it short. She had gained a couple of pounds since I had seen her last, and they had done nice things to the way her white blouse curved and dipped over her breast. But though I realized Sally would not seem remarkably attractive to someone else, to me as she sat before me she had a kind of shimmering magic, as though she were bathed in a spectral radiance, a phenomenon which surely did not exist outside my mind.

"Do you ever see Judson Graver?"

She looked up quickly. "See him? Yes, of course. We work together now and then."

"How is he?"

Again the quick upward glance. "He's fine." She reached across the table and took my hand. "Dana, how about *you*? How are you? *Really*?"

"Oh, I'm fine. Like Judson, I'm fine."

Her thin smile was reproachful. "How are things going for you at the *News*?"

"Pretty good. I'm now handling all the international stuff, both straight news and think pieces."

"I'm not surprised. You know, Dana, you have too much talent to spend the rest of your career in Denton. You belong in the mainstream, the big leagues."

"I wonder."

"No, I *know*. Every week I deal with one or more of the big names in New York and not one is better than you. You could be a topflight foreign correspondent."

"Really? Well, before I take that on let's order some lunch."

Later, over her fruit dessert Sally talked about her job as features editor for a children's magazine and explained that Judson Graver, who was an advertising salesman, sometimes worked with her on advertising tie-ins. Then she put her spoon down and asked brightly. "What's next? What do you usually do on Sunday afternoons?"

"Spring and summer I usually play golf. Now, I usually listen to the New York Philharmonic at three o'clock and read a book."

"Sounds lovely to me but I propose one slight change. Instead of reading your book, talk to me."

When I let ourselves into my apartment Sally excused herself and found my bathroom. I tuned the radio to the station for the Philharmonic broadcast which would begin in about fifteen minutes. Sally emerged shortly, her hair fluffed up and fresh lipstick on her mouth. She came to me and put her arms around my neck. "Do you remember how you used to get lipstick all over your face? You used to lick your handkerchief and scrub it off and sometimes I had to help you. Remember?"

"I remember."

"It began like this," she said and pulled my mouth down to hers. At first, I was numb and scarcely responded but suddenly the memory of thousands of kisses came flooding over me, washing away restraint, and I kissed her back. But then good sense took charge and I pulled away.

She looked up at me questioningly. "I thought we had agreed that that was all over."

Sally shook her head and smiled forgivingly. She took my hand. "Dana, dear Dana, come sit down with me." She led me to the sofa. "Ah, Dana, honey. We share such wonderful memories of our time together. A big, beautiful warehouse full."

I looked into those gray-green eyes. Their expression now was warm and caressing but I could remember when they were cold and dismissive. "Some of those memories are painful."

"Perhaps, but think how they are outnumbered."

I braced myself against the pleading affection in Sally's eyes and the warm promise of her mouth. "Sally, have you forgotten you broke us up? And I seem to remember the words 'this is final'."

"No, I remember. And I find it painful too." Now, those gray-green eyes looked at me through a mist. "But, darling, that was three long years ago. I've changed. And I came home just to see you."

Sally talked on in a low, soft voice, and while she talked the New York Philharmonic broadcast began with the orchestra playing Sibelius' Fourth Symphony. Through the somber, doom-threatening music I heard Sally's voice speak of Judson Graver and infatuation and something about her compass swinging wildly. At one point she said, "I still like some things about Judson but they are not the solid, wonderful things I love about you."

This went on for all the first movement of the Sibelius's Fourth, and despite the symbolic warning of the dark, somber music I began to weaken. That old Sally magic bent and broke my stern resolves, and I took her in my arms and soon we were thoroughly involved. She broke away suddenly, her eyes swimming with desire. "Let's go in your bedroom," she whispered.

I followed her as a stag follows a doe and then went on into the bathroom. When I came out about two minutes later my eyes met Sally standing like a small nude statue beside the bed. But this statue was not white stone; it was pink and soft and breathing and those few more pounds had visibly enhanced both her roundness and softness. She came to me and wrapped her arms around my neck. "Dana, do you remember that fiasco we had when we tried to make love in the back seat of your father's car?"

"Painfully."

She took my hand and led me to the bed. "This time we will make it real." I was still on my knees and throwing pillows over the side when the music from the radio abruptly stopped. Then the announcer in New York said in a voice God might have used when he gave Moses the Ten Commandments, "We interrupt this broadcast with a special news announcement. Japanese war planes have attacked Pearl Harbor in Hawaii and have inflicted severe damage on US Navy facilities and vessels stationed there." I looked down at Sally while the announcer gave out a few more details but my eyes did not take in the lovely vision of the nude young woman below me. A Japanese attack on the US Navy in Hawaii could only mean the United States was going to war, and I needed to get to my newspaper office at once. I jumped out of bed and started dressing. "I'll drop you off on the way downtown, Sally. I've got to get to the *News* office."

After hurried goodbyes and a quick peck I drove on

down to Fourth and Lillow. When I walked into the newsroom Walt Murphy was standing behind his desk waving his arms and shouting. Three reporters and a couple of copy desk men were also taking turns at shouting. When Murphy spotted me he yelled, "Where the hell have you been? I've been trying to get you on the phone. We've got an extra edition to get out."

"Came as fast as I could, Walt." I put out of my mind the cause of my delay: a nude and ready Sally waiting on the bed and the subsequent wild scramble. "What do you want me to do?"

"Do? Christ! Someone's got to write the lead story!"

"I'll do it. Any restrictions on length?"

"God, no! This is the story of the century. Keep writing until your fingers are bloody."

Leaving his office I ran into a copy-boy. "Get me all the Pearl Harbor take on the AP, UP and INS tickers and keep on feeding it to me as fast as it comes." I sat down at my desk and fed a sheet of paper into the Underwood. While I waited for the ticker tear sheets my mind wandered briefly back to Sally O'Shaugnessy and fondled the memory of our brief and broken afternoon. But then thoughts of Sally faded away, shoved back—well, almost back—to the neglected niche they had occupied for the past three years. The boy arrived with the yellow ticker sheets and after a moment I began to write, "Japanese war planes in a savage surprise attack bombed and devastated US Navy ships and installations in Pearl Harbor at dawn in Hawaii today."

The following days and weeks were frantically busy. Walt Murphy seemed almost to take the war personally and drove me relentlessly to produce more and more copy. It seemed during that time that I did nothing but pound away at my typewriter, eat hurried meals, and catch a few hours sleep. Then one day Murphy called me into his office and motioned to a chair. "Sit down, Brown. I've got something to talk over with you."

I sat down, noting that Walt seemed unusually serious. Calm but serious. "Brown, the chief thinks we got to have our own man down in Washington, and he expects me to pick someone from the staff to go. It's a big job working down there with all those big boys, and it's going to take someone with brains and education to handle it. Well, I've looked over the outfit, and you're the only guy we've got who graduated from college. Some of these other slobs went to college for a couple of years but you're the only one with a degree. And you've been handling the foreign stuff for some time, so it looks to me like you're my best choice." He gazed across the desk with what almost seemed a kind expression on his face. "Well, whaddya say? You want the job?"

I took a deep breath. Washington, the capital of a nation at war, press conferences, military briefings. Suddenly I remembered Sally O'Shaugnessy's remark at lunch on December 7th, "You belong in the mainstream, the big leagues." Of course, I wanted it. To Murphy I said, "I'd like to take a crack at it, Walt."

"Okay, it's yours."

I wandered back to my desk in a happy daze. After staring at nothing in space for several minutes I picked up the telephone and called Saul Zollerman. "Saul? Come have dinner with me tonight. The drinks are on me."

Two

Seven years earlier, on a hot June afternoon of 1934, I was leaning against a stanchion of the broad-decked ore freighter, *Samuel F B Morse*, watching her labored progress down the tortuous channel of the Cuyahoga River. I was the newest crew member of the *Morse*, having boarded her only an hour and a half earlier while the drop buckets of the Cleveland Central Furnace docks were still scooping the red iron ore out of her hold. Now, in later afternoon, *Morse* was extricating her 500-foot self from the barely navigable Cuyahoga on her way to Lake Erie and onward up the Detroit and St. Clair Rivers to Lake Huron, the St. Mary River, the locks at Sault Ste. Marie, Lake Superior and westward then to Duluth where again she would be loaded with ore destined for South Chicago, Gary, Lorain, Cleveland, Ashtabula, Conneaut, or Buffalo. At the moment, one bustling tug was pushing her bow hard against the bank on the starboard side while another tug was shoving her port flank in order to line her up for another 300 yard stretch of river.

I had been on board long enough to be directed to my bunk in the deckhouse amidship by the hunchbacked second cook and to meet the two stokers I was to help, Don, a strapping blond man in his late 20s, and

John, a short fiftyish man who spoke with a Bavarian accent. As the third man in the six-to-ten firehold watch, my title was "coal passer." Other than the obvious fact that the job had something to do with coal, I had no notion of the duties of a coal passer, but at the moment it did not much matter. I was reveling in the strangeness of everything around me: the chuff of the tugboats as they bustled about, their whistles uttering short, gruff toots as they signalled to each other and to the pilot in *Morse's* wheelhouse; the stark industrial landscape along the river, the cranes, warehouses, tanker depots, and railroad sidings with stubby switch locomotives and coal gondolas; and the broad steel deck of *Morse* with the yawning hatches now being covered with wooden hatch leaves by the deckhands.

The afternoon was sliding slowly into dusk as *Morse* finally broke free from the confines of the Cuyahoga—a river so polluted with industrial waste that it once caught fire—and headed out the channel past the breakwater into Lake Erie. The sea was dead calm as the ship gathered way and moved northwestward quietly. It was the quiet that impressed me most; a steamship in calm water moves in near silence. But then, unexpectedly, *Morse* spoke with her great, hoarse voice, two short blasts signalling to an incoming ship. By then, I could see the running-lights, some red and some green, of ships moving either east or west on the broad, shoreless waters of Lake Erie, and could occasionally hear their distant whistles as they signalled to one another. I took a deep, deep breath of satisfaction. Life was once again on track and no longer looked hopeless. Just then, Don called from the hatchway leading down to the firehold, "Hey Brown! Time to go to work."

The previous four months had been the darkest days of my life. It began the week before Christmas, my freshman year at college. I had walked back from Psych 1 class with Wayne Wilkins, whistling together the frisky tune of "Margie" as we trudged down the cinder path leading to Fishel Hall. I stopped by the rack of post boxes to check on the mail. A small single envelope sat diagonally in the little slot, and for one brief, bright moment I thought it was a letter from Sally O'Shaughnessy. It was not. It was a letter from Mother, who seldom wrote, and the message was stark. "Your father has been put on indefinite furlough by the Denton Rubber Company. We won't be able to send you any more money for your schooling."

It was no consolation for me that hundreds, perhaps thousands, of college students all across the United States received letters similar to mine in the grim year of the Great Depression, 1933. To me, though, it was an especially savage blow. After high school graduation I had spent a dismal year working at a cut-rate filling station to make and save three-fourths the money needed for a year at college. My father undertook to provide the rest. College, when I entered Maumee University in September of that year, had been a release, a joyous deliverance from my life at home where bickering and mean-spiritedness were triumphant. Then, it seemed, the bright, happy days of college life were about to come to an abrupt, shocking end. Unless, unless...

The next weeks while I did my damnedest to fend off the inevitable were difficult to remember in later years. Only disconnected, disparate scenes remained:

—the confident assurance of my square-faced, square-toed roommate, solid old Jim Blodgett who said, "Aw. hell, Brownie. You'll find a way to stay, somehow." No one except Blodgett called me "Brownie" and it would have been offensive from anyone else;

—the warm sympathy in the blue eyes of Mrs. Finley, the manager of the University's dining halls, as she told me my name was still far down the waiting list for waiter's jobs.

—the impassive expression on the face of the University Bursar, Oliver Bunkel, as he told me with the demeanor of a Victorian vicar, that the University's student loan funds were exhausted.

—the hollow cheer in the voices of Blodgett and Wayne Wilkins as they helped tie up my trunk and carried it down to the front entrance;

—the kindness of my freshman English professor, Harold Innman, a moist-eyed romantic man, who drove me over to the Cincinnati turnpike "where you can hitch a ride to Denton more easily."

—the thin-faced, defeated young man who picked me up in a limping, clattering Chevy truck and assured me "they ain't no jobs anywhere so I'm a 'gonna join the Army."

—the hour-long waits on the sparsely travelled road while the January wind probed icily around my collar and whipped my pant legs taut around my ankles.

—the smirk in the voice of my fifteen year old sister, Irene, as I walked in the front door, "Well, here comes the college man. Now we'll have to watch our grammar and our p's and q's."

The next three months were a dark pit into which I sank. I made the rounds looking for a job once or twice every week, and each negative response pushed me deeper and deeper into the pit. The future looked to be utterly without hope, and the tensions at home grew more and more rasping and binding.

The letters I received sporadically from Sally O'Shaugnessy who was attending North Wesleyan College did little to relieve my drowning depression. Mine to her were passionate and sensuous, recalling the nights we had parked in the wooded nook I had discovered near the Wamplertown graveyard. Hers in response were gay and superficial accounts of fraternity parties or moonlight hayrides. More and more the name of Judson Graver, my best friend in high school, appeared in the accounts of these happy parties. The letters were quintessential Sally, perky, witty, and slightly offbeat, but I became more and more aware that they did not truly *engage*. They no longer conveyed the sense of a bond between us, the bond we had forged during the previous three years. They were letters that could have been written to Sally's cousin, Jane.

Now and then I got a letter from Jim Blodgett. These were straight-forward accounts of a recent basketball victory by Maumee or of Wayne Wilkins' latest blind date with non-productive results. But somehow Blodgett's letters, despite their unadorned simplicity, conveyed friendly affection and a sense of continuing friendship.

And then one day a letter arrived from Blodgett that opened a window in my life and let in a little sunshine. "Dear Brownie," it read, "I just got a letter from my Dad saying he thinks he can get us both jobs on an ore freighter on the Lakes this summer. The pay is not bad and the food is real good. What do you say? If you are interested we can go up to Cleveland together when school lets out the last week of May. Sure hope you want to do this with me. We ought to have a great time as sailors with a girl in every port. Ha-hah!"

On the day Blodgett and I left Denton for Cleveland, my father, his shoulders bowed and looking more defeated every day, pulled a worn $5 bill out of his pocket and wished me luck while Mother tearfully urged me to be careful. My sister, Irene, cracked in her taunting voice, "Try not to fall overboard, sailor boy!"

Blodgett and I made our way to the Union Station by trolley and took the 10:40 Big Four Limited for Cleveland. Blodgett was his usual cheerful self as we sat side by side in the green velour upholstered seats in the day coach, while I tried as best I could, after four months of soul-drowning depression, to regain the level of banter and good humor we had shared as college roommates, As the Ohio landscape streaked by the train window, Blodgett bubbled, "We'll have a ball, Brownie, Dad is going to fix it so we'll ship out on the same boat, and we can go see the sights while we are in port."

But it did not work out that way. Three days after we had arrived at Blodgett's home a ship came into Cleveland in need of a cook's helper, and Blodgett's father advised Jim to take it. "Jobs are scarce this season," said Mr. Blodgett, "but we'll get you fixed up in short order, Dana."

Actually, it took twelve days, and during that time, as a reluctant guest, I did my best to help Mrs. Blodgett with household duties and went along nightly with Mr. Blodgett to girls' softball league games, watching the athletic teenagers with their thighs chubby and pink below their shorts. And then the call came, "There's a job for a coal passer on *Samuel F B Morse.* She's unloading here in Cleveland down at Central Furnace. I don't want to push you but I would advise you to take it. What do you say?" Within an hour I was climbing the wooden ladder up the steel-plated side of the *Morse* and reporting for duty.

When Don called me that first day, I followed him down the steel-runged vertical ladder to the firehold with its smell of hot metal and the hiss of air rushing through the drafts. Separated on either side by an open space about twelve feet across were banks of six furnaces. Just as my feet touched the deck John opened a furnace door and threw a scoop of coal on the white hot bed of coals which stretched eight feet toward the side of the ship. "First thing you do," said Don. "Go get a big monkey wrench off the tool-board in the engine room."

As I stepped over the coaming in the hatchway to the engine room I saw before me a magnificent sight, an enormous, gleaming brass and steel reciprocal steam engine, its great cams thrashing around and around as its giant pistons lifted and plunged. It was the biggest and most beautiful machine I had ever seen, and I was spell-bound as I watched its motion. I reached with half an eye toward the toolboard and picked off a wrench.

When I got back to the firehold and handed over the tool, Don exclaimed, "My God, we've got a college boy that doesn't know the difference between a stillson and a monkey wrench!" Chagrined, I found that with my attention riveted on that gigantic machine I had got the wrong tool. Of course I knew the difference. My handyman father had seen to that. As I replaced the stillson on the toolboard and picked off a monkey wrench I nearly ran over a sharp-faced man wearing a soiled cap slouched over his left ear. "Who are you? The new coal passer? The collitch boy?"

"Yes, I am."

"Some problem with the tools?"

"No. I just took a stillson instead of a monkey wrench by mistake."

"Don't know the difference between a stillson and a monkey! Jesus Christ! What the hell do you dopes in college learn?"

Well, I—"

"Go on. Cut out the horseshit. Get back to your job!"

When I got back in the firehold, where the temperature was a good fifteen degrees higher than the engine room and the smell of hot iron seared my nostrils, I asked Don, "Who's that guy in there wearing a cap?"

"Cap? Oh, that's the new third engineer, Smelcher. This is his second trip. Better watch out for him."

"Why?"

"I'll tell you later. Take that wrench and climb up onto the catwalk up there and open the valve."

Standing on steel grating suspended over the boilers, I opened the red-handled valve and heard a loud hissing above my head. After a couple of minutes, Don called, "Okay. Close her up and come back down. You've just blown the flues," he told me. "First thing we do every watch."

My next task was to pull the burning coals of two furnaces out onto the firehold deck. The tool for this was an iron hoe which felt as though it weighed at least forty pounds. The white hot coals, snapping and crackling and seemingly almost singeing my eyes, were shoved into a round hole in the deck where a steam jet sluiced them through a tube out over the side of the ship. "Now we pull the ashes on those furnaces," said Don, "and shoot them out with the ash-gun." With the iron hoe at shoe-top level, now seeming to weigh at least fifty pounds, I reached far back under the furnace grates and pulled ashes out onto the deck and then pushed them into the hole while Don turned the valve on the ash-gun.

"We do this at the start of every watch," he said. "Keeps clinkers from building up and burning the grates." He turned and gestured toward the forward bulkhead of the firehold where coal spilled out of the eight foot hatch of the coal bunker. "On the night watch tomorrow, or maybe next morning, you'll have to start shovelling coal out of the bunker so we can get at it. For now, it's running free." He glanced around as though looking for something else to explain and then turned back. "And that's the job. Nothing else for you to do right now. You can go topside if you want but stay close nearby in case we need you."

I climbed up the steel-runged ladder and stepped out into the soft, humid air of the Ohio night. Below me, alongside the ship, the water rippled and broke away in wide streamers with gurgles and splashes. Off to port, another freighter moved northwest on a parallel course, her green running lights and white lamp at the top of her mast flickering in the early evening dark. Once again, the newness and the strangeness of it all struck me and delighted me.

Then, as so often in those days when I was in love with Sally, my mind sought her out, wishing in vain she could be sharing my pleasure. Where, I wondered, was

Sally at this moment? What day was it? The days of waiting at Blodgett's house had been so featureless that I had almost lost the sequence. Was it Friday? It *was* Friday, the night Sally and I usually had a date. So where was she now? Probably, and I winced at the thought, somewhere in a car or perhaps at a party, lighting up the place with her impish gaiety, her rippling laugh, her offbeat wit. God, I missed her! From deep within me a pulse of love and longing surged toward faraway Sally, out across the calm waters of Lake Erie and down across the gently undulating Ohio plains to Denton. It was so strong a pulse that I could imagine Sally, in mid-sentence, pausing in surprise and looking around for me.

And just then, Don came up the ladder and took me by the arm. "C'mon, have a cup of coffee in the night lunch."

The night lunch was as strong a tradition on Great Lakes freighters as was the super-abundant food at meals. Each night at eight the cook set out platters of cold meats, cheese, bread, pies, and cakes. Sailors off-watch gathered there as they would have at their neighborhood tavern ashore. It was the only recreation the ship offered. Don and I poured ourselves coffee and sat down at a bench beside the oil-cloth covered table. There were five other men swapping stories about adventures and misadventures, their speech as festooned with obscenities as flies on fresh cow plops. I listened and amused myself by counting the number per sentence and decided the average was three or four. The steady beat of conversation was suddenly broken when the galley door was opened by Smelcher, the third engineer. He looked around the suddenly silent group and then stared at Don and me.

He scowled. "Aren't you two fuckers supposed to be standing watch?"

"Just having a cup of coffee, Third," said Don.

"Yeah. Well, have it off watch. And get the hell back down in the firehold."

Don looked at him evenly. "Okay."

Smelcher left, slamming the galley door behind him.

"Son of a bitch," said the 10-to-2 stoker across from me.

"Who is that sucker?" asked another man.

"Either a company spy or a labor organizer. CIO," said a man beside Don.

"He's no company man," said Don. "My guess is he's a labor union guy but he's also a first-class shit."

"You got it right that time," said the stoker. "Good man to stay clear of."

"Yeah," Don agreed. "You about ready to go back down, Brown? No sense looking for trouble."

When we were relieved by the 10-to-2 watch, I was more than ready for my bunk. As I walked up the slanting red deck toward the deckhouse I was swatted in the face by large, clumsy insects, and I noticed piles of wriggling, large-winged bugs collecting under the lights on the side of the deckhouse. The late night air was cool and moist on my face, and the freighter that previously had been slightly ahead off to port was now directly abeam. A man was walking aft alongside the lighted, white superstructure. I opened the door to the deckhouse, quickly undressed, and fell gratefully into bed.

The next sound I heard was the harsh voice of the humpbacked second cook yelling from the doorway, "College boy, get up!" It was 5:30. I threw cold water on my face in the small lavatory, and when I emerged into the wan morning light I found that the ship was inexplicably sailing through a lush, green meadow, in a channel that serpentined in graceful curves. We were in the St. Clair River which links Lake St. Clair with Lake Huron. Off in the distance a black self-unloading freighter loomed high above the green meadow, seemingly floating on grass.

My arm and shoulder muscles winced when I grasped the heavy iron hoe and began the ritual of pulling fires and hauling out ashes. The last ashes were just disappearing through the ash-gun when the third engineer, Smelcher, yelled from the hatchway into the engine room, "Hey, collitch boy! When you finish there, haul your ass back aft. Got a job for you."

The job was wielding a pushbroom up on deck while Smelcher played a hose, sluicing the piles of dead insects toward the gunwales. The size of the piles under the deck lights was astonishing. "What are there things?" I asked Smelcher.

"Jeez, you *are* a dumb bastard! First, it's stillson wrenches and now this. Canadian soldiers. Ain't you never heard of Canadian soldiers? They fly across the lake from Canada. That's why they're Canadian soldiers." Smelcher turned to look back and as he did swung the hose so that the stream struck me across the chest. "Over here, Brown," he gestured. "Oh, got you wet, did I?" He chuckled. "Good thing. Wash some of that firehold stink off you."

When I got back down in the firehold I was seething. "What the hell's the matter with that bastard?" I asked Don.

The husky, blond stoker looked at me impassively. "Smelcher?" He shrugged. "Just keep clear as best you can."

Throughout the morning the blunt-bowed freighter pushed silently up the St. Clair River, occasionally breaking the quiet with a hoarse blast of the whistle to signal a downbound ship. Along the banks were cottages with waving children and an occasional fisherman with a chugging outboard. A fair number of *Morse's* crew sat on the hatches watching the passing scene. Now and then they would sight a woman in a bathing suit, sometimes on a dock, sometimes tending a clump of flowers beside a cottage. Regardless of the age, shape, or size, the crewmen would murmur, "There's one! Hey, have a look at that ass!"

About noon the ship's northward passage carried her

out of the river and into the broad reaches of Lake Huron. By early afternoon the shoreline of Michigan off to the west dwindled in the distance and then sank below the horizon. Except for a distant plume of smoke from another ship the deep blue, gently rolling sea of Huron was empty, stretching away into an infinity that belied the designation "lake."

The evening watch passed routinely. My back and shoulder muscles groaned silently while I wielded the iron hoe, hauling the searingly hot, white coals out of the long firebox onto the firehold deck. After shooting the ashes I walked over to the hatchway to the coal bunker and saw that the black chunks were still forming a small pile at the entrance. Don came over beside me. "Squat down and look up into the corners of the bunker," he said. "See those big donnikers up there, big as your head? Well, before you start shovelling tomorrow morning you'll have to crawl up the sides and knock them down. Otherwise, they'll come banging down on you later. Might break a leg."

"Okay, Don. Thanks."

When I stepped out of the deckhouse next morning in the cool, gray morning light the ship was nosing her way silently up a deep blue river which threaded through a thick evergreen forest. The air was sharply clean, smelling of the river and pine resin, heart-lifting and exhilarating. It was in essence a virgin smell, as though God had created sky, river, and forest only moments before and no human being before me had ever breathed it. I paused by a stanchion holding the steel cable running waist high along the edge of the deck and watched the passing wilderness, impenetrable beyond the river's edge. Long, blue ripples arced out away from the ship and lapped against the shore, the wash and splash waking the primeval silence. An elegant, haughty heron walked with exaggeratedly high steps along the edge, head cocked and tense for the strike at his prey. It was a pristine moment, one I savored for years still to come.

Breaking the spell, the coal passer on the 2-to-6 watch came clumping down the deck. He was a swarthy, dumpy fellow who walked with a pronounced swagger, seeming to proclaim toughness. "Hey, Brown," he said as he approached, "ain't none of my business but I guess I oughta warn ya. Smelcher, the Third, is out to get ya."

"Where did you get that?"

"Last night in the night lunch. He was talkin' about collitch boys like you taking jobs away from workin' stiffs. Said he was gonna throw your ass off the boat."

I gazed at the dark-hued face with its small, black eyes. "Hey, Joe, thanks for warning me."

"Don't say nothin' 'bout me tellin' ya."

"I won't." I walked thoughtfully aft and climbed down the steel-runged ladder to the firehold. Later, I took a long poker Don handed me and climbed up the steeply slanting pile of coal toward the top of the bunker, twenty feet high. Perched in the corner was a black boulder as big as a watermelon. I poked at it from one side and down it tumbled and bounced, landing with a crash on the steel deck of the bunker. This was fun. I moved around and dislodged four or five other potential leg-breakers. Then I climbed down and began shovelling coal out of the bunker onto the firehold deck. The ship burned over a ton of coal each hour, and I found I had to shovel pretty steadily to keep ahead of the firemen as they fed the big furnaces. By the time the watch ended my back and shoulders were a massive ache.

Just before noon the *Morse* entered the locks at Sault Ste. Marie and lifted silently twenty-two feet as the water rose beneath her. Just before entering the gigantic, black-sided locks, the ship had paused to take on a drum of oil for the engine room, two ten gallon cans of buttermilk for the galley, and mail for the crew. I had rushed back to my cabin after watch to finish my letter to Sally, a letter full of aching love and longing. I had added a brief description of the St. Mary River in the silent, early morning, saying, "How I wish you were beside me to see it!" The violent incompatibility of the feminine persona of Sally with the harsh steel-girded world then around me made the concept inconceivable but my longing transcended reality entirely. I watched the mail sack as it was swung aboard the mail launch, and I thought, sentimentally, of the letter which was soon to be touched by Sally's fingers. As I said before, I was desperately in love in those days, a malaise I now find difficult to understand.

The northern Michigan shore fell slowly away as the *Morse* took a northwest heading into Whitefish Bay in Lake Superior on her 400-mile passage to Duluth. Late that night, as I came off the 6-to-10 watch I could see the flashing light at Whitefish Point off to port. The air was sharply cold and the stars in the black sky glittered and hung astonishingly low overhead. No other ships' lights were visible through the darkness over the broad sea, and looking down at the menacingly black, cold water beside the ship I felt a sudden shiver of apprehension. I hurried into the deckhouse and climbed into the warmth of my bunk.

Next day, when I walked down the deck at 5:45 a.m. the early June morning felt like raw November. The air was bitingly cold, and the water rippling alongside the ship was a deep sea-green. The sea extended from horizon to horizon in all directions without sight of land. Superior, the greatest of the Great Lakes—coldest, deepest, meanest—held *Morse* like a floating chip on its wide expanse. All that day the ship plowed steadily ahead at her unloaded pace of twelve miles per hour, turning to a course slightly south of west after passing Manitou Island lying off the Keneewaw Peninsula of Michigan. It was midnight when the lights of Duluth rose slowly up out of the sea.

Within an hour *Morse* was tied up at an ore loading dock, the great bins rising beside the ship as high as her masts. Very shortly the red rocks and chunks began flowing down chutes into the hold with a roaring rush. The first mate, in charge of the loading, paced up and down the deck, checking the balance of the load by peering over the side of the ship at the Plimsoll marks, and directing the flow into one hatch or another. Several hours later, in the early northern Minnesota dawn, *Morse* backed away from the dock and headed easterly with her heavy cargo destined for the steel mills of Pittsburgh or South Chicago.

Three

Even during my first week aboard *Samuel F B Morse,* I began, characteristically, to analyze the personalities of my ship-mates. They were not an attractive group of men, and most of them I found difficult to like or take much interest in. Our values, the things we knew and thought important, were so unlike that I could almost view the whole ship's crew as belonging to a separate phylum, and so perhaps find them interesting as I had found termites interesting in Zoology I.

Individually, of course, they varied greatly, and some of them I managed to like. Take Joe, the 2-to-6 coal passer, for example, the guy who had warned me about Smelcher—acting, I suppose, out of a kind of group loyalty, perhaps crewmen against officers. Joe's icon for behavior was Tough Guy. But so transparent were his gestures and actions in this role that he became in my view a great innocent, a child who would be a man. On that first trip, for instance, as we headed east toward Sault Ste. Marie, a hard driving northwest wind picked up and gained strength throughout the morning. Green waves began to gather and break into seething foam off the *Morse's* port quarter, and soon there were long ranks of waves advancing like charging cavalry with flowing white manes.

Despite her heavy load the ship began to roll slowly. I met Joe walking down the deck with his Lorain swagger, his black eyes snapping with excitement. "Hey, Brown," he said. "I hope it gets real rough. I like da t'rills!" I met him again after lunch at almost the same spot on the deck but this time we did not speak. By then old *Sam Morse's* roll had become an ungainly wallow, and Joe was absorbed in depositing his lunch over the side of the ship into Lake Superior.

Don, the fireman on my watch, was almost an exact opposite. Blond, tall, and strong, he carried his strength with the ease of a man who had always been strong. He seemed entirely unselfconscious, so completely at ease that he seemed oblivious to relationships with other people. He was always kind to me, and very helpful, but he acted, I felt, out of an impersonal feeling of duty or decorum. His code of behavior told him it was the right thing to do.

John, the older fireman, seemed most of the time to be nursing a grudge. Maybe the old Bavarian carried within him some residual clannishness, or pride of race, and resented the motley collection of Slavs, Finns, and Swedes—not to mention mongrelized Americans—he found around him. Maybe he just resented being fiftyish. At any rate, on only two occasions did I see him smile. Once, while he was leaning on his shovel between intervals of feeding the fires, he told me a story about a trip he had made aboard a ship transiting the Welland Canal which runs between Lake Erie and Lake Ontario. His ship tied up for a while on Sunday afternoon, and a number of curious visitors came on board to inspect the ship. One was an old Canadian farmer who climbed down into the firehold where John was working. He looked around in amazement and walked over to a bulkhead—here John mimicked his action—and rapped it with his knuckles. "All iron!" he exclaimed. "How does she float?" And John broke into a high-pitched giggle, "Hee,

hee, hee!" while his square, broad face creased in wrinkles. "How does she float?"

On one other, much later, occasion his smile was wan and grateful. It was a steamy hot Ohio afternoon and *Morse* was plowing down a soupy, flat Lake Erie toward Ashtabula. I had been up on deck letting the humid, soft air wash against my sweat-laden shirt, but then I went back down into the firehold to check the state of the coal pile. John was alone while Don was topside doing his laundry, and when I stepped off the ladder I found old John swaying on his feet, his face a ghastly white. "Go get Don," he muttered weakly.

"Let's get you up on deck, first," I said. He looked to me as though he was about to pass out from heat exhaustion. I pushed him toward the vertical ladder and climbed up closely behind him, my hands holding the sides of the ladder so that I could try to hold him if he fell. It was a sweaty, slow climb with my heart beating anxiously until we reached the top. I got John over to the rail and then turned to go back down. "You get Don," I said, "I'll stoke the fires until he comes." It was then that John smiled for the second time, a weak, apologetic smile.

"Okay," he said "Thanks."

Incidentally, it was during this incident that it was impressed upon me that in all human activity, no matter how basic or menial, there are elements of craft, of knowing skill. Back down in the firehold, I saw that the needle of the steam gauge was quivering on 232, eight points below the required 240. I opened a furnace door and threw on a scoop of coal. The needle continued to drop, now on 230. I opened another door and threw on another scoop and then another and another. The needle maintained a steady downward course, and when Don arrived it was riding on 225. "I'm sorry as hell, Don," I said. "I threw on plenty of coal."

Don opened the door of a furnace I had just fed. "But look in there," he said. "See that black spot on the firebed? That's your scoop of coal. That black spot cools down the fire. You've got to fan the coal as you throw it." He demonstrated then, flipping his wrist with the skill of a major league baseball pitcher, or perhaps that of a casino croupier, and the coal fanned out over the width and depth of the fire.

"I see," I said humbly.

The lay-out of ʷorking and living quarters aboard *Samuel F.B. Morse* exactly imaged the sociology of the crew and the officers. Like all Great Lakes ore freighters, *Morse* had a forecastle near the bow and a large superstructure near the stern with 150 yards or so of open deck in between. The forecastle contained, or course, the pilot house and the steering and navigation equipment. The after deckhouse contained the propulsion machinery. The captain, his three mates, and the navigation crew (wheelsmen, watchmen, and deckhands) all had quarters forward and were known then to us grimy propulsion guys as "sharp-enders." The chief engineer, his three assistant engineers, and the propulsion crew (oilers, firemen, and coal passers) lived in the after section, except that on *Morse* there was the rare exception of a mid-deck deckhouse where I lived with the other coal passers.

Because of this physical separation and its caste-like implications I had few contacts with "sharp-enders." One day, though, I was stopped on deck by a man whom I had learned was the second mate. Like the other mates, he wore a tie and jacket. He was a pleasant-faced man with intelligent eyes beneath his cap. "Are you the college boy?" he asked.

"Yes, I am."

He nodded and gazed at me for a moment. "I never went to college. Thought I would when I graduated from high school, but then didn't make it." He looked at me thoughtfully for another moment. "Hope you enjoy it," he said and walked on up the deck.

It was the first—and only—moment of all my days

aboard the *Morse* when I had what could be called a genuine human encounter. Then I was left to speculate as to its meaning.

And then, of course, there was Smelcher, the third engineer. Despite my best efforts to keep my distance, he found daily opportunities to harass me. We were, after all, on the same watch, and although my immediate services belonged to Don and John, Smelcher was the officer in charge of the watch. He gave me every dirty, nasty job he could find in the engine room, and even ordered me once to clean out the toilet in the engineer's head. "How do you like the work, collitch boy?" he would ask. "Am I helping you get an edjucation?" The animosity was unrelenting and to me mysterious in origin. Was he a union man acting on principle? Or was he in Don's phrase, just "a first class shit" acting out of some complicated set of internal grievances and grudges? I could not find the answer.

The voyage back down the chain of lakes and rivers to Lake Erie after our loading at Duluth was uneventful, and I began to fall easily into the rhythms of the two watch days. The combination of heavy physical labor and the head-cleansing sea air gave me a prodigious appetite. My back and shoulder muscles, unused to the hard labor of shovel and firehoe, gradually lost their soreness and took on tension and strength. By the time we tied up at the unloading dock down below I was already thinking of myself as a seasoned Great Lakes sailor.

We were berthed at Conneaut Harbor, having been directed there by a dispatcher who came alongside in a launch on the Detroit River as we were passing the city. He yelled through a megaphone to the officers on *Morse's* bridge, "C O N N E A U T!" Old hands on board had groaned at the news because Conneaut, a port created by the United States Steel Company for trans-shipping ore to the steel mills in Pittsburgh, was at the farthest eastern edge of Ohio, and the long passage from Detroit would give us an after midnight arrival, probably two or three a.m. when all the stores and bars—most especially the bars—would be closed.

My watch read 2:15 when the chuffing of the deck engines snubbing up on the dock lines fore and aft woke me. The ship lay still, as though she were dead, without even the gentle vibration of her engine to give her life. Outside the porthole I could hear voices of men on the dock as preparations began for lifting the enormous load of iron ore out of the hold with the giant Hulitt cranes. I swung my feet out of bed and put on my dungarees, blue work shirt, and heavy work boots. As I stepped out of the deckhouse door I found myself looking straight into the blue eyes of a Hulitt crane operator. He was sitting in the tiny cab which was fitted into the shaft of the giant machine about fifteen feet above the enormous clam-shaped scoop and was riding right down into *Morse's* cavernous hold. I watched as he maneuvered down below to gather half a freight car pile of red ore, rise quickly, swivel to the ship's side, and deposit the load gently into a gondola car sitting on the dockside track.

As I stood watching, the door to the deckhouse head, situated between the portside cabin for the coal passers and the starboardside room for the firemen, opened behind me, and Don asked, "Going ashore?"

"Thought I might. Are you?"

"Nothing there to interest me at this time of night. If you go, watch yourself and get back by 4:30. We'll probably sail around 5, 5:30."

I nodded and walked aft where I found a wooden ladder down to the dock. I picked my way across the railway tracks and around the huge bases of the busy Hulitts, and on through the unloading yard to the gate. In a few minutes I was walking down a sidewalk of the small

Ohio town beneath a leafy canopy of poplar and maple trees. After an iron-bound week aboard the ship surrounded by gray and blue seascapes the green overhead was refreshing, and I breathed in the raw green smell of the leaves gratefully. The night was noisy with cicadas, tree frogs, and crickets while the modest, white-sided houses on the street were dark and silent.

Inevitably, being alone in the night, my thoughts turned to Sally O'Shaugnessy. "Turned"? Hell, plunged whooping with joy toward Sally. Poignantly, I remembered how she looked when she came to the door to meet me on the night of our dates, eyes crinkling above her smile, her lips gleaming red with fresh lipstick, her dress bespeaking fresh daintiness, her entire presence breathing the glowing promise of young femininity. And then walking hand in hand out to my father's car and asking as I started the engine, "Where shall we go?"

"Oh, let's just ride out into the country somewhere."

Together we had discovered quiet back roads just west of Denton, and we would cruise slowly along the gently curving by-ways, relishing the sudden coolness washing in through the open car windows as we dipped down into brushy hollows, often shrouded with light mist, and sometimes turning into a lane and stopping to murmur and kiss. Usually, we would stop somewhere during the evening to sip a coke—paid for out of my meager funds—and then we would move on, talking and loving and fondling. Both of us read a lot, and Sally would urge me to read Rostand's *Cyrano de Bergerac* which she was just finishing while I would tell her to read Munthe's *Axel's Castle.* We would agree that on our next date we ought to see the movie, "Desire Under The Elms," which was just opening at Loew's Denton Theater. She might ask, "Don't you love that new song, 'Sweet and Lovely'? I heard Hal Kemp play it on the radio last night." "Sure. Makes me think of you." And I would whistle the song while Sally giggled and leaned closer to me. Immersed in the memories of those halcyon hours, I began then, alone on the early morning streets of Conneaut, to whistle the lovely nostalgic tune, "Sweet and Lovely." When I reached the bridge of the song, the *b* of the a-a-b-a structure, I sang, "When she nestles in my arms so tenderly, / There's a thrill that words cannot express. / There's a song of love that's haunting me, / Melody, haunting me." I blush now to recall that I sang those saccharine phrases with an emotional intensity that would have been appropriate for the poetry of John Keats.

I must have wandered about the streets of the little northern Ohio town for nearly an hour, passing Kroger's grocery, Rexall's drug store, the Sohio filling station, the Ashtabula County First National Bank—all dark, the windows blank in the wan light of the single-bulbed street lights suspended on criss-crossing lines at each street corner. Even Billy's Tavern was dark, though the pungent smell of spilled beer seeped out under the door.

But some place where spirit-lifting drinks were available must have been open because I saw ahead of me on the dark street two figures, one a man seemingly staggering from side to side while the other man tried to steady his course. They were making slow progress, and I soon caught up with them. At the sound of my footsteps, the two swung around and peered at me. Through the gloom I could make out that the staggerer, wearing a cloth cap slouching over one ear, was the third engineer, Smelcher. The other man, seemingly sober and in control, was the second mate, the man who had confided to me that time when we met on the deck, that he had planned to go to college but for unstated reasons had not.

Smelcher lurched, trying to get a better visual fix on me, and blurted, "Who zat? The fucking collitch boy?"

"That's Brown, the six to ten coal passer," said the mate.

"I know his goddamn name, all right, the pissin' son

of a bitch." Smelcher lurched again, this time in my direction, but was held back by the mate. "C'mon closer, Brown, you bloodsucker. I want to beat the shit out of you." He swung a right punch in my general direction, and as he did so the force of his momentum tore him from the grasp of the mate, and he fell face down on the sidewalk.

"Go on back to the ship, Brown," said the mate. "He's had a few too many straight whiskeys with beer chasers. Go on along. I can handle him."

I stepped around the struggling man on the sidewalk, trying without success to get back on his feet unaided, and walked quickly back to the dockyard and climbed aboard the *Morse*. The deck watchman, a sullen Finn, nodded at me silently as my feet hit the deck, and I walked forward to the deckhouse. It would be less than two hours before I had to go back on watch, but I undressed and crawled into bed. I lay in the dark, with the noises of the unloading machinery outside, trying to dispel the image of Smelcher's snarling, drink-contorted face and the inexplicable hatred it conveyed. I finally wrenched my thoughts away and turned them tenderly toward Sally. The next thing I knew I was being shaken by the hunchbacked cook. "Wake up, you dumb bastard! Time to go to work."

When I met Don in the firehold just after six, he asked, "How'd you make out last night ashore?"

"All right. Had a good walk. But I ran into Smelcher on the way back. Drunk as a piss ant."

"Trouble?"

"He wanted to punch me out. But the second mate was with him, and he held him back."

Don shook his head. "He's bad trouble, Brown. *Bad.* Like I told you before, stay away from him."

"I'm doing my best."

Four

The inevitable explosion with Smelcher occurred on my fourth trip aboard the *Morse*. We were unloading at Lorain, a choice of ports that had created great joy among the "after end" crew, many of whom lived in Lorain. This included Joe, my coal passer friend, who stopped me on deck while we were still going down the Detroit river shortly after we passed the dispatcher's launch. "Hey, Brown. Ja hear the good news? We're going to Lorain!"

"Yeah?" I greeted this tremendous news calmly. "Well, okay."

"Okay, *shit*! We'll get in there about three this afternoon, an' I'll go find some girls and get me some pussy." His face took on a leer so exaggerated it was nearly a caricature. "You like pussy, Brown?"

There is only one answer a man can make to that question, regardless of his experience or lack of it, and I made it.

"Well, okay then. C'mon with me and I'll fix you up with some Polack girls who fuck like minks."

I declined this handsome offer, pleading that I had some essential shopping to do. Actually, what I needed was stationery to maintain the very active correspondence I was carrying on with Sally, Judson Graver, and Jim Blodgett. A quick trip to Kresge's Five and Ten on Lorain's main street took care of that. I spent another half hour in the town, wandering around the streets of the grim industrial city and then headed back to the ship. It was after 5 and I was going back on watch at 6.

Down in the firehold at 6 I found Don doing some minor mechanical maintenance, tightening nuts on valve seats and other odds and ends. He sent me back to the engine room toolboard for a small monkey wrench. I picked the tool off the board and turned to go back through the hatchway into the firehold when a hand grabbed my shoulder violently and spun me around. It was Smelcher, eyes red-rimmed and breath rank with beer and whiskey. "Lessee what tool you got, collitch boy," he rasped. "Prolly got the wrong one, you stupid bastard."

I showed him the small monkey wrench. "This is what Don asked me to get."

Smelcher staggered slightly and grabbed the wrench out of my hand. "Nah, you pissing shit, thass the wrong wrench. Thissza one." He took the biggest stillson off the board and shoved it at me. "Take that one, you fuckhead."

Reason clearly was useless in this situation, so I said, "Why don't I take them both and let Don choose."

"No, goddammit! Thissza one. Take it! Take it!"

"Okay, and I'll take the other one too." I reached for the smaller wrench in his hand.

"Like hell you will. Take this one like I tell you, goddammit!" He raised his arm holding the stillson and for an instant I thought he was going to throw the heavy tool at me. I raised my arm to block the throw just as he lunged at me and smashed the wrench down across my elbow so hard I was knocked backwards onto my back. Reeling forward toward me, he raised his right arm again to swing the stillson down at my head. Flat on my back, I saw the big tool with its massive head outlined against the white-painted girders of the engine room overhead. Smelcher's arm started to swing down, and almost instinctively, I pulled my legs up against my chest and kicked back with all my strength. I caught him smack in the belly and he went flying back, legs crumpling under him, and slammed into the block of *Morse's* huge engine. Smelcher's head crashed into the massive steel housing with a heavy thunk, and he slumped down, eyes open and staring, and lay still. He was out cold.

I got to my feet, and before I could decide what to do or where to go, Pinsky, the oiler on my watch, came around from the other side of the engine. "You okay, Brown?" he asked.

"Think so but my left arm and shoulder are all numb."

"Go on back to the firehold. I saw the whole thing. I'll go get the Old Man."

Dazed and holding my left arm, I walked through the hatchway back to the firehold. The instant Don saw my face, he asked, "What happened?" I was in the middle of my explanation when the Old Man, the chief engineer, came through the hatchway.

"You all right, son?"

"I think so, sir. How's Smelcher?"

"Still unconscious. We've sent for a doctor. Pinsky tells me he watched the whole thing, and that you were just defending yourself."

"That's right, sir."

The heavy-set, bespectacled man shook his head. "It's a bad business, Brown. Very bad. But let's go forward and see the captain and let him decide what to do."

I followed the Old Man up the long deck to the Captain Neilson's cabin on the starboard side just below the bridge. He was sitting at his desk, reading the front page of *The Toledo Blade*. The banner headline read: JOBLESS NUMBERS MOUNT. He folded the paper and said, "Hello, Ed. What's up?"

"Fight back in the engine room, Nels. Brown, here, knocked the Third, Smelcher, out cold."

Captain Neilson swung his blue eyes toward me. "What happened, son?"

"Well, sir, I went back to get a wrench and—"

"Pinsky, the oiler on watch," interrupted the Old Man, "saw the whole thing and said it was self-defense."

"Let's get Pinsky up here, then." Captain Neilson turned and swung his head toward the door. "Brewster!" he called. The second mate looked in. "Have someone bring Pinsky up here. He's on watch in the engine room." Captain Neilson turned back to the Old Man. "What about Smelcher? Is he being treated?"

"Still out cold when I left back aft. I sent for a doctor."

Neilson nodded. "Well, Ed, why don't you go see what the doc has to say while I hear Brown's story. Then I'll hear what Pinsky has to add."

The Old Man left and the Captain said to me, "Sit down, son. Start at the beginning and tell me what happened."

With his cold blue eyes fixed on me, I told him about the many times Smelcher had harassed me out of some inexplicable enmity that had culminated in the engine room brawl. I was describing the brief fight itself when Pinsky appeared in the doorway. "Wait outside a minute or two, Pinsky," said Neilson. "I'll call you."

When I finished, Captain Neilson ran the fingertips of his right hand down the side of his long face "Sounds pretty straightforward to me. If Pinsky backs you up, you're in the clear, unless—*unless*—the man is seriously injured. If his life is in danger I'll have to call in the police. *That* would tie my hands." He swivelled around in his chair and looked out the doorway at the early evening sky. After a long pause, he turned back. "You're one of Henry Blodgett's boys, aren't you?"

"Yes, sir. Mr. Blodgett is the father of one of my friends."

He nodded. "I'm just thinking what's best for you, Brown. Either way it goes, you probably ought to leave the ship. Safest thing for you. After I get the doctor's report, if it's okay I'll go ashore and telephone Henry. He'll get you on another boat right away." He smiled assuringly. "So you go back to your room and start packing."

Stunned, I walked back down the deck to the midships deckhouse, feeling my left arm as I walked. The numbness was gone but there was a lump the size of a walnut on my elbow. The deckhands were hard at work covering the open hatches with heavy wooden covers, picking the sections up at the side of the ship and swinging them into place with their hatch clubs. I had to pause several times and step around them.

In my room, I pulled my suitcase out from under the bed. I had got about half packed when Joe came in. "Hey, Brown! What the hell happened? They say you slugged Smelcher with a stillson and he's prolly dead!"

I shook my head, too confused and stunned to answer.

Five

One day later I was side-stepping alongside an open cargo hatch across from a fellow deckhand. Together we were swinging an 125-pound wooden hatch cover leaf into place. Each of us held baseball bat-sized hatch clubs with steel hooks at the fat ends fitted into transverse steel rods embedded in the wooden slab. "Okay put 'er down, Brownie," said my new shipmate, Felix Horst, a shortish broad-shouldered German from Milwaukee.

As we walked back to the edge of the deck to pick up another leaf the familiar grimy industrial banks of the Cuyahoga River moved slowly by while my new ship, *Maunaloa*, struggled to clear the slimy, snake-like river and move out into the blue waters of Lake Erie. Though new to me, *Maunaloa* like her sister, *Mataloa*, had been built in 1895 and was just emerging from six years of idle storage. She was shorter than *Morse*—450 feet to 500—and was having a somewhat easier time negotiating the tortuous curves below the Central Furnace docks. She was also more nicely shaped, as ore freighters go, with a lifting sheer to her bow.

At the moment my attention was concentrated on maintaining my grip on the hatch club as my elbow yelped with pain every time I flexed it. The open hatch, about 10 feet across, yawned above the bottom of the hold 25 feet down. One slip and the massive hatch leaf would go slamming down through the gap, possibly pulling one of us with it. After a couple more lifts and carries the pain in my elbow was getting out of control. "Gotta rest, Felix," I said.

"Let me take over, Brownie," said the third deckhand, Ralph Dean, a tall 19-year old with an uncertain, somewhat unformed face. "You're not used to it yet."

I walked over to the side and sat down on a squat, steel bollard. Rubbing the lump on my elbow I remembered the warning of my former shipmate, old John, the Bavarian stoker: "sitting on that cold hunka steel will give you piles every time, sure as anythin'." I was fond of John but not fond enough to accept medically dubious advice when I needed so badly to sit down.

I had not told my new shipmates about the knot on my elbow. Had not had time really. From the time the doctor had told Captain Neilson that Smelcher's injury was just a concussion, needing only a couple of days' bed rest, and the captain had returned after his telephone call to Mr. Blodgett with the news that *Maunaloa* was lying at the Central Furnace docks in need of a deckhand, I had caught the first train out of Lorain for Cleveland, taken a taxi from the Cleveland Terminal to the dockside, and had been on board only long enough to get unpacked and go to work. Now, sitting on the bollard and nursing my elbow with the sounds of the chuffing and hooting tugboats around me and a new ship bound for Lake Superior under me, I blessed Mr. Blodgett and my good luck in landing on my feet so quickly.

As my first week passed aboard *Maunaloa* I blessed my good luck again and again. Unlike *Morse*, she was a happy ship. My fellow deckhands were not remarkable men in any way, but they were socialized people, accustomed by their upbringings to give-and-take instead of unrelenting confrontation. Felix came from a solid German family where grandmother presided over the dinner table and German was invariably spoken in her presence. Learning that Felix spoke German, I tried out some of my one semester's command of the language and confused him immediately by using the pronoun *sie*—"you"—instead of *du*—"thou." Around the family dinner table he had heard only *du*, the familiar form of the pronoun.

When Ralph learned that I had spent half a year at college, he immediately regarded me as a superior being, a "college man." His respect approached awe and was embarrassing, but nothing I could say would restore equal status between us.

Now that I was a "sharp-ender," part of the ship's navigation crew instead of the propulsion unit, I had less strenuous duties and, for the most part, better hours. Having just emerged from a six-year storage, *Maunaloa* needed scraping and painting from her bow to her fantail. On the days we were at sea, and not making a dock or transiting the Soo, we put in an eight hour day with scraper and paint brush. We started at 8 and stopped at 4:30. On fair days we painted outside—everything on the long red deck: hatch coamings, stanchions, bollards, and hatch covers—and the white superstructure fore and aft. After such a day in the open air with the wide sea around us or the ever-shifting scenes along the river shores, we showered, ate a belly-gorging supper, and returned to the small deckhands' room and listened to Ralph's radio which brought in Benny Goodman with Harry James' flaring trumpet and Gene Krupa's tom-tom drums, or Glen Gray's Casa Loma band with its haunting theme, "Smoke Rings," and Kenny Sargent's falsetto crooning, or the wit and chuckles of Jack Benny's or Fred Allen's comedy hour.

My initiation into the other duties of a deckhand on a 1930s ore freighter came as we entered the Soo. It was a late July night in Sault Ste. Marie, and the air had the tang of northern Michigan forests and ice-cold lakes commingled with the sharp green smell of the newly mown grass along the stone walkways beside the locks. Lights on tall masts transformed the scene into a stage setting and cast an unnatural shade of green over the grass. As the ship glided into the lock, the first mate summoned us to the port side just aft of the forecastle where a bosun's chair hung suspended from an 8-foot arm that pivoted out over the side of the ship. "All right, Brown," he said and pointed to the chair shaped exactly like a child's swing. I put my legs through and immediately two crewmen pulled on the rope which lifted me off the deck, swung me out over the side, and dropped me onto the dock. The ship was still sliding forward at three or four miles an hour. I hit the dock running and pulled the ropes of the swing over my head. The mate ordered me to move aft where the second mate threw me a line attached to a steel cable with a loop which I swung over a bollard. Felix had been put on the dock to handle the line forward and soon the deck engines fore and aft snubbed the lines taut and *Maunaloa* came to rest, the long ship lying quiescent beside the gleaming black wall of the lock. I watched while the massive gates swung closed behind the ship's stern, and the icy water from Lake Superior flowed into the lock, roiling and tumbling, and *Maunaloa* began almost imperceptibly to rise. "Better come aboard, Brown, before she gets too high," said the second mate and gestured to a small ladder. I climbed the four feet to the deck from the dock which fifteen minutes later was twenty-odd feet below us. Then the front gate swung slowly back, *Maunaloa's* great gruff voice spoke a short blast, a lock-keeper on the dock loosened the lines fore and aft, and the ship nosed out into the waters of Whitefish Bay and Lake Superior.

This docking procedure, lowering the deckhands onto the dock from a still moving ship with a bosun's chair, was repeated twice a week as we passed through the Soo and each time we tied up before loading in Lake Superior and unloading in either Lake Erie or Lake Michigan. Night or day, cold or hot, wet or dry, my feet hit the dock three or four times each week, and I trotted forward several steps until I could release the bosun's chair over my head. It soon became routine, but sometimes, as I later learned, the routine became highly dangerous.

All in all, the work of a deckhand was more varied and exciting than a coal passer's. But beyond the work I found real delight in the offbeat personalities among my new shipmates. One night when we were steaming northwest on Lake Superior I decided, as I had sometimes when I was aboard *Morse*, to take a short walk on deck before going to bed. I climbed the short ladder leading up to the foredeck and walked up the passage beside the forecastle to the bow. It was a brisk moonless night with the stars spangling the black sky in lavish numbers. Through the darkness I could make out the figure of the watchman who, in those pre-radar days, kept a lookout for danger ahead. On *Morse* the watchman on the 10 to 2 watch was a sullen Finn who never spoke so I was mildly surprised when the man turned as I approached and said, "Hey, who's there?"

"Brown, the new deckhand."

"I'm Henderson. Aren't you the college boy?"

"Well, in a way." I stood quietly beside him, the steady wash and swish of the sea around *Maunaloa's* bow sounding in my ears and the cold northern air tingling against my forehead. I looked up into the diamond-dotted black sky. "My God, there are a lot of stars!"

"Any idea how many? What would you guess?"

"I don't know. More than I can count."

"No, that's wrong. I counted them one night. Got exactly six thousand eight hundred sixty-five."

"Wow." My eyes had begun to adjust to dark, and I could make out Henderson's burly figure against the faint star-shine. "There're so many you'd think they'd bump into each other."

Henderson grunted. "Not up there, not in space. They're ruled by laws."

"Laws?"

"Sure, natural laws, the kind we ought to have here on earth. In college you must have read Herbert Spencer and found out the difference between natural law and man-made law. What does Spencer say about that?"

I was stumped. Until then I had not even heard of Herbert Spencer, a 19th century English philosopher, let alone read him. "I don't know."

"Hunh! I'm surprised. I'd think his *Principles of Ethics*'d be required reading in college."

"Not yet."

"That's amazing."

We stood silent for a while and then I said, "Guess I'll turn in. 'Night."

"Okay."

As I walked back to the companionway leading into the crew's quarters I marvelled over the erudition of my shipmate, an ordinary seaman. But in later conversations on dark nights up in the bow I discovered that his thorough knowledge of Herbert Spencer was an isolated peak in the geography of his learning. Otherwise, large areas of reading and enlightenment lay unexplored. Like other self-educated men I later met, he regarded the books he had chanced upon as unique sources of wisdom when academically-trained men, with their broader perspectives, would compare those same books with their peers and contemporaries and place them appropriately among them. Still, he was a highly intelligent man, if firmly opinionated and rigid about what he knew. We had many fine talks at night as the ship pushed her way through the dark waters of the Great Lakes.

Another shipmate, Shorty, the wheelsman on the 2 to 6 watch, Shorty Bellau, was utterly different—earthy, funny, quivering with jerky energy and a constant delight. I first talked with him when he came bursting into our room one night, and said "Oh, hell, I wish I was home under da bed eatin' catshit!"

That was the most unusual and powerful metaphor for boredom I had ever heard, and it tickled my delight in expressive language. From my bed where I lay reading I grinned up at him. "What's the trouble, Shorty?"

"Hell, I don' know. Nothin'. Everythin'." He looked around the room, jerking his head with the quick nervous motion of a ferret and spotted a calendar picture on the wall of a blonde girl who stretched her green bathing suit in all the anatomically appropriate places. "Jeez, look at dat!" he said admiringly. "Any man who wouldn't take a bite outa dat is a coward."

As the days passed aboard *Maunaloa* I had many more conversations with Shorty, and each time he delighted me with a vivid, quirky expression, each delivered in his staccato, high-pitched voice and French-Canadian accent. One day he invited me to come up to the pilot house while he was standing watch at the wheel. I stood beside him, looking out over *Maunaloa's* blunt bow at the broad blue-green waters of Lake Superior as the ship plowed steadily northwest, and listened as he talked to soothe his boredom. He told me he lived at Sault Ste. Marie, two blocks from the locks, and had a wife and two small children. "Gotta picture of da family here," he said. He pulled his wallet out of his pocket and fished out a snap-shot. As he handed it to me I missed taking hold and it fell to the deck. "God, Brown," said Shorty, "you're as clumsy as a bear cub fumblin' with his prick!"

After I had dutifully admired the picture of the plump, hot-eyed woman and the two small children with eyes like black marbles Shorty sighed deeply and said "Christ, I hope it's night-time next time we go troo da Soo."

"What difference does it make?"

"*Difference*! When it's day-time and I go running up

to da house for a quick one wit' da wife, the kids are all over me. I have a hell of time shakin' 'em off so I can get da woman upstairs to bed."

"But that's only natural, Shorty." I said helpfully. "The kids are just glad to see their daddy."

"Yeah, yeah, I know dat. But that don't make it any easier for me to get some nooky. But when we come troo at night, you see, the old lady comes down to da locks and we go out behind some dark bushes. Providin' it ain't rainin' or snowin'. She won't do it in da rain."

I could think of nothing helpful to say to that so I merely nodded and kept on looking out across *Mauna-loa's* bow at the rippling green sea ahead. After a moment or two, Shorty asked, "Would ya like to steer some?"

"Sure."

"Here." He pointed at the dial of the gyro-compass just beyond the large, wooden-spoked steering wheel. "Just keep her readin' 283. But ya gotta watch her. She's a little down by the bow and takes a sheer."

"Okay." I took hold of the wheel and almost at once the dial read 283.5 and the gyro-compass clicked once. I swung the wheel to the left and the dial passed through 283 down to 282.5 and the gyro clicked twice.

"Keep 'er steady."

"I'm trying." I swung the wheel back to the right and the gyro began a steady click-click-click-click.

"Aw, hell, Brownie," said Shorty. "Let her go on around and catch her when she comes back!"

At this point the first mate came into the pilot house and sighted back over the long deck at the wavy line of the ship's wake I had left as a record of my wheelsman-ship. "Take over, Bellau," he said and that ended my first effort at steering an ore freighter.

As it turned out, contrary to Shorty's wishes we did not transit the Soo at night on our return trip down. Instead, it was high noon on Sunday when we eased into the lock and tied up. But Shorty had only one thought, one carnal destination in mind, and he did not intend to be deflected from the path leading to it. He stood tense and ready by the rail as the ship's side brushed the edge of the lock. He was first to get himself into the bosun's chair, then hit the dock running, sprinted across the grass beside the locks, and ran up one of the side streets of Sault Ste. Marie toward his house. From the deck, I watched him as he ran, his small figure diminishing in the distance while I thought about the reception he would get as he burst through the front door: the eager little kids hugging him around the knees and Shorty struggling to get to his plump little wife standing slightly apart and smiling.

Meanwhile, *Maunaloa* proceeded about her business. She sank slowly inside the lock to the level of the St. Mary's River, moved sedately out, and stopped to pick up the mail bag, a drum of oil, two 5-gallon cans of buttermilk, and a box of fruit. By then, nearly 40 minutes had passed since Shorty had jumped over the side and he had not returned. The ship lingered a while longer while the mate and captain watched on the shore for the wheelsman-lover to appear. Time passed. Finally the captain reached up in the pilot house and pulled the lanyard which blew the whistle. In the pristine quiet of a Sunday noon in the little Michigan town, *Maunaloa's* gruff great voice sounded and echoed. After quiet had returned the captain waited another five minutes, and blew the great whistle again. In my mind's eye I pictured Shorty, at some stage or other of the proceedings in his bedroom, hearing the steamship whistle, knowing exactly what it meant, and resolutely closing his mind to the blast while he turned back to the sweet task at hand. *Maunaloa* loitered in the small bay for another fifteen minutes, again and again raising her raucous voice to call her missing boy who was joyfully otherwise engaged, and then moved off downriver minus one wheelsman.

We deckhands were aghast, wondering what would happen to Shorty and how the ship would operate with only two wheelsmen. We had seen one or two displays of temper by Captain Boyce, a swaggering, aggressive Irishman, and we kept glancing up at the pilot house looking for signs of how he was taking Shorty's unsanctioned absence.

Meanwhile, *Maunaloa* proceeded quietly down the St. Mary's River with the virgin pine forest lining the banks and glistening in the golden sunshine. At one point we passed a log cabin cottage where a boy stood on the dock yelling through a megaphone, "Captain, give me a salute!" He repeated the call twice before someone in the pilot house pulled the whistle lanyard and blasted two longs and two shorts, the standard salute. Herons and gulls lifted off the water and circled as the sound shattered the pristine quiet. Then the boy on the dock yelled, "Thank you, Captain!"

The passage down the river from the Soo to the northern entrance to Lake Huron took about three hours, and we had stopped worrying about Shorty. Just before moving out into the lake and passing the coaling station at Detour, we saw a launch moving out from the dock toward us. Aboard it was the renegade Shorty, grinning up at us as the boat came alongside the ship. The mate dropped a rope ladder over the side, and Shorty scrambled up on deck. The mate escorted him briskly up to the pilot house, reminding me of a wayward pupil being taken to the school principal, and we saw nothing of Shorty until after supper. He came into our room looking as relaxed and at peace as I had ever seen him. He glanced at the calendar picture of the voluptuous girl and looked away, smiling shyly.

"What did the skipper say, Shorty?" I asked.

"Nuttin' much." He grinned mischievously. "Tell da troot, I t'ink he was jealous."

Six

The flow of mail from Sally, Judson Graver, and Jim Blodgett, in answer to my steady stream of letters, was of course interrupted by my transfer from *Morse* to *Maunaloa*. When the flow did resume it came in a flood, and its volume mightily upset the first mate who passed out the mail to the crew. A bony, angular Swede—a typical "squarehead" my shipmates called him—1st Mate Alrik Gustafson stood on the bottom step of the starboard ladder to the foc'sle, shortly after we cleared the lock at the Soo and headed westward on Whitefish Bay, and called out the names in Swedish sing-song as he read them off the letter envelopes. All but one was for me. "Donna Bra-oon," he would say in his rugged accent and hand me a letter. Then again, "Donna Bra-oon." On the third time, "Got Tamm! Donna Bra-oon." And then, "Son of a pitch! Donna Bra-oon!"

I took my treasure of letters to my bunk. Two of them, I recognized by the delicate, feminine script and the faint hint of Tweed perfume, were from Sally. "Dearest, darling Dana," the first one began, "I am home alone tonight and my longing for you is an ache that starts with my lips and goes to my toes. You are so very, very dear to me, my Dana. You are always in my mind and my heart, ever in my blood." Then, after some brief bits of news about her friends, Jane and Vicky, she wrote, "Work hard, darling, be a success, and marry me."

I looked up, my eyes misty, my mind a glowing radiance, and saw Felix, dressed only in his skivvies, earnestly examining his toes and picking stocking lint out of them. I looked back down quickly, wanting somehow to express the tide of love those words released. I looked up again and found Felix staring at me. "Somepun wrong, Dane? Bad news?"

"No. Just a letter from my girl. Says she misses me."

"Oh, that's okay." He looked reflective. "I don't have any reglar girl. But, boy, I'll tell ya, I sure miss havin' a woman. Gonna get me a piece of ass next time we get into port Down Below."

In my heightened state, my mind overflowing with love of the purest, virgin strain, that comment was as painful to me as a slap across the mouth—Sally's mouth. I got up and walked out on deck and stood by the cable rail. Staring down at the blue-green water eddying along the steel plates on *Maunaloa's* flank, I dreamed for several minutes of being with Sally, remembering the flooding joy of holding her slender body in my arms and kissing her soft, caressing mouth.

A little later I read the second Sally letter, dated about ten days later. It was cold water on glowing fire. "Dana, dear old thing," it began. "August is half way through, and I am panting with impatience to get back to college. Juddie and I were talking about it last night—the parties after the football games at the fraternity houses, sneaking away to Columbus and having manhattans at the Deshler-Walleck Hotel bar, going on hay-rides out into the countryside. Such fun!" The letter ended: "Hope you're not working too hard. Juddie says you'll come back a grizzled sailor with a dock-side girl at every port. Be careful you don't fall off the dock! Hah! Meanwhile, Sailor Boy, as Miss Gautier taught us to say in our French class, *Au revoir*. Sally."

Like the shadow of a heavy cloud moving across a field, my mood shifted from glowing to somber. "Juddie" would have to be Judson Graver, my high school best friend, but how did he become "Juddie" to Sally? That was troubling enough but there were resonances that were worse. How did Sally's joking about picking up girls at dockside jibe with "marry me"? I tried to tell myself I was being too sensitive to nuance, but I could not escape the tone of detachment underlying the whole letter. Whether a passing mood or something permanent, the letter certainly bespoke change.

Perplexed, I opened Judson's letter. "Dear Dane, How I envy the life you must be leading! This has been the dullest summer of the century. I work half days at my Dad's office, filing letters and crap like that, and then I go out to the country club and hang around the pool looking for babes. There's some new stuff around and some of them hang half way out of these new low cut bathing suits, but they're all so damned pure. I can't wait to get back to school and those night-time hay-rides. I'm telling you, boy, when you get a babe lying down there in the hay after a few beers there isn't anything she won't do. Like I've always said, there isn't a woman in the world who won't do it if she feels certain no one will find out."

I recognized that last statement as one of Judson's maxims, one I had heard many times along with "Women are cats: stroke them anywhere and they'll purr; stroke them in the right places and they'll screw." I must admit I had always been fascinated by Jud's cynical sophistication—at least it seemed like sophistication to me at the time and I never thought to question how a guy my own age could have had all the experience such cynicism implied—but now I found it jarring when I encountered it right after Sally's letter. I knew that Jud's sleepy good looks and his slow, knowing smile were very attractive to girls, and although I had only his word for it I took for granted he had been successful many times with his so-called stroking technique. But I had always felt confident that the unspoken code between best friends would make Sally out of bounds for him. Now I was considerably less confident. In fact, I was besieged by doubt and miserable.

But the work rhythm of the ship did not allow me much time for brooding. Once we were well under way out of the Soo the second mate assembled us deckhands and gave us painting assignments. I was sent down to the anchor chain locker, a small enclosed space in the very nose of the ship. A fairly vigorous chop was rolling westward across Lake Superior, and *Maunaloa* began to lift her bow and drop it swiftly down in a regular sequence: up and down, up and down, and up and down. It was like riding in a tightly enclosed, berserk elevator which had somehow been saturated with the overpowering smell of red lead paint. Keeping my mind focused on fighting back welling nausea as I rose up and down in a bent over position inside the enclosed space left me no time to dwell on Sally and her wayward fancies. It was a close thing, the nearest I ever came to seasickness, but by keeping a tight grip on focusing my mind I kept the threat at bay and by suppertime worry over Sally had been pushed back into a far corner.

An incident two days later made such worry seem almost irrelevant. The ship had gone into Two Harbors, Minnesota to load, and when we tied up we found ourselves tucked in between two other ships in a slip that ran at right angles to the main throughway. By three o'clock in the afternoon we were loaded and ready to depart. Captain Boyce called for a tug to help us back out of the narrow slip but was told that the tugs were all assigned to other ships and it would be a two hour wait for his turn. The over-riding principle for skippers in the Great Lakes ore trade was to keep the ship on the move, avoid all delays, in order to qualify for a season-end bonus for the number of round trips made. To Captain

Boyce, two hours delay was intolerable, and he decided to extricate *Maunaloa* from her narrow berth with the ship's own resources.

The 1st mate called the other deckhands aboard and left me on the dock. Then he ordered me to put the aft line on a bollard at the end of the dock and to stand well back. The captain put the ship in reverse with her rudder set to swing her stern around the end of the dock. But of course she could not make so tight a turn, and the line to the aft deck engine paid slowly and grudgingly out while the woven steel cable hawser vibrated with the tension and strain as the ship's stern moved farther and farther away. I had heard stories of men being cut in two by the backlash of a snapped cable so I crouched behind a girder, my heart thumping hard as I watched the straining quivering line. When the cable was almost paid out, the captain eased the ship slowly forward while the deck engine pulled the ship's stern toward the dock. This maneuver succeeded in bringing the ship only about a third of the way around to line her up with the throughway. The captain repeated the operation three more times, each time the cable jumping and quivering under the strain while I stooped down behind the girder.

After the fourth try, the ship was sufficiently lined up to head out but was fifteen or twenty feet off the end of the pier where I stood. The captain ordered full speed ahead, and the ship began to slide past me headed for the open sea. Up to that moment I had given no thought as to how I was going to get back on board. Was the ship going to park at the end of the dock while I stepped aboard like a passenger? Not likely. To Captain Boyce, getting enough way on to give the ship steerage-way was the prime consideration. I had only an instant to consider the possibility of being left behind in Two Harbors before the 1st mate grabbed a 30-foot ladder and with the help of Felix and Ralph pushed it over the side of the ship toward me. "Put the end on the dock," he ordered.

I positioned the end of it several feet from the edge. "Now come aboard."

The ladder was horizontal, with one end on the dock and the other end held high over the heads of my fellow deckhands who were walking aft to keep the ladder in place as the ship moved forward. Appalled, I hesitated while I watched the black water eddying and swirling between the ship and the dock. "Come aboard!" the mate shouted. Nearly paralyzed with fear, I began to crawl slowly across the space between dock and ship, my hands clutching the rungs of the ladder and my feet groping for the supports I could not see in that crouching position. I had advanced only a few feet when one of the deckhands stumbled and the ladder lurched. I froze, staring at the roiling black water below. "Oh, gotdammit," said the mate and took the end of the ladder himself. "Come on! Come on!" I scrambled the rest of the way across and fell off the ladder onto the deck. My relief was so great I would willingly have hugged and kissed the raw-boned Swede but before I could say anything he said to me and the others, "Get that gotdamned ladder aboard." He strode off forward without looking back.

"Jeez, Brown," said Felix. "You're one brave son of a bitch. I woulda stayed on the goddamned dock and let the ship go without me."

Seven

The batch of letters the 1st mate handed me as we left the Soo, downbound for Ashtabula, was smaller than the previous one but still gratifying because there were letters from Sally and Jim Blodgett. Hesitantly, I opened the familiar small envelope with its faint hint of Sally's fragrance and read, "Darling, darling, Dana, why aren't you with me tonight and not hundreds of miles away on some grimy old freighter? My longing for you right now is a deep down ache. It seems a year or more since you kissed me goodbye and walked away, and I'm deathly afraid you won't come home until I have left for college and it will be many months more before you hold me in your arms again. Oh, Dana, Dana, I *need* you! You must come—come *now*!"

I looked up from the page at the slowly passing shoreline of the St. Mary's River, and at that moment the tall, green pines lofting at the water's edge, which had previously seemed evocative of a peaceful wilderness, free of the noise and the stench of an industrial world, now seemed alien and symbolic of separation, distancing me from the truly meaningful part of my life. The Sally magic had snared me once again, and it did not occur to me in that spell to wonder at this latest transformation or to question its permanence. Sally's passionate cry had so fired my love that I was nearly ready to jump over the side of the ship and start swimming south.

Blodgett's letter did nothing to quench the flame. "Dear Brownie," it read, "I've decided to make one more trip after this and then quit. That will be about August 30. How about you quitting then too and coming to stay with me here while we bum around for a few days? Then my Dad will drive us down to Maumee and we can work out getting a room together again. What do you say?"

What my heart said loud and clear was "yes"! And for the next day and a half as we cleared St. Mary's at Detour and plowed southward down Lake Huron I dreamed constantly of joining Jim and then being together again with Sally. I saw neither the paint brush in my hand or the red lead paint as I daubed it on *Maunaloa's* fantail housing. Instead, in my mind's eye I ran up the walk to Sally's house and took her in my arms as I met her at the door. It was not until we were passing Detroit and I was staring at the tall office buildings and the traffic along the streets that reality finally took charge. And then I knew suddenly and for certain that I could not leave the ship after one more trip. It was out of the question. From my monthly pay envelope I had saved by then only three hundred dollars despite rigorous frugality, spending money only on necessary things like work gloves and on stationery and stamps. Three hundred dollars would not see me through a college year. I would need at least twice that much, and I could save up the money only by staying aboard the ship another two or three months. There was no other way. As I stood at the railing and watched it pass, Detroit's skyline suddenly became bleak and cheerless.

After supper that night I wrote letters to Sally and Jim to be posted the next day in Ashtabula. They were brief because I could think of little to say beyond saying "no." And so began the next three months aboard *Mauna-*

loa, three of the longest months of my life. By that time the romance and excitement of shipping on the Great Lakes had worn away, and I was left with the drudgery of the daily routine and the stupefying dullness of my time off watch. After September 15 had come and gone there seemed to be a sagging of spirit throughout the ship. Every task became harder because of the cold and the blustery winds of October and November. The ship heaved and rolled and bucked, and green seas leaped over her flanks and splashed across her deck in long streaks that swiftly transformed to sheets of ice. Before September was out the 1st mate had us rig a lifeline running from the forecastle to the after deck house to hang on to while walking the deck. I learned its value one brisk October afternoon as I walked aft for supper. I came out of the lee of the forecastle and a heavy blast staggered me sideways onto a patch of ice. Before I knew that was happening I was splayed against the three-cable railing at the edge of the deck with the grey surging waters of Lake Michigan just below me. I crawled back to the forecastle on my hands and knees and grabbed the lifeline before starting aft again.

Shorty, the wheelsman, whose capacity for boredom was always near a screaming peak, seemed to be teetering on the edge of madness. "Christ on the Cross!" he exclaimed as he burst into the room one night. "Won't this fuckin' season never end?" He paced up and down in short jerky steps. "Each goddamned year I swear I'm gonna quit shippin' and get a job with one of those sawmill outfits up in Chippewa County. But then spring comes and I get the itch to have steel deck under my feet all over agin." He walked over and examined the engaging bulges and curves of the bathing suit girl on the calendar. "I still say a man ud be a coward not to take a bite outa dat." He wheeled back and pointed a stubby finger at me. "You know what we gotta hope for, Brownie?" I shook my head. "We gotta hope we get iced in on Whitefish Bay next trip down."

But we did not get caught in an ice pack the next trip down nor did we on succeeding trips although the northwest winds blasting down across Manitoba and Ontario lashed Lake Superior into gray-green and white fury and plunged the thermometer into the twenties. Like the rest of *Maunaloa's* crew I hunkered down and counted the days as October plodded by and November inched glacially on. While the ship was at sea, we deckhands painted the interior of the cabins, and I found the chore of painting inside a steel enclosed closet off the captain's room about as hard on my internal stability as painting the chain locker had been.

Working the ship's lines as she came into the lock at the Soo or made a dock Up Above or Down Below was considerably more challenging in the heavy fall weather. Lines were stiff and hands were cold, and there was the ever-present risk of hitting a sheet of ice that could flip you into the water between the dock and the crushing side of the ship.

It was Thanksgiving Day when I, crammed with turkey, oyster stuffing, candied yams, and cranberries, decided that I was on my last trip. Rumors were already flying around the ship that *Maunaloa* was going into port the first week of December to lay up for the winter. My bank account had swollen to $620. Moreover, I just felt in my bones, somehow, that the time had come to leave. It was a sort of premonition, some general feeling of looming disaster, and there were moments on that last trip as we were making the dock at Ashland, Wisconsin that I thought I might have made one trip too many and that the threatened disaster had arrived.

It was a black, moonless night as we threaded our way through the channel off Chequamegon Point and arrived at the head of Chequamegon Bay just around nine o'clock. I was standing ready beside the bosun's chair as we neared the Ashland dock, and I could see by the glare of the dock lights that it was an entirely wooden structure with a narrow catwalk, open of course on the sea side and bordered by a two-by-four hand railing on the shore side. "All right, Brown," said the mate, so I climbed into the chair and was swung out over the side and lowered onto the catwalk.

There had been a gusty, offshore wind blowing as we had approached but just as my feet hit the planking it suddenly became a blinding snow squall. I could barely see to catch the line the mate threw me through the swirling whiteness and within seconds the catwalk became coated with slippery wet snow. It took three tries for the mate, throwing against the blustering wind, to get the line to me, and then I had to pull the heavy steel cable across the steadily widening gap between the ship and the dock as the gusts shoved *Maunaloa* farther and farther out. I grabbed the two-by-four railing with my left hand and was just barely able to reach with my right to drop the loop of the bowline over the bollard.

The catwalk was by then treacherously slippery, and I could see and hear through the open planking the thrashing of the waves against the pilings below. It quickly became clear that although we had the ship's nose snubbed to the dock with the bowline, the wind beating against her port side, rising high in the water after her ballast had been pumped out, was swinging her stern dangerously far out. Still, the mate, again after several tries, got a line to me off the bow, and we both walked aft, I slithering and sliding on the snowy planks, holding the line between us. The mate took the stern cable, fastened the woven steel line to the rope line and told me to pull it over to the dock.

As soon as the steel cable cleared the side of the ship its weight strained heavily in my grasp, and as the ship pulled farther and farther out from the dock the strain increased rapidly. I could feel my grasp on the two-by-four railing starting to slip, and I realized that unless I let go soon the mounting strain was going to pull me into the turbulent water below.

I let go.

Through the squalling wind I could hear the mate cursing in Swedish and broken English. But then he yelled at me to go forward and release the bowline which I did. While the forward deck engine reeled in the cable the skipper backed the ship out and I waited on the dock. The ship receded into the blackness and then slowly came in again. By this time the squall had eased and although the catwalk was still treacherously slippery it was fairly easy to secure the lines. The mate scowled blackly at me as I came aboard but said nothing. Back in the privacy of our room Felix and Ralph told me I had done the right thing. "I woulduna let that stupid cable pull me in that goddamned water," said Felix. "Me neither," Ralph said.

We cleared Ashland around two in the morning, and it took the three of us another hour to put the hatch leaves back on the hatches. Then the mate ordered us to break out the tarpaulins, fit them over the hatches, and secure them along the hatch coamings with battens and wedges. The open deck was bitter cold in the biting wind as we cleared Chequamegon Point and moved out into the mounting seas of Lake Superior. Our hands in our stiff leather gloves grew numb and clumsy, and we grumbled about having to put on tarps in the dim light of the deck lights. "Damn mate could have waited till daylight to make us do this," complained Ralph.

"Naw, Dean, the mate's right," said Felix. "See how that water is humpin' up out there? A coupla those seas come over the side and slop down through the cracks between the hatch leaves, and we'd be in trouble. Get very much water in the hold and this tub'd go down like a rock."

We were all stiff and aching with cold when we jammed the last wedge in beside a batten. Felix straightened up and said, "Let's go in the night lunch and have a cuppa coffee."

We had just arranged ourselves on the benches, each with a thick white mug of steaming black coffee, and Felix announced, "I'm gettin' tired of this shit. 'Bout one more trip and I'm headin' for Milwaukee."

"Well," said Ralph, "I think I'll ride her into her lay-up port. It'll probably be Conneaut, only 15 miles from home."

"I was going to tell you fellows tonight, I said. "This is my last trip. Soon as we get her tied up at Lorain or Conneaut I'm going to grab the first train for Cleveland and then grab one for home—Denton."

But at the Soo we learned that our destination was not a Lake Erie port, as I had hoped. Instead, we were bound for Lake Michigan and South Chicago. At Detour we headed west for the Straits of Mackinac and then south toward Chicago. Lake Michigan is only one degree less grim and menacing than Lake Superior in the winter months. The fierce Dakota prairie winds roar across Minnesota and Wisconsin and rip the blue water of Lake Michigan into gray and white streaks and shreds. A heavy following sea built up behind *Maunaloa's* stern about the time we were opposite Ludington and chased us the rest of the way down the lake. When we turned to starboard opposite the breakwater for South Chicago, old *Maunaloa* rolled from one beam end to the other, and heavy seas broke over the side and washed harmlessly off the green tarps onto the deck.

Inside the breakwater the water was calm, and Felix and I tied the ship up with no difficulty. I climbed up the ladder over the ship's side with a great sense of relief. The long ordeal was over. I was on my way home—home and Sally. But Great Lakes shipping had one more scare in store for me. I was walking toward the forecastle, hearing the rumble above me of an overhead crane positioning itself to unload the ship, when suddenly there was an explosion of sharp cracks and the pinging of flying pieces of metal striking the deck. I looked up and saw that the crane operator had rammed his machine into the ship's forward mast that carried her running lights. As the mast bent, the steel wire stays snapped or ripped the metal fastenings loose, and they flew around the deck like shrapnel. When I was sure I had not been hit, I scurried down into my room, tore off my work clothes, and threw them out the porthole.

My suitcase was packed and ready, and as I started to say goodbye to my shipmates, Felix grabbed my bag and said, "C'mon, Brownie, I'll walk you out to the gate. After a trip like this I'm gonna put down three boilermakers and then get me three pieces of ass—one, two, three!"

"G'bye, Dana," said Ralph solemnly, "Sure's been a pleasure workin' with you."

Walking down the deck I met Shorty standing by the railing, "Hey, Brown," he said. "Take care yaself and keep your pecker up."

"You too, Shorty," I said in what I felt certain was unnecessary counsel.

Eight

Spring had come trailing radiant glory to Bedford, the tidy village in southwestern Ohio where Maumee University had held a place of honor for well over a century. It was my fourth spring in Bedford, probably my last, and I greeted it with the mingled joy and apprehension with which most college seniors face those last months before graduation and their entry into the unknown outside world. The dream I had first held firmly in mind four years earlier while shovelling coal in the firehold of *Samuel F B Morse,* the dream of finishing four years of college, was soon to be realized.

On this particular April day, I was sitting at my desk in the little office of the editor of the University newspaper, *The Student Record,* trying to compose an application letter for a job with *The Denton Daily News*. I intended to send identical letters to *The Columbus Dispatch* and *The Cincinnati Enquirer,* but the *News* was my prime target. I was hopeful that the letterhead of *The Student Record* with the line below pronouncing "Dana Brown, Editor-in-chief" would carry some weight with a managing editor.

It took four tries before I got what seemed to be the right tone and amount of information in the application. I ended it with the sentence, "If you should wish, I will be happy to send you clippings of my work." For good measure I included passport size copies of my picture in the forthcoming Yearbook. Gazing at the prints before placing them inside the folded letters, I recognized once again my mother's brown eyes and my father's full, sensuous mouth, mother's round face and father's dark-to-almost-black hair, mother's straight nose and father's large ears.

It was nearly four o'clock and the sun was dyeing the campus lawns with that young April green which brings new hope and springing joy each year. I decided to walk uptown in the glorious afternoon and mail my letters at the village post office. The air outside Irving Hall was tinged with chill but the sunshine glowed on the old red brick buildings around which my life had centered for four years. Rain or shine, sleet or snow, it was a lovely campus with its widely spaced academic halls and resident dormitories standing in quiet serenity under the shelter of graceful elms and heavy-barked oaks. The quiet, well-ordered campus embodied the new life I had found there, a life free from family bickering and petty tensions, a world in which I had found enduring satisfaction in study and campus achievement. I would miss it, come graduation, miss the structural order of academic life, but I knew the time had come to take the knowledge and skills I had acquired at Maumee out into the everyday world.

Walking past Walker Library, I recognized among the several students on the walk ahead the fondly familiar figure of Mit Daley—"Mit" for Millicent. "Hey, Mit!" I called, "Wait up!"

She turned, gray eyes smiling. "Hi, Dane." Her strong high-cheek-boned face was squarish and she was slightly above medium height and robustly made. There was, as my Phi Delt fraternity brothers said, not critically but with an admiration erotically tinged, "a lot of girl there." Mit and I were close friends, a closeness that had steadily grown since my "final" break-up with Sally O'Shaugnessy. Close but not lovers. Neither admiration, erotically tinged, nor ardor was lacking on my part but when we kissed, as we did sometimes in the secluded trophy room of the fraternity house, Mit would break sharply away at the first movement of my hands across her shoulders. "I won't be mauled!" she would say, and then after few minutes she would let me kiss her again. Still there was warmth and fondness between us, and I treasured her company more than anyone's I knew.

"Walk uptown with me while I mail my letters. I'll buy you a milkshake."

She looked at me appraisingly and at the letters in my hand. "Sure," she said. "Let me stop first at the dorm to drop my books."

Her dormitory was Deacon Hall, next to the Library, and I waited briefly while she went inside. When she skipped down the steps to join me I watched with fond pleasure. She was good to look at. Dressed smartly in the sweater and skirt and silk stockings and low heels the college girls of my generation wore, she could have posed as a model for collegiate clothes of the late 1930s. "Let's go," she said and took my hand in her warm, strong one. "What's all this letter writing about?"

"I'm applying for a job next year with a couple of newspapers."

"Oh? Where?" I told her the *Daily News*, the *Enquirer*, and the *Dispatch*. "What do you suppose the chances are? Are newspapers hiring people these days?"

"I really don't know, but I've got to try."

"And if nothing turns up?"

I shook my head. "Guess I'll have to go back to shipping out on ore freighters." I said this with far greater ease and calm than I really felt. I had set my heart on working on a newspaper and eventually becoming a foreign correspondent. I yearned to get into newspaper work with a quiet desperation, but even though the

Depression had lost some of its rigor I was aware that unemployment was still rampant and jobs scarce. Looking back, I realize that my notions about newspaper work and the life of a foreign correspondent were romantic almost to absurdity, but at that time my vision was as fixed as a mariner's sextant on the North Star.

"Hmmm," was all Mit said. We walked along past Welborn Hall, the physical sciences building, and on up to the Angle Walk, the broad walkway that sliced across the campus on a diagonal. The Angle Walk was thronged with students strolling uptown in the sunny afternoon, seeking a coke or milkshake or some other diversion. On Spring Street, the main street of the village, several couples turned in to a squat building where a sign said "The Teepee." Passing it, I could hear the Campus Hawks, a student dance band, playing a passable rendition of Benny Goodman's arrangement of "Stompin' at the Savoy."

"I can't imagine going into that dark place to dance on a lovely afternoon like this," said Mit.

"Me neither."

In the center of the village was the town square with a large silver water tower in the middle; on one side stood the Post Office with the American flag waving gently in the breeze and on the other stood the Bedford Volunteer Fire Department. We stepped inside the musty smelling Post Office with its banks of gilt-numbered postal boxes, knurled knobs on their faces, and just before I slid the letters into the brass slot marked "Letters" Mit said, "Let me kiss them first for luck." She touched her lips to each envelope and muttered, "Luck."

"Can't miss now," I said.

Outside the Post Office we stood hesitating for a moment in the waning sunshine. Mit turned and said, "Instead of a milkshake, let's walk down to Buster's and have a toasted roll."

"Fine by me."

We passed the Village Rexall Drug Store, the Bedford Paint and Varnish Store, and the Odeon Movie Theater where signboards in blazing colors proclaimed that Katherine Hepburn and Cary Grant were starring in "Bringing Up Baby." Then, sauntering slowly down Spring Street under the newly budding maple trees with their faint new-shoot-green smell we passed the New England style cottage of the Alumni Center and the square white mansion of the University president.

"You know," Mit said as we walked along hand in hand, "I've been giving some thought to this upcoming Senior Ball. I hear Duke Ellington is playing. I believe I'll go."

I was slightly puzzled by this remark because I had assumed that Mit and I would go to the Ball together, but I decided to play along with her gambit, whatever it meant. "Oh, do you have a date?"

"Not yet."

"How can that be? How can a knock-out girl like you not have a date for the Senior Ball?"

"Simple. The dumb lug hasn't asked me."

Now I got it. "Well, Miss Daley, since *he* hasn't done right by you may *I* have the honor of escorting you to the Ball?"

"I'll give it some thought, Dumb Lug."

Buster's, the campus hang-out, was a dark room with wooden, high-back booths, and the specialty of the house was a toasted sweet roll. In the late afternoon, the place was packed with chattering students, trying to hear each other over the juke box booming with a Tommy Dorsey record, "Dipsy Doodle." Buster himself, a round little man whose large dark-rimmed glasses made him resemble a rotund owl, came up to us. "Hi, Brown. What'll you have?"

"Two toasted rolls, two small cokes."

Mit and I sat side by side in the high—backed wooden booth, waiting for our order. I took her hand

and held it with the back of my hand resting on her warm, firm thigh. "You know what we haven't talked about, Mit? We haven't talked about what *you* plan to do after graduation."

"Oh, well not much has been decided. My father thinks I ought to take a stenographic course and my mother thinks I ought to get married."

"*Married*! What a thought! Does your mother know you have a thing about 'being mauled.'?"

Mit snatched her hand out of mine and turned to me, gray eyes blazing. "*That*," she said, "is *not* funny! Not a damned *bit* funny." She glared at me for several long seconds.

I reached for her hand again and held it though it was clenched in a fist. "No," I said, "I think you're right. Just thoughtless. Said by a thoughtless, dumb lug."

Her stern look gradually softened and the edge of a smile gentled her mouth and eyes. "You nut," she softly said. "No wonder I like you."

Nine

Each day during the weeks when budding April ripened into blooming May, I anxiously scanned my mail slot in the letter box beside the front door of the Phi Delt house, hoping for a reply to my job applications. These were my last few weeks of classes and I was feeling some regret that I was soon to leave the company of my professors, thoughtful, learned men. At one of those last few classes, Howard Nicholas, my modern European history professor and one of my favorites, a brilliant lecturer, talked about the gathering forces of war in Europe, and I went straight from class to my desk at *The Student Record* and wrote an editorial, ripe with rhetoric like "the mad dance of alliances" and "the flames of armed conflict," predicting that war would come "within the next several years. But come it will!" The words were accurate enough in expressing my newly acquired intellectual conviction but they fell far, far short of expressing any realistic understanding of what the oncoming terrible war would mean, and eventually did mean, to the world and to me and my life.

And then one day I found in my mail slot an envelope headed "*The Cincinnati Enquirer.*" I ripped it open and found nothing but disappointment inside. The killing words were: "thanks for your interest" and "no vacancies at this time." But Mit Daley, when I told her, was full of optimism. "One down," she said. "but still two to go. One of them is *certain* to say yes, so your chances are 50-50."

"Interesting statistical theory," I said.

"Not statistics. Woman's intuition. Known since the dawn of time to be infallible."

It was another week before the next shoe dropped, this time a letter from *The Columbus Dispatch*. The words were not quite the same as those in the *Enquirer* letter but the message was identical: no. "Good," said Mit. "That leaves just *The Denton Daily News* and that's where you wanted to go all along."

"You know," I said, "without the support of your infallible woman's intuition I probably would be discouraged by now."

"Wait and see."

"Well, while I'm waiting, the guys at the house are organizing a beer picnic Saturday afternoon. How about our joining in?"

"Sounds swell."

Beer picnics had become a springtime tradition at Maumee after President Roosevelt ended prohibition in 1933. In fact, picnics of whatever kind had become a tradition on a campus which was bounded on two sides by open meadows and gently flowing, shallow streams. The saying on the campus was, "All you need for a picnic is a blanket and a date." Mit and I had both as we gathered with ten other couples in a grassy meadow beside Tollander Creek where a keg of beer had been set up.

All afternoon the beer flowed freely from keg to paper cups to the mouths of the romping twenty-year olds. While the consumption of beer was steady, physical activity was equally so. Softball, boy-girl chases, splashing in the knee-deep water of the sandy-bottomed creek, wrestling on the soft meadow grass—all matched pace with intake and as a result inebriation never exceeded joyous hilarity. In the early dusk wood was gathered and fire lighted for grilling hot dogs. Along with potato chips they were washed down with more beer.

Then as dusk began to gather into night, the couples moved apart and sat or lay together on the blankets. Lying beside Mit, holding her hand in mine, and gazing up through the small-leaved branches of an overhanging tree at stars just beginning to glimmer in the darkening sky, I thought about my fraternity brothers nearby and the girls they were lying with. Off to the right, Harry Baker and his Mary June were a dedicated couple, as near to being married as their present status would permit, but, I suspected, entirely chaste. They were too pious about their relationship and the sanctity of marriage to be otherwise. There were other dedicated couples, who I suspected though I was never told so, were not always as abstemious as Harry and Mary June, feeling that their commitment to one another gave sanction to full intimacy. Jeff Letvold and Larry Whittaker, farther away, were in a different situation. They were with girls they dated casually and occasionally. What was going on under their blankets, I suspected, was an essentially good-humored contest between male and female in which he would make advances which she would accept or reject until together they reached the point where she would say, STOP. And he would stop—at least on that occasion. Still farther away, in isolation from the group, was Jimmy Tate, star halfback of the champion Maumee football team, lying with Mary Lou Betters, and what went on under their blanket, I was pretty certain, was a little more earthy. Mary Lou, sultry eyed and a ripe beauty, had the reputation of a girl who "could be had." She and Donna Sanders were the only girls on campus I knew who had that reputation. And then, continuing the survey, were Mit and I whose sexual activities never progressed beyond some fairly active kissing. And this, I realized as I remembered the occasion years later, was probably a representative sample of sexual mores among college students in the 1930s. For most of us, the outer permissible limit was "heavy petting" and that line was established and maintained by the girl. To have sexual intercourse required, for most of my contemporaries, a prolonged and deep commitment, or what was known quaintly then as "being in love." *Quaint* is indeed the word as subsequent experience has taught me.

But on that evening, lying under the stars beside a handsome young woman, and given happy release from restraint by uncountable cups of beer, I began to emulate Jeff and Larry's amorous exploration. I turned to Mit and kissed her gently at first and then with mounting intensity. It seemed to me that Mit was accompanying me without restraint, and in that happy realization I moved my caressing hand from beside her face down across her shoulder and over her lovely rounded breast. In a flash she broke away and shoved me aside. "Don't *do* that!" she whispered fiercely.

I pulled up on one elbow, frustrated and irritated. "I know, I know," I said. "You *'won't be mauled!'*"

Mit sat up straight and faced me, her face angry in the twilight. "Listen to me, Dana Brown," she said in a low undertone. "You seem to think that that's some kind of a joke. Well, let me tell you once for all that it is *not*."

"Mit, I didn't mean—"

"I don't care what you meant. I want you to get this straight. I'm not a prude. Don't you *dare* think so! And I'm not cold and frigid. But I have a very deep reverence for love—*real* love. To me it's too sacred to play with. When I finally find real love—real, deep down love—then I will hold nothing back. I want very much to love someone passionately, love him with all my body and soul, but until that happens I'm going to wait." She stopped and gazed sternly at me in the near darkness. Then she got to her feet. "Let's go home. I've had enough beer." I got up and threw the blanket over my arm. We walked silently up the leaf-canopied street toward her dormitory and before we got there she let me take her hand in mine. At the door she turned and said, "Goodnight, you dumb lug." and pecked me on the cheek.

During the week after the beer picnic I followed Mit's advice to wait for good news from *The Denton Daily News*—what choice did I have?—but one day my anxious survey of my mail slot turned up not a letter from the *Daily News* but a great surprise, in fact a shocker—a letter from Sally O'Shaugnessy. We had broken up "finally" six months earlier after a bitter argument about Sally's relationship with Judson Graver. But there on a small envelope faintly carrying Sally's scent was the familiar, dainty hand-writing, and my heart defied my head by skipping a beat. My head had said, "What the hell does *she* want?" but my heart said, "It's from Sally! *Sally*!"

An impartial reader would never gather from Sally's letter that there had ever been a breach between us. "Dearest, darling Dana," it began and went on conveying tenderness and longing with every sentence. The business part of the letter came toward the end. "My sister, Jeanne, has a date for your Senior Ball and plans to drive down from Denton. I could come with her if you asked me, dearest Dana, so please, please, *please* do! You mean everything in the world to me, Dana, and I can't wait to be in your arms again and tell you so with all my heart and soul."

I looked up from the letter and stared out the window while a storm of turmoil began to rage inside. The forces of bitter experience and good sense arrayed themselves against fond nostalgia and reawakened affection and they fought a battle that went on all the rest of that day, most of the night, and for several more days until both sides were exhausted. Then a truce was declared and a negotiator named Rationalization undertook to deal with the dispute. The central question, whether or not to invite Sally to come, was difficult enough in its own right but it was complicated further by my having already asked Mit Daley to be my date for the Ball. To that clever fellow, Rationalization, however, this was scarcely an impediment. "Go ahead, invite Sally down," he counselled. "It will be fun to be with her again and what harm can it do? As for Mit, make it a double date and get one of your fraternity brothers to be her partner."

"Done," I said to myself, and the next time Mit and I were together I tried it out on her. I knew Mit to be a calm, sensible girl and I expected no problem. I found the part where I explained why I was inviting Sally down for the Ball fairly heavy going but then I rounded the bend and set sail for home with the plan for making the occasion a double date and getting Mit a date with someone else. When I finished there was a long, long silence. I looked at Mit and she was staring at the table in Buster's booth. I waited while the silence lengthened further and then Mit turned and looked at me, her face wearing an expression I had never before seen and could not quite decipher. It seemed to be a mixture of several emotions but when she spoke her voice was calm and low. "I don't know whether to pity you or despise you," she said. "You have a disease, Dana, and it seems to be incurable."

"But Mit," I protested, "it's just for one night and we will all be together."

She shook her head gently. "Wrong," she said. "It will not be one night or *any* night." Her gray eyes were unsmiling. "And now, if you will please let me out, I must get back to my room to study."

"Mit!" I said. "Please think it over."

She smiled wryly. "I don't need to think it over. You've made everything perfectly clear. Let me out, please. And by the way, I can't keep our date for Friday. I have an exam Saturday."

I slowly slid out of the booth and let her pass. She looked at me calmly and then turned and walked away. "Goodbye, Dana," she said. "I'll see you around."

Ten

Living with myself for the next week or so was hard. Waves of regret and spasms of self-righteous irritation washed alternately over me each day. Sitting in Professor St. James' class as he droned away on British constitutional history, Mit's face would suddenly emerge behind my eyes, wearing a mixed and indecipherable expression. It was the signature of that moment when I had told her Sally was coming to the Senior Ball, and it released a wounding sense of personal failure. Then, later, in my next class, while Professor Joseph Knight read with appropriately martial passion Othello's brusk command to Desdemona's angry father and his armed supporters, "Keep up your bright swords, for the dew will rust them!", I would suddenly recall how reasonable it had all seemed as I explained the situation to Mit. Had I not made a reasonable proposal, one that would accommodate both Sally and Mit? And then indignant irritation would surface. Why was Mit being so unreasonable? Was what I suggested so unfair to ask of a *friend*? Did Mit have any stronger claim on me than *friend*? But indignation, unlike remorse, was a hollow commodity, compounded of reaction not substance, and its more powerful counterpart soon took charge.

One day during those trying weeks a letter from *The Denton Daily News* appeared in my mail slot. With mixed hope and apprehension I tore the envelope open and read, "Although we have no immediate opening, one may occur during the course of the year. We would like to interview you and discuss the prospects." Not a clear-cut victory, I told myself, but still not a defeat. Whether or not I would have to ship out on an ore freighter next summer was a decision to be deferred.

Later that day, I passed Mit on the Angle Walk between classes. "Hey, Mit, I got that letter from *The Denton Daily News*. You were right. Woman's intuition scores again."

She stopped, her mouth wearing a thin smile which her eyes did not share. "Good, Dana. I'm glad for you." But that was all she said. She turned and walked on, leaving me watching her proud-backed figure disappear amidst the throng of between-class students.

The Saturday of the Senior Ball arrived at last. On that day I was sitting at lunch alongside Mrs. Lunday, the white-haired and kindly house mother of Phi Delta Theta, when one of the freshman pledges tapped me on the shoulder. "Telephone call for you." I took the call upstairs at the house telephone in the front entrance and through the receiver bubbled Sally, a joy-voiced, super-animated Sally. "Dana. I'm here, Dana, I'm *here*!"

Still chewing on a slightly stringy morsel of cold roast beef, I said, "Fine. Where are you?"

"With my sister's friend, here at Philby Hall. I've got the family car. When can I pick you up?"

"We've got a house meeting this afternoon, officer's elections. So tonight about 8."

"Not till then?"

"Afraid not."

Now the voice was pouty. "That's lousy, Dana. I've come all this way—"

The reaction still brewing within me from the hurtful incident with Mit had armored me somewhat against Sally's wiles and that, combined with a dim feeling that Sally was to blame for the misunderstanding, gave me the assurance to say firmly, "That's the best I can do."

The telephone was silent for a moment and I could almost hear the little wheels revolving in Sally's mind. Then she said, "See you tonight at 8."

That evening the fraternity house was jumping with Prom night anticipation. One or two more worldly brothers were having a drink in their room, usually a gin-and-ginger-ale Tom Collins with a slice of lemon, and the festive, let's-have-a-party smell of fresh-cut lemon and gin perfumed the hallways. Other guys were standing before the washroom sinks, wearing only their skivvies, as they shaved their cheeks and chins close in anticipation of some end-of-the-dance smooching, while behind them showers hissed and steamed against young male bodies. Tom Bingham wandered up and down the hallway, pantless and wearing his stiff-fronted tux shirt, looking for someone to tie his black bow tie.

About 8, dressed and ready and feeling a little sullen, I went out onto the front porch to wait for Sally. It was a soft May night, gently scented with fragrance from the candle-blossomed horse chestnut trees lining the front sidewalk. Sally was uncharacteristically punctual and soon I saw the O'Shaugnessy family car, a big black Oldsmobile, stop at the front curb. I opened the car door and as I did the Sally magic engulfed me in a rush. She was wearing a white, tiny-pleated evening gown cinched with a gold belt, and her joyous smile was ravishing. "Dana! Darling Dana!" I slid into the seat and soon had her in my arms, close, soft, and clinging. She kissed me with an abandon that overwhelmed all my reservations and drowned my determination to stand off. Sally was back. She was mine.

We parked the car in front of Winston Hall, the new men's gymnasium, and walked through the open doors into the enormous hall where the Ball was in full cry.

Duke Ellington's sixteen piece orchestra, resplendent on the raised dais in tuxedos, was playing a medium tempo piece, the saxophone section sounding rich and creamy. I took Sally in my arms and we danced out into the middle of the swaying crowd. I was in bliss but I soon became aware that Sally was tense, supercharged and tense. We said little but I could feel the rigidity and tension through the palm of my hand on her back. We paused for a moment while the piece ended, and then Duke, foot stomping to set the rhythm, led off an upbeat, fast number. After a half dozen steps, Sally pushed back. "I don't want to dance to this, Dana. Let's go out to the car for a while and talk."

I agreed and soon we were in the wide back seat of the big Oldsmobile but we did not talk. Just as I closed the car door behind me Sally reached her hand behind my head and pulled my mouth down to hers which was open and caressing. From then on, things moved very fast. Sally was passionate, almost frantic it seemed, and soon she was lying down across the seat and pulling me down onto her, murmuring and panting. I was swept away myself at first, my conscious mind on the verge of submerging itself in waves of blind, joyous sensation, but then some part of me began to wonder and to question. Beneath me I suddenly realized Sally's long dress was above her hips and she was writhing as her hands were busily pulling down whatever she was wearing underneath. The frantic pace, the frenzy, the writhing and panting were all too much—they were unreal—and suddenly the questions in my mind quenched the passion and took charge. "Sally, what's happening here?"

"Oh, Dana," she moaned. "Take me, Dana. Take me!" She pulled hard against my shoulders and tried to kiss me again.

"No, Sally, wait. Wait. I don't understand. Why are you so frantic?"

Suddenly she was still. She turned her face toward

the back of the seat, and in a moment I realized she was crying. There was a long moment of bewildered silence for me. Finally, Sally sat up slowly and pulled her clothes together. Then she reached out and came sobbing into my arms. "Oh, Dana, I'm so unhappy, so scared. I'm so scared."

"Scared?"

She nodded her head against my shoulder. Then, after a pause she said, "I'm afraid I may be pregnant. I'm two weeks late with the curse."

"*Pregnant*! My God! But—" The questions now whirling in my mind were too many to give voice to. If Sally thought she was pregnant, then why—?

"It's Judson," she said in a low voice. "We got careless, and I'm afraid it happened."

This baffled me even more. "But if it's Judson, what does *he* say? What is he going to do about it?"

She shook her head against my shoulder. In a voice so low I could scarcely hear her, she said, "Nothing. He laughs and shrugs his shoulders. He says it's *my* problem."

I thought about this for a moment as the meaning of it all began to take shape. "And so you came to me."

She nodded and snuggled closer against me. "Yes, Dana. You've always been so good to me."

And those words suddenly clarified for me the whole carefully contrived arrangement—the wangled invitation to the Senior Ball and the passionate love-making in the car. If Sally's pre-arranged scenario had played out to the climax she had in mind, then I, not Judson, could be made to bear the responsibility for her pregnancy. I would have had no way of knowing otherwise. And Sally knew, knowing me, that I would accept that responsibility regardless of the wreckage it might make of all my plans for the future.

All of a sudden, I was flaming mad, deeply angry. I shoved Sally away and got out of the car, slamming the door behind me. I was so angry, so shaken with rage down to my shoe-tops, that I did not know how to express it. I thrashed back and forth beside the car, cursing with all the vehemence and variety I had learned aboard Great Lakes ore freighters. In the midst of this explosion of rage I suddenly thought of Mit Daley—wholesome, clear-eyed, endearing Mit, whom I had hurt and alienated for the sake of *this*! That deepened the anger further, and I turned away and started to walk back to the fraternity house.

Then I heard the car door open and Sally cry, "Dana!"

I stopped.

"*Dana*!"

I could hear genuine heartbreak in that cry, heartbreak and total abandonment. It touched an old chord. Sally *did* need help. I turned back but before I reached the car anger had taken charge once again. "Listen, Sally, *listen* to me! I'm sorry you're in the mess you're in, but I will never, *never* forgive you for what you tried to do to me tonight. *Never*!"

"Dana, please don't say that. I *need* you. I *need* your help."

"Listen, Sally, you"—I hesitated a second before saying the word I had never previously thought I could ever apply to Sally—"you *bitch*. You *could* have had my help. All you had to do was ask. I would have found some way to help you. But instead you tried to be clever; you tried to trick me. Well. *That* does it. As far as I am concerned you can go to hell and you can rot there!"

Sally stiffened, a small, defiant figure standing beside the black car in her white evening gown, "You can go to hell yourself, you damned holier-than-thou Boy Scout. I don't need you or your goddamned help. And don't worry, you never *will* see me again!"

She got in the car and drove off, tires screeching as she flipped around in the parking lot. I walked slowly back to the fraternity house, my anger slowly ebbing.

Of course, as it turned out, neither Sally's retort nor

my angry speech stood the test of time. My anger eventually dissipated as my life moved on, and it finally became so faint that affectionate nostalgia had taken its place by the time I saw Sally again three years later on Pearl Harbor day, 7 December 1941. Sometime after that night of the Senior Ball—I can not remember when or how—I learned that Sally's feared pregnancy was a false alarm. That should not have had any effect on my harrowing feeling of betrayal but I must admit that somehow it lessened it.

After the Senior Ball the rest of the college year moved to a stately close: final examinations, Commencement Day with its black academic gowns, Wagnerian marching music, and long advisory speeches, and regretful farewells to professors and student friends. Mit Daley gave me a quick handshake and a cool smile and was gone, taking with her some of the deepest regret I have ever known.

My interview with Walt Murphy at the *Denton Daily News* turned out to be unexpectedly positive. Two weeks after graduation I was a fully installed cub reporter, a *professional* newspaper man, with a salary of $25 a week. Looking back over the slogging, grinding days I had endured to get there—the back-aching hours in the firehold of *Samuel F. B. Morse*, the episodes of high danger on *Maunaloa*, the midnight-to-early-morning hours spent at The Bedford Press to win the editorship of *The Student Record*—I had a feeling of final achievement. I had made it. Now my life could assume its lasting shape.

Eleven

Three years had passed. For three years I had served Walt Murphy's bidding when he told me I was going to Washington as special correspondent for *The Denton Daily News*. Now one week later, I had arrived and Washington overawed me at first glance. I had taken the Big Four to Cincinnati where I transferred to the Chesapeake and Ohio. I watched out the soot-and-rain-streaked window as the broad, muddy water of the Ohio River rushed past and then gazed as dusk fell on the forests and gorges of West Virginia. I had a dinner of liver and onions in the dining car and then fell asleep in my berth with Hemingway's *For Whom the Bell Tolls* on my chest.

Next morning, after the train had glided to a stop, Ben, the smooth-skinned black porter, brushed me down with deft strokes of his big whisk-broom and handed me my Gladstone bag as I swung down off the Pullman car steps. I had tipped him the obligatory quarter, walked through the marble grandeur of the Union Station's enormous waiting room, and there, rising in imperial splendor just across an avenue and beyond an expanse of trees and green grass, was the great glistening white dome of the United States Capitol. Its visual splendor so far exceeded the images I had previously seen on postcards and movie newsreels that I gasped. Still gawking, I accepted the bid of the nearest taxi driver and said, "The YMCA."

The ride up Constitution Avenue, past the white-fronted classical buildings with the red brick castle of The Smithsonian Institute looming through the trees across the Mall to my left, only added to the spell the noble city was casting upon me. I caught a fleeting glimpse of the White House as we went up 17th Street alongside the intricately facaded State Department and then turned left into F Street and pulled up before the YMCA where I found a closet-sized room with a linoleum-covered floor and a metal-framed bed.

The first press conference I attended in the State Department auditorium did nothing to diminish my feeling of insignificance in the presence of so much national grandeur. From my seat well back and to one side I could see and recognize the giants of the press and radio: Walter Lippman, Westbrook Pegler, Elmer Davis, Hans Kaltenborn, Lowell Thomas. None of these luminaries, I felt certain, would have the slightest interest in meeting the newest member of the Washington press corps, the correspondent for *The Denton Daily News*. I listened in a kind of daze to the presentation of the State Department spokesman and the later rapid-fire questions from the press. I made several notes, which I later found indecipherable, and then watched, after the press conference ended, as the several press stars were escorted by the State Department spokesman to his office for what I supposed were "off-the-record" discussions. In my befuddled state I had recorded nothing newsworthy, nothing to put on the wire for Walt Murphy, so finally in desperation I picked the Associated Press account off the ticker and paraphrased it before turning it over to Western Union for transmission to Denton. If my first day as special correspondent was any measure of what was to follow, it was clear that I was not going to be a success.

And indeed, as the days passed and my frustration mounted, the fact became ever clearer. I could attend the daily briefings along with the rest of the press corps, and I could write an accurate account of it, but what I wrote was essentially the same as the Associated Press or United Press story and could as well have been written at my desk at my home office. What I lacked was contacts among top officials and the access to establish those contacts. I was uncertain what to do about it. I did not want to admit defeat but I certainly could not continue as I was for long. Besides, I was deeply lonely and the narrow, linoleum-floored YMCA room offered no solace.

And then I met by chance two men out of my past who did not solve my problem, at least not immediately, but did provide diversion. The first I met was Judson Graver and the second, who I encountered several days later, was my Maumee University modern European history professor, Howard Nicholas.

I was standing in line at the Pennsylvania Avenue branch of the Hamilton National Bank, waiting to cash my weekly pay check, when I noticed a familiar figure two places ahead of me. The back of the handsome, narrow head and the familiar set of the shoulders belonged to only one person out of my past: Judson Graver. When he finished his transaction and turned away from the teller's window, I reached out a hand as he passed. "Judson."

"Dana! My God, what are you doing here?"

My responses were a bit stiff and awkward—Judson and I had broken off contact three years back because of Sally O'Shaugnessy—but Graver was his characteristic self, smooth and urbane. "Great to see you, fella. I'm in a terrible rush right now but we must get together. Here's my card. Call my office and we'll set up a date." With a parting pat on the shoulder he was off.

My initial impulse was not to call him but loneliness finally won out. Using the pay phone in the hallway of the YMCA I called the office of "Caleb Jones Associates,

Public Relations Specialists, Judson Graver, Representative." A crisp-voiced female answered and I asked for Judson. "Mr. Graver is in conference just now but if you will leave your number I will arrange for him to call back."

I said I would call again and hung up. It took three tries but at last I got Judson to answer. "Hey, fella, It's great to hear your voice! How about dinner sometime? How about next Tuesday?"

"Okay."

"Great! I'll meet you at the Iron Gate on N Street at 6:30."

"The Iron Gate?"

"Yes, it's a restaurant on N Street, east of Connecticut. Okay?"

"Fine."

The slight pleasurable anticipation I had for seeing Judson again—it was nine-tenths curiosity—had wilted substantially by 6:30 Tuesday but I arrived on time at the Iron Gate, a grotto-like restaurant with amber lights along the walls and heavy, dark-wooded tables. Judson was fifteen minutes late but he came up to me, hand outstretched and emitting gracious charm. "How great to see you, old friend. Tell me what brings you to Washington?"

I explained my special correspondent status with the *Denton Daily News*.

"Denton. How is the old dump? I left for New York right after college and I've never gone back."

"About the same. Changed some by the war—busier. But what about you? What's this 'public relations' thing?"

"Caleb Jones. We met in the magazine trade in New York. There's a guy that can spot a fresh angle faster than anyone I ever knew, and he saw as soon as Roosevelt declared war that a zillion manufacturers and distributors of military supplies would be trying to get the attention of officials in Washington. So we set ourselves up here, and that's what we do."

"How's it working out?"

"Fabulous. The money's rolling in by the bagful. Hey, Dane, maybe you ought to drop that low-paying newspaper job and join us."

I looked at him speculatively. At the moment, anything besides special correspondenting looked attractive, but there was a lot of bad history between Judson and me and most important there was Sally.

"I'll give it some thought." By that time we had ordered, and I was making strong headway with Swiss steak and mashed potatoes. After a while I looked up and asked, "What do you hear from Sally?"

He almost permitted surprise to surface on his face. "O'Shaugnessy? Nothing. Why do you ask?"

"Why not? The last I heard you and Sally were—"

"Oh, that! Oh, no, that's all over."

"Over?"

He looked at me a little suspiciously. "Sure. Over." He lit a cigarette and looked off into space. "You know, Sally's not a bad kid. We've had a lot of fun together, and I know you have too. I'll say this for her, she's a hot little piece. Stroke her once or twice on the box and she's hot to trot. But, hell, I'm not telling you anything. Didn't she come out to Denton last year to see you? You must've gotten some of that good nooky then."

I said nothing but my memory suddenly unreeled an image of me scurrying out of the bed, leaving Sally waiting and untouched, as the announcer broke into the Philharmonic broadcast with the stunning news of Pearl Harbor.

"But she's so goddamned possessive. Didn't you find that so?"

This was becoming a little too much. The implicit suggestion that we were two guys mutually recalling previous flings with the same woman rubbed me the wrong way. Graver's relationship with Sally and mine were poles apart in every respect. It grated on me to have him imply they were comparable. "Can't say that I did."

"Hmmh. Well, I sure as hell did. God, she clung to me like a leech. I finally had to brush her off. Tell her to get lost. Kind of tough to do since she was such a great lay."

Ambiguous as my current feelings about Sally were, this was finally more than I could take. I put my napkin down and stared hard at the table, frowning. "Maybe I'd better be going."

Now Judson *was* surprised. "Hey, what's the problem, old friend? Did I say something wrong? You're not still crazy about that babe, are you?"

The question was a stumper. The correct answer was yes-and-no. Alternatively, Mit Daley had said I had an incurable disease. But neither of these was an answer I could make to Judson. "Let's just say I find the subject disagreeable."

"Okay, we'll drop it. But Jesus, Dane, I don't understand how you can still hang on to these romantic ideas about women. They're all the same, man. They're all leaky bags with all their brains in that furrow between their legs. Pat them once or twice on the ass and they'll screw you, the guy next door, or the garbage man. Sit down, fella, and have some coffee."

I looked across the table at my great friend of high school days, his handsome, boyish face wearing a cynical smile, his eyes hooded and weary, and suddenly I seemed to see through the facade into a shallow, mannered immaturity. Even Judson's good looks seemed superficial, a mannequin-like glossy surface over a trivial interior. It was a startling revelation. I suddenly felt immeasurably older than Judson. I might not be fully mature by any standard but I knew I was farther down that path than he. And I knew then, sitting in the semi-darkness of the Iron Gate restaurant on N Street in Washington, hundreds of miles and thousands of hours from Stowell High School in Denton, Ohio, that—lonely or not and friendless or not—I had no further need for Judson Graver. I had outgrown him.

I got to my feet. "I've really got to go. I'll probably see you around." And I walked out the door of the Iron Gate into the fading twilight.

The warmth of Professor Nicholas' response to my greeting took me by surprise. He was one of my favorite teachers at Maumee, to be sure, but I had never seen him socially outside the classroom. I had spotted his short somewhat round figure trudging energetically toward me in the corridor of the State Department. I reached out a hand to touch his arm. "Professor Nicholas."

He stopped and wheeled around, peering at me through his horn-rimmed glasses. "Brown!" he said. "Dana, isn't it? That's it. Dana Brown. You were in that wonderful class with Phil Cronsky and Dick Blaisinger. Sure, I remember. We used to have some rousing discussions."

"It's good to see you, sir. A familiar face."

"Same here. But what brings you to Washington?"

"I'm special correspondent for the *Denton Daily News*."

"Say, that's great!"

"Well, uh—"

He cocked his head like a terrier. "Oh, *not* so great?"

"Not so far. I'm having trouble making contacts."

He frowned, brown eyes peering at me earnestly. "Umm. Look, Brown—Dana. I'm already late for a meeting." He took a card out of his pocket and wrote a number on it. "Call me this afternoon and we'll get together."

That evening we had dinner at a brightly lighted cafeteria on Pennsylvania Avenue, a block from the White House. I had loaded my aluminum tray with baked hash and poached egg with peaches for dessert. The professor, I noted, was nourishing his roundish figure with hamburger steak, mashed potatoes, and cherry pie a la mode. After a few eager bites he plunged into conversation. "You say you're having trouble making contacts for news sources. Is that it?"

I pushed a lump of hash to one side of my mouth with my tongue. "Yes, that's it. But there's more to it than that."

"Oh?"

I swallowed the lump. "I guess I'm not really convinced there's a real job here. I'm not certain that the *News needs* a special correspondent in Washington."

"Isn't it a sort of prestige thing?"

"Exactly. And if that's what it mainly is, then I'm just a figurehead. I'm not contributing anything that the wire services have not already provided."

Professor Nicholas nodded and continued to make heroic headway through the hamburger and mashed potatoes. "Leaves you feeling rather useless."

"That's right." Conversation lapsed between us while we worked our way through our meals. I began to wish I had picked up a cup of coffee.

"You know, Dana, there are a lot of interesting things going on just now in this town. Some that might interest you. Would you consider taking a leave of absence from your paper and doing something in the war effort?"

"I might. Depends."

My companion moved his plate aside and addressed the bright red pie with its crown of melting ice cream. "I have a friend I met while I was in graduate school at Harvard, fellow I tutored. He's helping to set up a new organization which will work primarily overseas. That's all I can tell you, but why don't you go see him?"

The next afternoon, after filing my re-write of the AP story, I walked west on E Street to 26th Street and found the address I had written down, It looked from the outside to be some sort of arena or skating rink, but at the doorway was an armed, uniformed guard and beyond him was a pleasant-faced receptionist, a woman of 45 or so. I gave her the name Professor Nicholas had provided and shortly a very tall man about my age with deep-set blue eyes came striding toward me. "Dana Brown? Come on in. Come in to our palatial quarters."

The ensuing interview took place at Mercer Radcliffe's small, battered desk amidst a sea of equally battered desks in the large open arena—it *had* been a skating rink. Telephones jangled and typewriters clacked on every side, but Radcliffe was as urbane and undistracted as though he were occupying a deep pile carpeted office in the Chrysler Building in Manhattan. He was also friendly and jovial. "Before we get down to business, let me tell you a cute story I heard at lunch today." He reached over and patted my knee. "This Catholic priest, you see, was late for his appointment, and he wanted to telephone ahead and say he was coming. There was a telephone booth on the street corner there but all the priest had in change was a dime and he needed a nickel. He saw people coming and going from a nearby house, so he assumed it must be a place of business. It *was*. It was a cat house. So he walked in the door and there facing him were three of the buxom girls, naked to the waist. The madame of the house came running up and said, 'Oh, Father, you should not be in a place like this!' 'Oh, that's all right, my dear' he said, 'doesn't bother me a bit. If you'll just give me two nipples for this dime I'll be on my way.'" And Radcliffe slapped his knee and threw himself back in his chair with a loud guffaw.

Then he leaned forward with an engaging smile and said, "Well, Mr. Brown, this is the Office of Special Services, and we're selecting people for a variety of overseas posts. Tell me about yourself."

Twelve

In the middle of a warm, comforting dream, a hissing in my left ear scissored through and split the dream into fragments. I groped my way to wakefulness and the hissing in my ear became "Sah'ib! Sah'ib!" In the smothering darkness I became aware of a black Tamil face close to mine. The mouth was saying, "Wake up, Sah'ib. Wake up. It's five o'clock." With this, my mind fled the scene of my lovely dream, the Maumee University campus, and resumed its workaday presence in Kandy, Ceylon. I had been dreaming that some misfortune had sidelined the editor of the University student newspaper, *The Student Record*, and the president of Maumee was begging me to return to the job of editor I had held as a senior and take over the paper for the remainder of the college year. Just as I was accepting this proposal with unalloyed joy, the bearer at the Transient Quarters of the Office of Special Services in Kandy had yanked me awake and back into Ceylon and the middle of World War II.

"*Tikay, tikay,*" I mumbled. "*Tikay*" was the word I had learned to indicate assent to Badam, my bearer in New Delhi, and I assumed it would do in Ceylon as well.

"Five o'clock," the Tamil repeated. "Train leave at six, Sah'ib."

I crawled out of bed and stumbled down the dimly lighted hallway to the latrine. There by the light of a 25-watt bulb hung next to the fifteen foot ceiling I sloshed some tepid water on my face. Shaving in that dimness would be hazardous, I decided, so I brushed my teeth in more tepid water and went back to the bedroom and got dressed.

A staff car delivered me to the Kandy railway station, a square, white building with its two yellow-lighted, grimy windows glimmering in the warm, enveloping darkness. Despite the pre-dawn hour, the station was teeming with people. Whole families of eight or ten squatted on their heels or sat cross-legged in circles around mounds of baggage, piles of blankets, thread-bare carpets, cooking pots, water jugs and miscellaneous bundles of indecipherable shapes. The air was thick with a rank smell compounded of cheap tobacco, aspirated garlic, curry and cumin, commingled with the fragrance of well-seasoned sweat-saturated clothes. The shrilling of several babies crying in acute disharmony bounced off the high ceiling.

I had only recently learned what lay behind this extraordinary scene, this assemblage of people in this unlikely place in the waning night hours. It was simply that in a land where Time flows so slowly and so uncertainly as to be almost indiscernible, the gentle and patient people—such as these travellers in the Kandy railway station—make their way to the Place Where The Train Stops, well in advance, sometimes several days even, and patiently await its coming. They make the railway station their village and cook, eat, and sleep within its walls until The Train arrives.

So densely covered was the station floor with bundles and bodies that I picked my way to the ticket counter with considerable difficulty, unavoidably nudging several backs with my knees. "Second class compartment to Colombo," I said to the bespectacled clerk behind the brass bars.

I shared my compartment in the second-class coach

with a saffron-robed Buddhist monk, a slender dusky young man who kept his eyes meekly fastened upon the floor. Promptly at six there was wild shouting on the station platform and then with a massive jerk the train began its eighty mile journey down from the mountain slopes of Kandy to the shores of the Indian Ocean at Colombo. The light on the ancient landscape gradually shifted from black into a thin grey and then a wan yellow. Off to the left the mountain-sides lifted toward the pale lemon sky, their slopes latticed with layer upon layer of intricate terracing, tangible remains of the labor and sweat of generations and generations of mankind.

As the train jolted and swayed along at its modest twenty-five or thirty mile per hour pace, I reflected upon the cosmic change my life had undergone in the past six months. Six months before I was sitting in Mercer Radcliffe's office in the one-time skating rink on 26th Street beside the Potomac River, and now I was—of all places on God's green earth—riding in a Ceylonese train bound for Colombo and on to my current residence in New Delhi. No one could be more surprised than I, and no one, at least at the moment, more content.

Elbow on the thin ledge beside the dirt-streaked window, while my eyes gazed unseeingly at the exotic countryside slowly swimming by, my mind wandered back to my broken dream of returning to edit my college newspaper. The warm glow of pleasure I had felt was almost palpable, and I wondered why. What was there about the prospect of returning to Maumee and *The Student Record* that was so pleasing, so fulfilling? But before the answer came, if one indeed existed, the sliding door into the passageway screeched open, and a severely officious conductor in a dark blue uniform barked, "Your tickets, Sah'ib." He examined my ticket so suspiciously and minutely that I thought he might be about to refuse it, but at last he gave it a vicious punch with his nickel-plated tool and handed it back.

"What time does the train arrive in Colombo?" I asked.

Grudgingly, tight-lipped, he said, "Ten ten a.m."

Over four hours to cover eighty miles! But I made no comment. I recalled the parting advice of Paul Matteson, chief of the South Asia Division of Special Services in Washington. He had grown up in India as the son of missionary parents and was saturated with knowledge of the alien ways of the sub-continent. "Everything out there takes at least twice as long, and sometimes three or four times as long, as you think it should. The worst thing you can do, both for the situation and your own peace of mind is to become impatient or, far worse, *show* your impatience. Then everything will grind to a halt while the people you are dealing with will smile gently and reassuringly and say with perfect innocence, "Soon coming, Sah'ib. Soon coming."

I had been sent to Matteson by Mercer Radcliffe, the personnel man I had first interviewed, when my previous orders for a post in London were abruptly cancelled. "Sorry, old fella," said Radcliffe, "but we've got this top priority request for a liaison officer with the British Viceroy's staff in New Delhi and you're the nearest warm body."

"Liaison officer?" I asked. "What does a liaison officer do?"

"Search me. But I reckon you'll find out soon enough. Besides, you'll love India. I understand those dusky Indian dancing girls, with bangles on their ankles, are something special. Even their wiggles have wiggles." He grinned reassuringly. "That reminds of a cute story about dancing girls." While he was telling that and two other innocently bawdy stories, I was trying to master my dismay at the thought of going to India. Virtually all I knew about that country I had learned from reading Katherine Mayo's *Mother India*. Her depiction of the filth and poverty and degradation were stomach-turning. But Radcliffe had made it clear the choice was no longer mine so I had braced myself for a grim time in a sordid land.

The trip out in the bowels of a troop ship was probably, I thought at the time, perfect preparation for life in over-populated India, but that thought did nothing to relieve the acute discomfort of living with 2000 men, packed like cattle in a slow-moving ship. But then, to my surprise, my first impressions of India, as seen from the bus that took me to my billet at the cantonment of the Allied Southeast Asia Supreme Command, were delightful. It was a brilliantly sunny day in early November, the air light and dry, and the broad boulevards we travelled were edged with massive beds of bright flowers. The people I saw on the streets, riding bicycles or strolling along, wore clothes nearly as bright as the flowers—pinks, purples, greens, yellows and oranges. And there were no dense crowds, no teeming masses, but instead a flow of traffic not unlike Pennsylvania Avenue in Washington. These initial impressions were modified on by later experience, to be sure, but on the whole I had found India, and New Delhi in particular, a pleasant surprise.

The tedium of the four hour journey from Kandy to Colombo was relieved by the fascination I found in the exotic landscape swimming slowly by, and at last the train pulled to a stop at the Colombo station. I selected a pedicab from amongst a crowd of clamoring pedicab drivers and said, "To the airport." To my surprise a Delhi-bound military transport was loading as I arrived, and within minutes I was airborne and returning to my post as Special Services liaison officer with the Viceregal Council for External Affairs. I had completed a two-day consultation in Kandy and was returning to New Delhi armed with new instructions.

Thirteen

Angus MacLeod, Chairman of the Viceroy's Council for External Affairs, his round face shaped by a short, pointed beard, focused his gaze on me across the large, open square of tables around which the members of the Council sat. He was wearing an expression of exaggerated resignation as he sighed and said, "I guess now we'll have to listen to the twanging of our American friend, Mr. Brown. Come now, Brown, tell us what word you bring from your masters in Kandy."

Angus and I had downed too many late night scotches together for me to be put down by this bit of British schoolboy ragging, and a glance at my fellow committee members, especially my good friend, Captain Monty Gilpin, Royal Navy, told me they found it more tiresome than amusing.

The Council was holding its weekly meeting in the high-ceilinged, open-windowed conference room of the Indian Parliament building standing in the center of the magnificent complex designed by Sir Frederic Luytens to proclaim the imperial majesty of the British Raj. Outside the windows the late January sunlight shone golden on the red sandstone walls, and the gentle, sunny fragrance of bougainvillea drifted into the room on a cool breeze.

Nearly a thousand miles from the savage jungle fighting in Burma, the work of the Council in this serene and majestic setting seemed academic and remote. I had joined the Office of Special Services with the expectation that I would be blowing up tunnels or bridges, like Hemingway's Robert Jordan, but instead I was serving my country in time of war by attending meetings.

Leaning forward in my chair, I responded to the chairman's cue. "I'm ready to report at any time about the plans of the Office of Special Services for a black propaganda operation against the Japanese in Burma."

Before MacLeod could speak, the British Army representative, Colonel Dalton Danders, banged his fist on the table and said, "For God's sake, Mr. Chairman, when are we going to stop fighting the war with words and paper? Why doesn't the American representative bring us word of some plans for real action, like blowing up a few bridges or an ammo dump or two? Let me ask the gentleman directly, when are you Americans going to give us some real help in this war instead of frigging around with your radios and leaflets?"

There was a sudden deep silence in the room while I stared at the scowling face of Colonel Danders, his black moustache a straight line above his set mouth and every line of his figure and his meticulously correct uniform declaring his Sandhurst training and tradition. I had some sympathy for his point of view, but I knew the other Council members were looking at me expectantly and I had to make some suitable response. Probably in an American committee meeting the chairman would at this point try to smooth the situation over, but the British style was to let the attacker and the attackee sort it out between themselves, especially, it seemed to me, when the attackee was an American. The next move was unavoidably mine, so after a pause, I said in a low voice while looking directly at the scowling colonel, "Colonel Danders, my Service stands ready to help in any way it can. If you have a specific request for a sabotage operation; or plans for any, I will rush them to my headquarters at once and demand a prompt reply."

Colonel Danders stared at me grimly for a moment but said nothing. In the momentary silence several chairs creaked as members leaned back, and Chairman MacLeod said cheerily, "There you are Dalton, a fair offer."

Danders grunted and leaned back, "Thank you, sir."

Angus MacLeod patted his broad hands on the table. "Well, now, Brown, about your black propaganda thing. We appreciate your giving us this information about the planned operation. I will give you a buzz in a day or two and we'll get together to prepare a minute for the Viceroy."

"Thank you, Mr. Chairman."

Since I was always the last to be called on, the meeting ended shortly after this. On the way out, Angus took me by the arm. "You handled Dalton just right, Dana. He's a good chap. Means well. Just gets carried away sometimes."

I restrained an impulse to quote my father's favorite maxim: "Hell, if a fellow don't mean well, he should be in jail. Just meaning well ain't good enough." Instead, I said. "I suppose you're right, Angus, but this is not the first time Danders has blasted the Americans."

"I know. I'll have a word with him. But don't let it upset you."

Outside in the corridor, Monty Gilpin, tall and striking in his Royal Navy white blouse, white shorts, white knee-length stockings, and white shoes, was waiting for me. "Well done, old boy. Well done. Handled that chap neatly. See here, I'm having a few people around for drinks this afternoon. How about joining us?"

"Fine. Love to."

"Good show. Shall we say six?"

"I'll be there."

Captain Gilpin stalked rapidly away, and I strolled slowly down the walkway. The sun was warm and caressing as it shone through the crisp, cool air of a late January morning. Once again I marvelled at the unexpected beauty of the New Delhi autumn and winter weather. Was this the scorching plain of India where British soldiers for over two centuries had perished in droves from the searing heat? I recalled the words of Paul Matteson, the missionary's son, who had briefed me in Washington on what to expect in India. "For six months of the year," he had said, "the weather in Delhi is the weather people go to southern California for. From October to March, sunshine all day every day and temperatures in the day ranging from 70 to 80 and at night from 40 to 50. And dry, dry, dry." At the time, I had not fully believed him, putting it down to the enthusiasm of an Indophile, but each passing day since my arrival had borne him out.

With my attendance at the morning Council meeting accomplished, I now had to decide how to spend the afternoon. On the desk at my cubicle in the Viceregal office building was a small stack of dispatches from Washington, especially one on communal unrest in Kashmir that I wanted to read. Alternatively, I could make my weekly rounds of calling on the officers I was detailed to liaise with. Better still, I could tell myself I was badly in need of exercise and see if I could work up a golf game with someone out at the magnificent course of the Delhi Golf Club. I had learned to play golf during the long, hot summers of my high school days, begging my mother for the one dollar greens fee that permitted me to play as many holes—18, 36, 54, or 72—of the Denton municipal course as my legs could stand. I had loved golf instantly, especially the aesthetics of the game: the beautiful sculpturing and manicuring of the terrain; the handsome, well-crafted equipment—the gleaming white, dimpled ball, the graceful wood clubs with their varnished, shapely heads, and the gleaming stainless steel irons, flanged and grooved. I had continued to play golf in college at Maumee despite my grinding work schedule, rising at six and getting out on the dew-drenched course in the dawning April and May mornings. So I was delighted to find available to me in India the Delhi course, set off to one side of the city. It was a long, testing course, dotted here and there with ruined tombs memorializing 14th century sultans, and inhabited in the scrubby brush beside the fairways by screeching peacocks and marauding, ball-snatching monkeys.

At lunch I spotted Ian Ainsley, a young British MI-5 officer standing in the mess line two men ahead of me. I had played in a foursome with Ian the week before, and had found him almost comically languid and affected. Still, he played a reasonable game of golf. I followed him with my tray to the long mess hall table and sat down on the bench beside him. "Hello, Ian. Any chance I can get you for a round of golf this afternoon?"

He swung around to survey me with his pale blue eyes. "Oh, hullo. *This* afternoon, old boy? Frightfully short notice, but let me give it a think." Long pause while he gazed at the ceiling with his index finger on his mouth, pointing at his nose. At last he turned to me. "Why, yes, I believe I can do that. Shall we say two? Have to have a bit of a lie-down after tiffin."

"Fine."

It was an idyllic afternoon, on the golf course, the air bright and crisp, the green grass glistening in the sunshine, the yellow flags on the greens stirring gently in the mild breeze. Ian and I had a fairly even match, seesawing back and forth in the lead most of the round. He got his par and beat me 1-up on the last hole, a defeat that irritated me just a little. His golf style was like his personality, a carefully contrived swing ending with his right toe pointing daintily at the ground. The ball flew straight but not far. My swing was flatter and looser, and the ball went fairly far but not always straight. To redeem an otherwise mediocre round that afternoon, I did have one good hole, the 425 yard seventh. I hit a long straight drive, the club head meeting the ball with one of those perfect impacts in the exact center of the sweet spot, so clean a contact that my hands felt no shock and the ball seemed almost to be swinging on the end of a string. My drive bounced to a stop a good 240 yards out, leaving about 185 yards to the flag. I took out my three wood, and miraculously, this hit was as clean as the one before. The ball lifted high into the blue sky, flying straight for the green. It landed softly on the front apron and rolled on toward the cup, stopping just ten inches short." Now *that*," I said to myself like every true golfer, "is my *real* game. This other stuff is just mistakes."

"Nice shot, old boy," said Ian as I tapped in for my birdie three. It was the only consolation I could later find after letting this affected Brit beat me on the last hole.

We walked together from the 18th green to the pleasant little clubhouse and had a watery beer at the bar. Afterward, we found a half dozen pedicabs waiting outside, their drivers waving their hands and bidding raucously for our custom. I motioned to one of them, a lanky, dark-skinned young man, and Ian and I climbed into the buggy-like vehicle for the ride back to the cantonment. "Enjoyed it muchly," Ian said as we parted, and, waving a languid hand of farewell, "must do it again."

I muttered, "Yeah," feeling not only disgruntled by the loss of the match to Ian but also carrying an unsettling sense that I had substantially frittered away a day in my life. I had acquired in college, when every waking minute in my jam-packed days had to be put to some positive purpose, the guiding principle that each day had to count for something. When I felt it did not, I was uneasy and discontented.

It was in that vaguely dissatisfied mood that, a little after six, I climbed the front steps of Monty Gilpin's low white house, its veranda fronted with a line of square white pillars. A soft yellow light gilded the leaves and branches of the jacaranda trees along the edge of the garden, and a half dozen mynah birds pranced about on the smooth green lawn looking for supper. While Monty was shaking my hand in welcome, I gazed down the length of the veranda through the throng of chattering people and there I saw, radiant in a bright yellow dress, a throat-catchingly lovely girl, an *astonishingly* lovely girl. "My God, Monty, who is that?" I asked.

His eyes traced my glance. Turning back, he said, "Diana Ainsley."

I felt like quoting Shakespeare when Romeo first sights Juliet across a crowded room, "O, she doth teach the torches to burn bright!" I continued to stare at this delightful vision while asking, "Related to Ian?"

"Sister-in-law. Her husband was killed in France in 1940. She's out here with the Red Cross," He looked toward her and then back to me. "Helluva fine golfer."

"Ummm." For several moments I gazed down the length of the veranda at this arresting vision—small, golden-headed, nicely-made, animated quick gestures. I felt much as a trout must feel when a gorgeously shaped and colorful lure floats before his eyes.

"What will you have to drink?"

"Scotch-soda." Then, drink in hand, I moved slowly through the crowd toward Diana Ainsley, my mood of discontent suddenly gone and in its place a sense of discovery and excitement.

She looked directly at me as I approached, her blue-green eyes gently appraising. "Oh, hullo," she said, holding out a slender, tanned hand. "I'm Diana Ainsley." Her voice with its crisp English accent sounded like cool spring water running over silver pebbles.

"Dana Brown."

"Howja do." She paused, a quirky smile forming at the edges of her small mouth as she obviously became aware of my fixed, almost hypnotic gaze. "I was just telling Peter," she nodded toward the chunky man beside her, whose insignia on his white blouse, established his rank as lieutenant in the Royal Navy, "about my bad luck in losing my partner for the mixed foursomes tournament at the Club Saturday. Poor Michael was sent down to Calcutta for a fortnight."

"And you need a partner." I had to hold on tight to keep from adding, "I'll play! I'll play!"

"Yes, I do." Again, her greenish eyes appraised me. "Do you know any—or, maybe, do *you* play?"

"Yes. Played today, in fact. Not very well, I'm afraid."

"What did you shoot?"

"Eighty-seven."

She smiled sweetly. "What's your handicap?"

"Twelve."

She cocked her head, figuring. "Just three off." She nodded at me. "Not bad. I have an eight handicap—ladies' tees, of course—which sometimes I play to and sometimes don't." She smiled up at me winningly, indeed, irresistibly. "Would you be interested in partnering with me Saturday?"

I could think of a dozen or more words that would describe my feelings on the matter more aptly than "interested," but I restrained myself to responding, "Yes, I would."

"Splendid." The word as she spoke it was compounded of silver-plated vowels and diamond-edged consonants. She turned to the Navy officer beside her. "Peter, would you get me another gimlet, like a good chap?"

With Peter gone we exchanged information about where we had come from and what we were doing in India. For the next hour and a half I never left her side and seldom took my eyes off her glorious face. I knew with a certainty I had never known before that something remarkable, something unprecedented, was happening to me in the presence of this lovely creature. If it had been suggested that I was experiencing love at first sight, I would have scoffed, but I could not deny that I was dazzled, enchanted, and well nigh overwhelmed. Diana Ainsley was a stunning woman.

After the party that night, lying in my cot, I tried to recall an image of Diana's face with her dazzling smile, but all I could bring up was a vague outline suffused with radiance and a sheen of spangles.

Saturday afternoon found me beside the first tee at Delhi Golf Club with Diana Ainsley, swinging our clubs to warm up. Diana was wearing a knee-length, white, pleated skirt with white ankle-socks below her tanned, shapely legs. Our opponents were a married couple in their thirties, Bert and Joan Bingham, two roundish and grimly determined competitors. Diana and I won the toss for teeing off first to the evident displeasure of the Binghams. We were playing Scotch, or two-ball, foursomes which meant that Diana and I played the same ball, alternately taking turns.

She suggested I drive off the first tee. I placed my ball on the yellow wooden tee and, muscles twitching with tension and anxiety, telling myself to keep my head down and see the spot where the ball had been after I had swung through, I waggled a few times and then swung. There was a sharp crack and when I looked up I saw to my relief that the ball was on a straight trajectory but, because of my tight swing, was not very long. At least we were off the first tee. "Nice shot, partner," said Diana encouragingly.

After Bert Bingham hit an indifferent drive, a looping slice that found the rough on the right, the four of us set off down the first fairway preceded by four Indian caddies, all of them men aged between 35 and 45. The first hole at the Delhi Golf Club is a 515-yard par 5 of which I had made good only about 200 yards with my drive. We had a reasonably good lie so Diana took out her two wood, and with very little preliminary fuss, hit it. Her swing, like her person, was a thing of beauty: a very full arc, hands very high at the top and at the finish, and a lovely sense of ease and grace throughout. The ball rose in a good trajectory and rolled to a stop about 170 yards down the fairway. Meanwhile, Joan Bingham got their ball back on the fairway, and Bert then advanced it in the general direction of the green with another banana slice.

Diana and I surveyed the shot I had left to the hole, about 145 yards with a bunker to carry at the front edge of the green. "Four or five?" asked Diana.

"Five. Three-quarters five," said Dilpi, the caddy with great authority. "Nice easy swing, Sah'ib. Ball fly high and drop down soft."

"Okay." I took the 5-iron he handed me, looked once or twice at the flag, and swung, taking a small divot. It was a clean hit but I was still nervous and hit it a little harder than I meant. The ball landed about mid-green, bounced high once from the back-spin, and rolled slowly on about 15 feet past the pin.

"Well done," said Diana. We were on the green in three but the Binghams were four on the front edge and finally made a six. Diana put her putt within 18 inches, and I tapped in for the par five.

And that's the way it went for the first nine. My jumpiness wore off after the first few holes, and Diana was steady as a rock. We were three-up at the turn. "I think we've got them on the run, partner," Diana said. I was, of course, happy beyond good sense. Here I was playing golf, and playing it well, with an immensely attractive woman whom I wished to impress. And the brisk, golden sunshine glistened the grass and gilded the ruined ancient tombs of sultans long dead and forgotten. A soft breeze brushed the sparklingly crisp air across my face, and now and then I could hear in the distance the eerie shrieking of wild peacocks. It was a glorious day in every way.

But then things began to go sour. We halved the tenth, and then I topped my drive on the eleventh. "Looked up," said Dilpi almost before my club reached the top of the swing. This is a service Indian caddies invariably provide, wanted or not: an instant and ruthless analysis of your mistakes.

"Never mind," said Diana. "It's a short hole. A good second from me and a good chip shot from you and we'll still get our par."

But it did not work out that way. Diana's shot was fine, straight and far, but I bladed my chip—"Looked up again," said Dilpi—and the ball rolled over the back of the green into a bush and an unplayable lie. The Binghams took the hole with a bogey five and our lead was cut to two. Things continued to go down hill. On my next drive, I did not get all the way back on my back-swing, then hurried the down-swing and pulled the ball sharply to the left. "Too quick," commented Dilpi laconically. But Diana took me by the arm as we walked toward the ball, "You're hurrying your back-swing," she said. "Take it nice and slow back. We aren't beat yet. We'll get them."

This steadied me a little, and with a couple of good shots and a few lucky bounces we were all even as we came up to the 18th, a long par 4 with a large fairway sand trap about 130 yards out from the green. My drive was pretty fair, and as we looked over the next shot Diana said, "I can't carry that bunker so I'll lay up in front of it." But she hit her shot too well and it rolled into the trap and nestled in the sand. Meanwhile, the Binghams were just short of the green in three. "Damn, what bad luck!" she said. "I'm afraid that does it for us, Dana. My fault. Just do the best you can."

With 130 yards left, a 6-iron would ordinarily be the right shot, but I was hitting out of the sand, not off the grass. Yet, if I hit it clean, getting the clubhead on the ball before hitting the sand, it still might be the right club. I had made that shot once before, and maybe—just maybe. I anchored my feet solidly in the sand, placing them so the ball was back off my right foot, and then hit down hard and clean. The ball came off the sand in a low straight trajectory, bounced twice, and rolled straight for the flag. For one delirious second I thought it might go in, but it veered off slightly toward the end and stopped about a foot away.

You've done it, partner! You've done it!" Diana ran over and kissed me on the cheek, lifting on one tiptoe to reach my face. "I *knew* I'd be all right with a big strong Yank as my partner!"

We watched silently on the edge of the green while Joan Bingham put her fourth shot three feet past the hole. Diana tapped in for our par 4 and the match was ours. The Binghams congratulated us with a minimum of grace and stalked off.

"Let's have tea," said Diana, She was flushed and glowing and so outrageously lovely that my heart sang. As we sipped our tea, strong and acrid without the generous dollops of milk Diana used, she said, "You know what we should do this evening to celebrate our victory? Have a Maharajah Curry at Maiden's Hotel. My treat. Are you free?"

"Yes, but—" She cocked her head, eyes questioning. "I think I should take you. More proper."

"Tut tut. A gentleman does not refuse a lady's invitation. Or is that not the custom out on the prairie?"

"Why, ma'am," I drawled in a poor imitation of a Westerner's accent, "we don't allow our womenfolk any money for entertainin'. Makes them uppity."

She grinned. "In my village, we do. You're my guest." I gazed admiringly at the contours of her face, an aristocratic English face, slender nose, strong cheekbones, small mouth above a firm chin, tiny ears. It was only then, at that moment, having just achieved some equality of status as her partner in a winning golf match, that I had been able for the first time to look at her squarely and see her face clearly. Before then, it had been as it was when I was in kindergarten and was unable to look squarely at my teacher whose blonde beauty dazzled my eyes like the sun.

At dinner that evening I began to understand how widespread was my companion's popularity. Stopping by our table in Maiden's Hotel dining room, out of the gaily chattering assemblage of British officers, their female companions with skins color ranging from pinky-white to dusky tan, and a scattering of high caste Indians, was a succession of Reggie Sutherlands, Binky Smith-Hempstones, and Muffy Tattersalls who paused to murmur, "Di, darling," while kissing her on the check and to make obscure references to other Reggies and Binkies, all the while chittering away in that quick, staccato speech the English upper classes employ. When there was a pause in this parade of admiring acquaintances I looked up to find Diana smiling at me in some indecipherable way. I raised my eyebrows and said, "Yes?"

She shook her head, smiling still. "I was just thinking how different you are from those people."

"Different?"

"Yes. They're all surface manner, a glossy cover. One has to know them well to find the real person beneath. I have the impression that the real Dana Brown is what I see, right here." She patted my hand on the table.

"And is this the real Diana, right here?" I patted her hand over the top of mine.

She shook her head, eyes merry. "No, sorry. You'll have to know me better to find the real me."

"I hope to."

The Maiden's Hotel Maharajah Curry lived up to its high reputation. After gorging ourselves under the slowly turning, mahogany-bladed fans swishing overhead and quenching with a lemon ice the slow fire the curry had left behind, we strolled out through the lobby of the tradition-laden hotel into the street. A full moon was gliding up the sky before us, golden in the smoky atmosphere of downtown Delhi in early evening. Diana stopped, eyes glinting in the light. "Isn't that gorgeous?" She looked up for another moment and then turned to me excitedly. "You know what we should do, Dana? We should take a cab to the Lodi Gardens and go walking there. It would be breath-taking in the moonlight."

We found a tiny, wheezy cab parked outside Maiden's, and after hearing Diana's crisp, "Lodi Gardens, please," the blue-turbanned Sikh driver urged the tired, old vehicle westward and on out Safdarjang Boulevard. He stopped at one of the gates and we walked slowly into the spacious park. The tombs and mosques of the Afghan warrior-sultans who conquered the region and governed Delhi in the 15th century as though it were a military camp basked quietly in the light of the full moon. The air of India always possesses a fragrance and texture unique to itself. That night it had a pervasive musky, spicy scent, tinctured perhaps by the sharply piquant leaves of the overhanging *neem* trees and the gentle scent of jacaranda blooms. For nearly an hour Diana and I strolled on the serpentine walks beside the ponds and garden enclosures and paused to admire the tombs and mosques, their domes gleaming white under the moon, their columns casting sharp-lined shadows. We came to a large, circular tomb with steps leading up to a walkway that encircled it. As we sat down on the steps, Diana said, "This is the tomb of Sultan Ibrahim Lodi, the last of the Afghan rulers in the 16th century before the Mughals took over."

I turned to her and said, mockingly, "What erudition! How did you learn that?"

"Oh, I have my sources. Guide books, for instance."

I looked down at her upturned face, its loveliness enhanced by the soft, silvery moonlight. Our eyes locked together for a moment and then I bent and kissed her, gently at first and then more and more fully. She put her hand beside our mouths and pressed gently and then, after a moment, slightly away as our lips came slowly apart.

She looked up at me for another moment and then

looked down and rested her hand on my knee. "You know," she said, "that's the first time I've been kissed by an American." She looked up again with a soft smile. "You sort of bring the whole continent along when you kiss, don't you?"

"Whole continent?"

"Full commitment, nothing held back."

"Well, yes."

"Umm." She smiled thoughtfully. "Well, it may be new to me, but I can't say I dislike it."

I put my arm around her shoulder and hugged her close. All remaining doubt had just vanished. I was in love.

That night I had again that lovely dream of being called back to Maumee University to run the student newspaper for the remainder of the college year. This time no Tamil bearer hissed in my ear, and my happiness was unbroken.

Fourteen

News of the distant war reached me in New Delhi, if at all, through the daily BBC radio broadcasts. On the Monday morning after my golf tournament victory with Diana Ainsley—it was January 30, 1944—I listened while shaving to an account of fierce fighting between the Germans and the Allies on the beaches of Anzio, the slow advance northward of MacArthur's island hopping campaign in the South Pacific, and the fighting in Burma to re-open the Burma Road. I reached over and turned off the short wave radio and finished my shaving.

When the last stroke of the Gillette safety razor had skimmed the left side of my face, Badam, my bearer, gathered together razor, soap, shaving brush and metal basin and took them away. I finished dressing and set out on a leisurely stroll through the sparkling morning toward my office. I arrived at about the usual starting time, British time, 9:40, serene of mood and content with life, ready to resume my wartime duties consisting of reading reports and attending meetings.

As I opened the door to my office, I found waiting a stormy-faced American in civilian clothes, arms crossed, feet placed wide apart, posture rigid. "For Christ's sake, Brown," he barked,—"you *are* Brown, aren't you?"—

"what kind of hours do you keep? Is this the way you fight the war?"

I stopped dead and stared at this furious man, tall, dark-haired, and hard-featured. My years of working with Walt Murphy, my brass-lunged editor at the *Denton Daily News,* had given me training in dealing with such confrontations. "Three questions," I said calmly. "Let's take them one at a time. First, yes, I *am* Dana Brown. That's one. And now, may I ask, who are *you*?"

His face very nearly registered surprise but then thought better of it. "Ralph Rowley." He pulled an identification out of his pocket. "Special Services."

"Next question," I went on, "Yes, these are the hours this office keeps along with the rest of the Viceregal staff. And as for fighting the war—"

"All right, all right. I was a little abrupt. I've been waiting here since just after eight."

"Pit-ty." I gave the word the special condescending tone the British lay on it.

He glared at me briefly. "I've got something confidential to discuss. Let's take a walk outside."

We walked out into the brilliant morning and down the walkway onto the main esplanade running between the long rows of splendid, red sandstone structures housing the imperial British rulers. "I have in my pocket," Rowley said as we continued walking, "a cable from London which I would prefer not to hand you out here in the open but which I will leave with you. What it says is that Special Services London and British MI-5 have reason to believe that the Opposition has an asset operating here."

"What do you mean an asset? What's an asset?"

"An espionage agent."

"An agent? You mean a *spy*?"

"An *agent,* reporting to the Opposition."

"But what in hell could a spy learn here in Delhi?"

"Plenty if he had access to the traffic."

"Traffic?"

"Cables, dispatches. Messages to and from London."

"Oh." *Traffic* was apparently special terminology, jargon of the trade, in espionage. Every organized activity, I reminded myself, from fighting a war to playing sports or even running a restaurant, must create its own special terminology, its own jargon. I remembered how Buster at the Maumee college hang-out had insisted that his waiters, including me, must say "Strike one" not "One Coke" when passing an order for a Coke to the soda jerker manning the fountain.

"There is evidence to suggest that someone is reading this traffic and passing it to the enemy."

"What kind of evidence."

Rowley pursed his lips. "I can't tell you that. You're not cleared for it. But it's there."

Again I said, "Oh," while mystification flourished.

"We've got a prime suspect. What you can do to help the effort is to get to know him and learn his M.O."

"Em Oh?"

"His *modus operandi*. For God's sake, Brown, don't they train you new recruits in tradecraft at all before putting you out in the field?"

"*Modus operandi* I can understand. That's Latin. But 'tradecraft'? That sounds like something to do with plumbers or electricians."

Rowley snorted. "It means procedures and techniques in espionage."

"Oh." More jargon. More "Strike one."

"The suspect," Rowley went on in lowered voice after glancing about, "is a British business man, longtime resident in India, involved mostly in export-import trade."

"Name?"

Again Rowley glanced about before whispering "Rupert Wellstone."

"Wellstone." That rang a bell. "Oh, yeah."

"Know him?"

"I was introduced to him once at the Delhi Golf Club. He was sitting with some people at the next table."

"Great! So you know your target by sight. Now the next step is for you to move in."

"Get to know him and work out his M.O."

"Precisely." Rowley permitted a non-clandestine smile to cross his face. I could sense he was thinking somewhat better of me. "Now, look. Make secure notes and store them securely. I'll be back in about four weeks to pick up what you've got."

"Two fortnights," I said with intent to needle.

"Four weeks," he said firmly. "Don't mention any part of this to anyone. And watch yourself. We don't know whether this guy is dangerous but we do know he's very clever."

With this, Rowley gave my hand a brief, perfunctory shake and walked away, leaving me only a little less mystified.

In my office I sat down to think about how to deal with this new assignment. I soon realized that the task, call it establishing an M.O. or whatever, was basically the same as the investigating I had done as a reporter for *The Denton Daily News*.—Hey, look, I told myself, turns out I've been practicing tradecraft for years, like the Frenchman who discovered to his wonder that he had been speaking prose all his life and did not know it!—For a reporter the first item after establishing the name is to get the person's address. Next, get his age, but that did not seem significant in this case.

At lunchtime I went out to the Delhi Golf Club and ordered a sandwich and a bottle of beer at the bar. With no one around I knew, I ate alone. Afterward, I went to the office of the Club Secretary. He was a short, thin-necked, sallow-skinned Englishman who had stayed too long in India. He looked up from some papers on his desk as I knocked gently on the door-frame. "Y-e-e-s-s?"

"I have a small favor to ask, Mr. Tyburn."

"Y-e-e-s-s?"

"I'm sending out invitations to a party, and I need the address of Rupert Wellstone."

The Secretary grunted. He reached into a side drawer and pulled out a directory. "Wellstone, Wellstone." He put a finger down on the page. "It's 59 Ratendon Road." He snapped the book shut and slammed the desk drawer.

I made a note. "Thank you, Mr. Tyburn, I appreciate your assis—"

"Leave me, please. Leave me. I have work to do."

Back in my office I pursued my first venture into clandestine tradecraft by looking up Ratendon Road on my map of New Delhi. It turned out to be a street running along the north side of Lodi Gardens, and I learned from the symbols on the map that several foreign countries had diplomatic residences there. Now that I knew where the man lived, I wondered what to do with the knowledge. "Get to know him and learn his M.O." had been Rowley's instruction. Wellstone's fairly remote residence did not seem to offer much help here but there still was the Golf Club where I first met him.

Over the next two weeks I spent more time than usual at the Golf Club, hoping without success to encounter my "target". This is not to say that during that period I neglected Diana Ainsley, that bewitchingly attractive lady. I managed somehow to see her several times a week, sometimes meeting her as she left the Red Cross office to walk with her back to the quarters she shared with two other women. One such afternoon as we strolled through the slanting, golden sunshine—it was February and the temperature had flirted with the early 90s though the air was bone dry and very comfortable—Diana turned to me, a quirky smile on her lips, and said in that silvery voice, the consonants thin-edged and brittle, "You know, Mr. Brown, if I were an athletic thinker and inclined to jump at conclusions, I might think you are making a play for me, as the saying goes."

"No need to be athletic." I said. "I *am*. Flat out, *am*."

She looked up at me, her green eyes crinkled with smiling. "You Yanks," she said. "No beating about the bush for you chaps. You don't even notice a bush is there, do you."

I took her small, firm golfer's hand in mine. "I don't want any bushes between us, Diana. I am very, very serious."

She looked up quickly, eyes now intent and no longer smiling. She gave my hand a squeeze and withdrew hers. We walked on in silence.

Though I was able to see Diana fairly often during the week, I was unable to break into her regular Saturday afternoon foursome. I did manage, however, to get a game occasionally with her on Wednesday afternoons, and one Wednesday, about three weeks after my meeting with Ralph Rowley, we went out to the Golf Club for lunch at the bar before teeing off. The bar was crowded but we found a table for four near the door. We had just given our order to the waiter when Rupert Wellstone, appeared in the doorway with a slender, pale-skinned Indian. He looked around the room and, seeing no vacant table, was about to turn away when I, without consulting Diana, said quickly "Mr. Wellstone! Why don't you join us?"

He stopped and looked at us both with his eyes finally coming to rest on Diana. He turned to his Indian companion as though seeking assent and then looked back at me, smiling. "Very kind, if you are sure you don't mind."

"Please sit down," I said, while Diana smiled a neutral smile. "This is my friend, Diana Ainsley."

Wellstone bowed his head slightly, his eyes intent and searching. "Howjado? Umm, let me introduce Dr. Shankarin Rao." He looked at me, head cocked slightly. "Forgive me, but you are?"

"Dana Brown."

"Of course. Dr. Rao."

The two sat down with some scraping of chairs and jiggling of the table. Wellstone sat directly across from me and I studied his face, a rather heavy-lidded, thick-lipped affair, coarsely skinned. His eyes were large and intelligent and were at that moment devouring Diana. She seemed serenely unaware of his gaze, having no doubt experienced it hundreds of times in the past, beginning perhaps when she was thirteen.

"Dr. Rao and I came out on the spur of the moment," Wellstone said in his thick, rumbling voice, "hoping to pick up a match."

"Oh," I said and looked at Diana whose eyes met mine without expression. I turned to Wellstone. "There are just the two of us. Would you like to join us?"

"How very kind." He looked at the Indian doctor who gave him that ambivalent Indian head roll and waggle that can mean "Yes-no," "maybe," or "whatever you say." Wellstone turned back and beamed a high intensity smile on Diana. "I think that would be delightful."

When it came to comparing handicaps, it turned out that Wellstone's was 14 and Dr. Rao's 18. My 12 and Diana's 8 would seem to make for an unfair pairing against their higher handicaps, so I, feeling I was making a considerable sacrifice in pursuit of my clandestine assignment, suggested that Wellstone and I be partners. "I guess that would be the best arrangement," he said with a faint note of regret in his rumble and a lingering glance at Diana.

As a golf match it turned out to be what golfers call sardonically "a nice outing." The weather could not have been finer with the brilliant sun heating the dry, dry air into the high 80s and a gentle breeze washing the pungent green fragrance of the bordering trees and scrub bushes across our faces. But Wellstone did not come close to playing to his handicap. He was one of those golfers who raise the club slowly and then lash at the ball as though it were a galloping snake. But clearly he expected a better result than he got because each time he grunted furiously and smacked his club two or three times on the ground. Dr. Rao hit each ball neatly straight and short and met his handicap exactly while Diana played her usual effortless, economical round and finished with an 80. Intent as I was on my "target" my concentration went haywire, and I floundered from stroke to stroke. With Wellstone seemingly in constant despair over his game I found no conversational opening for finding out more about the man.

With Diana and Dr. Rao overwhelming winners, I was about to write the day off as a total loss and my artful arrangements with Wellstone a complete bust. But then, as the four of us strolled from the 18th green to the clubhouse, Wellstone turned to Diana and said, "I'm having a few friends in for supper and dancing to records Saturday night, and I would very much like to have the two of you join the party." His thick-lipped mouth managed a gracious smile.

Diana turned to me, her expression as enigmatic as the face of the Sphinx. I hesitated a moment, trying to get the signal, but then decided to plunge ahead. "Thank you, I think that would be fun."

We parted then with the customary inanities about "great match" and "must do it again." Diana and I were mostly silent as we rode home in a pedicab but as we arrived at her quarters and walked toward the door, she turned to me with a lips-pursing smile. "Can you give me any hint," she said with a sardonic edge in her voice, "as to what you find so compellingly appealing about your Mr. Wellstone?"

Sparring, I said, "What do you mean?"

"I mean," she said as one might explain something to a backward child, "that the man has all the charm of a toad."

"Oh, I don't think that—"

"He's a blithering vulgarian," she went on, "an

unsightly physical specimen, and he looks right through my clothes and undresses me one anatomical region after the other. If I have any physical secrets left it's no fault of that bloke."

"Ummm. Well, I—"

"Yes?"

"Well, look, Diana. I don't know—Well, I was just trying to be courteous. Kind."

"To whom. To me?"

"Well, no. I'm afraid I wasn't very thoughtful." I paused, looking down at her vexed, though still lovely, face. "Look, Diana, you don't need to go to this thing Saturday night if you'd rather not."

"Are you going?"

"Well, yes. I guess so." Pause. "I'm curious about what his place is like."

"Then I'll go too. I want to keep you from falling further under his magic spell."

Fifteen

It was a sprightly group of young people, 20s and 30s, that Rupert Wellstone gathered together for his supper and dancing party. We were about half Indian and half British, I being the only American. To my surprise, Ian Ainsley was there, squiring a gorgeous Indian girl whom he introduced, simperingly, as Kirin Rajiv. She was just Diana's height, full bosomed, with jet black finespun hair and large, lustrous, kohl-rimmed eyes. She wore a sea-green sari with gold edging, and the tawny skin along her delicately shaped arms and on the slender column of her neck was lambent against the shimmering green and gold. As she stood alongside my golden-headed Diana whose creamy white skin glowed softly in the subdued light, the contrast was stunning and enhancing to both lovely creatures.

We had been greeted at the door by Wellstone, expansive in a loud patterned Madras jacket. The gramophone was playing and several couples were already dancing in the high-ceilinged, broad room which was terrazzo-floored and adorned with marble columns at either end. Wellstone waved his hand grandiloquently toward the dancers. "Join the party. Go dance, my friends."

I took Diana in my arms, and to the sound of Glen

Miller's "That Old Black Magic" we whirled away. Across the room, as we moved in and out among the other dancers, I watched Ian Ainsley, a fatuous smile on his long, rather horsey face, dancing in a florid style with much arm moving and head nodding. I let Diana slip away to arms' length and said, "Not to be critical of your relative, but take a look at your brother-in-law. Did you ever see anything sillier than that?"

Diana looked across the room, smiled forbearingly, and said, "No, I guess not."

"I don't think I've ever met a more affected human being."

She looked up quickly. "He's certainly affected and sometimes silly, that's true. But it would be a mistake to underestimate him, Dana. Underneath that facade there is real substance. And he is very kind and very brave."

Brave got my attention. "Brave? How do you know that?"

She shook her head. "I'll tell you sometime."

Then the record ended and along with several other couples we walked over to the gramophone. There were several piles of records, maybe twenty or thirty in all, shiny black inside their spanking new sleeves and bearing names like Brunswick and MHV Victor. I leafed through one of the stacks, hoping to find a Hal Kemp or Guy Lombardo. Instead I found records with names like Artie Shaw, Tommy Dorsey, Vaughn Monroe, Freddy Martin, Glen Miller, Alvino Rey, and several others. and the tunes, mostly new to me, were "I Don't Want to Walk Without You," "Tangerine," "Moonlight Cocktail," "Sleepy Lagoon," "When the Lights Go On Again," and so on. Our host, Wellstone, came and stood beside me. "See anything there you like?"

"Sure. All of them. But they're mostly new to me."

"I just got a new shipment in. I have a record shop on Oxford Street in London which sends me out a new batch every three months."

"Very nice."

Wellstone turned to Diana. "Mrs. Ainsley, I have some chilled champagne ready. May I get you a glass to slake your thirst after dancing?"

"You're very kind. Yes, thank you."

Shortly after he left, Ian Ainsley approached. He first nodded at me and then said, "Dear sister-in-law, may I have the next caper with you?"

Diana smiled sweetly. "Certainly, darling," and off they swirled to the bounce of "Deep in the Heart of Texas."

My ears were still twitching enviously to that endearing "darling," when Wellstone arrived with two glasses of champagne. "Oh, the lady's dancing, I see. Well, I'll just join you until she comes back." He hoisted his glass. "Cheers!"

We sipped what was even to my inexperienced palate an excellent champagne. I glanced around the sumptuous room. "You have a lovely place."

"Thank you. I find it agreeable. Would you care to look around a bit?"

"Yes, indeed." He led me into the next room, a more intimate drawing room with softly glowing oriental rugs and beige velvet draperies. The room was adorned with small statues and gorgeously framed paintings. On a small marble table beside an amber-colored leather settee was a bronze statuette of an Indian dancing girl. She was wearing a tall conical head-dress and extravagantly large earrings. Nude to her hips, her breasts were, in the sensual Indian tradition, full, round globes with erect nipples while below a tiny waist her hips were flaring and her thighs luxuriant. "That's a lovely thing," I said, letting my fingertips explore her contours.

"Yes, isn't it? It's new to me. I picked it up last week at Agr—" He broke off. "Down in the country."

"A real find," I said. But I thought perhaps I had glimpsed a small opening in his hesitation over the name. Could it mean he had something he wished to hide? I decided to take a flyer. "Did you say you found it in Agra?"

His reluctance to answer was visible in another flicker of hesitation. "Ah, yes, I did."

"I've never been to Agra. I have yet to see the Taj Mahal."

"You must, my friend. It's the most glorious thing in this country. Indeed, it's the finest monument east of Suez."

"I must do it." I paused before launching the next probe. "Where do you usually stay when you're in Agra?"

Again a flicker of hesitation. "Well, usually at Maiden's Cottage."

"If I get a chance sometime soon, I'll take your advice and go see the Taj." I turned then to walk back into the room to rejoin the dancers. Just as I was passing through the marble columns between the rooms I heard a hurried mumble of conversation behind me. I looked back and saw Wellstone speaking rapidly to an Indian, his hand making sharp, chopping gestures. The man turned away but as he did I got a glimpse of his face, a strikingly handsome one. Indians taken as a whole are to my mind remarkably good-looking people but this man surpassed the national norm considerably. He was almost pretty but still masculine in his facial structure, much as movie star Robert Taylor was both pretty and masculine.

In an instant Wellstone was at my side, explaining. "One of my servants had a small problem," he said.

I had been in India a relatively short time but long enough to see and know the difference between servants and masters. That man was no servant.

On Monday morning I went to the Delhi Railway Station and bought a 2nd class ticket on the 7:35 train for Agra. It was to be an 110 mile journey but nearly four hours at the leisurely pace of Indian Railways, so I had brought along a copy of Somerset Maugham's spy novel, *Ashenden*, hoping to glean useful insights into the business the war had thoughtlessly immersed me. Promptly at 7:35 the train gathered itself and headed southeast toward Agra, the ancient capital and site of the Taj Mahal.

At first I watched as familiar landmarks like Humayun's Tomb swam by in the distance and we passed through outlying Nizamuddin and Ghaziabad. The morning sun slanted through a grayish haze that hung low over the parched and dusty land. Occasionally a cluster of mud huts passed by and now and then bony cattle or scrawny goats nibbling at low scrubby brush dotted the fields. After a while, I turned to Maugham's novel but very soon it became apparent that the gentlemanly hero, Ashenden, was engaged in matters totally unlike my problem with Wellstone, Agra, and M.O. So I turned back to the window and watched the sorrowing, brown land move by and thought about Diana Ainsley whose incandescent image shone in brilliant contrast with the passing scene.

Shortly before noon the train stopped at Agra station whose platform was so jammed with a shouting, arm-waving crowd that it resembled a budding riot scene. Hands brushed my sleeves and tugged at my suitcase as I stepped onto the landing while at the back of the mob ten or fifteen men raised their hands and cried, "Taxi, Sah'ib!" I chose a yellow-turbanned, big-bellied Sikh who took my bag and led me to a battered Morris, so small it seemed scarcely bigger than its driver. "Maiden's Cottage," I said and the Morris's clutch shuddered and grabbed and off we lurched.

After the flowered boulevards and broad vistas of New Delhi, the garden city, the dusty, cluttered streets of Agra were a shock. The roadway was so jammed with people, bicycles, wandering cows, and oxcarts drawn by massive, nodding water buffalo, that my taxi could only crawl, all the while bleeping its futile horn. The already narrow roadway was further tightened by a row of blankets and sheets lying on the ground along the side on which were displayed fruit, vegetables, shoes, and bright-colored clothing. Dust from the shuffling feet of people and animals lightly powdered the displayed fruit and goods.

Maiden's Cottage was a modest two story hostel on a quiet side street. The reception desk was a massive mahogany remnant of Victorian decor, flanked on one side by a scrubby potted palm and on the other by a gleaming brass spittoon. The clerk was a thin-faced Hindu who greeted me obsequiously, leaning forward over the high desk. "May we help you, Sah'ib?"

The registration ceremonies completed, a bare-footed peon wearing a white dhoti led me up the creaking stairway to a high-ceiling room facing on the street below. After depositing my bag on a stand, the bearer reached for a black box on the wall and overhead a large, wooden-bladed fan began a gentle, lazy whirl. Winter was dissolving into spring in India, and the thermometer marked each passing day with mounting degrees. This day promised to touch the middle 90s.

Now that I had reached the location of my proposed investigation, the next question was how to proceed. The first thing to do, I decided, was to try my chances with the Hindu desk clerk. After a nondescript lunch in the small dining room, I approached his desk. He smiled his oily, obsequious smile at me. "Yes, Sah'ib?"

"I want to inquire about my dear friend, Rupert Wellstone. I was rather hoping to find him here. Does he not stop here often?"

"Wellstone, Sah'ib? Oh yes, indeed."

"Has he been here lately?"

"I believe so. Let me look it up in the register."

I watched while he flipped through the pages of the leather-bound register, its edges frayed from wear. "Oh yes, here it is. It was last week, two nights." He closed the book and placed it precisely in the center of his desk.

"Do you remember, did he have any visitors while he was stopping here?"

The thin-faced Hindu's eyes dropped reproachfully and his smiled drooped. "Really, Sah'ib, we have so many guests I find it hard to remember."

I pulled a fifty rupee note from my pocket and laid it on the counter covered with my hand. As I took my hand away, I said, "I hoped you might be able to remember."

He looked thoughtfully at the note for a moment and then said, "I believe I do remember now someone who came to see Wellstone Sah'ib."

"What was his name?"

"I never heard his name, Sah'ib, but I believe he was a cinema star or an entertainer."

"Cinema star?"

"Yes, Sah'ib. You see, he was so very handsome. Very striking. Like Krishna Puri."

I recognized Krishna Puri as the name of the top star in Indian films, sort of a Hindu Clark Gable, but the clerk's description also reminded me of the man I had glimpsed in urgent conversation with Wellstone at the dance party. "Did my friend, Wellstone and his visitor stay in the lobby or go up to his room?"

Again the Hindu's face took on a look of mild reproach and his smile drooped. "Really, Sah'ib, it's so hard to remember every detail."

I took a twenty rupee note out and laid it between us. "I do wish you would try very hard."

Again he paused thoughtfully and then said, "Ah yes. Now I remember. I recall they chatted briefly here in the lobby and then took a taxi and went off for several hours."

"You don't know where they went."

"No, Sah'ib. But I believe the taxi driver was Patwant Singh. He would know, of course."

"How would I find him?"

"Well, Sah'ib, I—" As his smile began to droop I

placed another twenty rupee on the counter. the smile regained its full wattage, and he said, "He will be here at the head of the taxi rank at dinner time. He has purchased the right to be number one after 6 p.m."

"Patwant Singh?"

"Yes, Sah'ib. I will tell him you wish to speak with him."

I looked at my Bulova watch which read 1:25. I had a good four hours to kill before I could talk to the taxi driver. I turned to the clerk. "How far is it to the Taj Mahal?"

"About half mile, Sah'ib. Shall I call you a taxi?"

"No, I'll walk." Outside the rather dim lobby the day was dazzlingly bright, the sun casting sharp black shadows and beating hard on my head and shoulders. I walked slowly in the 90-degree heat, avoiding by halts and dodges the helter-skelter traffic of bicycles, sauntering people, plodding cows, and bleeping taxis. In something considerably less than a half mile I saw the outer gate of Taj Mahal, its sandstone walls glowing a pinkish red. A man in a brown uniform took my one rupee note in exchange for a ticket, and I stepped through the archway and stopped short, my breath an indrawn gasp. There before me, immaculate in all its purity and perfection was the fabled Taj Mahal. It stunned me. I was not prepared for its sublime elegance, its flawless symmetry, its quiet, assured beauty. I had seen dozens of pictures of the Taj. It was to me, as to most Americans, a cliche. But the magnificent structure before me, the classic gleaming white dome a lovely cynosure as four graceful minarets stood attendance on each corner of the surrounding esplanade, transcended all images of itself. It was simply too perfect in all its glorious aspects to be captured and represented in any form other than its own majestic perfection.

I stood for several minutes, transfixed by the vision before me, then walked slowly up the long walkway running alongside narrow pools and flanked by banks of flaming cannas and yellow asters. For the next two hours I walked about the broad surrounding grounds, gazing at the Taj from every possible vantage point. Like the perfect woman, she had no bad angles. The proportions, the symmetry, remained constant and pure. I finally left, with a regretful backward glance, more moved by the experience than anything I had previously known.

After a tub bath and a change of clothes I came down to the hotel lobby shortly after six. "Ah yes, Sah'ib," said the reception clerk, "Patwant Singh is here." He came from behind his desk and led me outside to the taxi rank before the hotel. Patwant Singh turned out to be the same yellow-turbanned, large bellied Sikh who had met me that morning at the railway station.

"You wish go somewhere, Sah'ib?" he asked.

"Later, maybe. First, I want to ask—" I turned and saw the Hindu leaning forward to catch every word. I stared him down and he excused himself and went back inside. "I want to ask whether you remember taking two sah'ibs, one English one Indian, somewhere last week." I had a fifty rupee note ready which I handed him.

He gazed thoughtfully at the note and said, "English sah'ib big man? Big, big with deep voice like tiger?"

"That's right. Name is Wellstone."

"Ah yes! I hear Indian sah'ib say 'Wellstone.'"

"Good. Do you remember where you took them?"

"Certainly, Sah'ib. To house in Firozabad. You want go there?"

"Later, after dinner, after dark."

The Sikh looked back at two other taxis waiting in the line. "But, Sah'ib. Maybe other mens want taxi."

I pulled another fifty rupee note out. "Wait for me," I said.

Around 7:30 I walked outside and found Patwant Singh, arms folded over his generous belly, leaning against his battered Morris taxi. "You go now to Firozabad, Sah'ib?"

"Yes." I found a portion of the back seat where the springs did not do violence to my bottom and we moved off, the Morris engine coughing and sputtering until it found its voice. "How far is Firozabad?"

"Twenty-two miles, Sah'ib."

"Do you have plenty of petrol?" I had nasty thoughts of being stranded on a back country road in India.

"Oh yes, Sah'ib." With that firm but to my mind equivocal, assurance—most Indian assurances are equivocal—I leaned back as we picked our way through the street traffic of Agra and then found the open road for Firozabad.

The night air rolled in through the open window, redolent with the fragrances of the Indian countryside: an indefinable musky smell intermingled with the dark brown odors of human and animal droppings. Now and then a dim, yellow-lighted window flickered in the distance but mostly the moonless night was black. In the faint, unsteady lights of the Morris the backs of bicyclists suddenly appeared, their chrome pedals rising and falling in the light, and from time to time an unlighted, high-wheeled bullock cart, its driver lying curled asleep on the flat bed of the wagon, jumped into view out of the night. Singh then bleeped his anemic horn, an almost comical "toot," and swerved out around the ancient vehicle drawn by the trudging beast.

In less than an hour the lighted outskirts of Firozabad loomed before us. It seemed a town much like Agra with dusty narrow streets. I had rather expected the Sikh to stop before a house within the limits of the town but he proceeded on through to the eastern outskirts. Then he turned off to the left, down a tree-lined lane, and stopped before a square white house.

"Go on!" I said. "go down a way and turn around."

"Ah-cha, Sah'ib." He moved down several hundred yards and then headed back.

"Stop here and turn off your lights." After the engine gave its final cough, I said, "Are you sure that's the house where the two sah'ibs went?"

"It is, Sah'ib."

"How long did they stay?"

"Half hour, maybe." In India, where time is too fluid to be precisely measured, "half hour," I knew, could mean anything from ten minutes to an hour. Still, it told me what I needed to know, the time was long enough to make a report, or a delivery, but not long enough for a prolonged negotiation. It was possible the visit was one of an extended series.

"Wait here while I look around." I closed the taxi door softly behind me and walked up the lane toward the house. It was very dark under the trees lining the narrow roadway, and I could see the lights of the house flickering through the branches. The air was pungent with the sharp, almost mint-like fragrance of the *neem* trees overhead. I advanced cautiously until I had the house fully in view. It was a solid, square, masonry structure probably built originally by an English planter—not luxurious but functional and comfortably spacious. I watched the windows for signs of activity but saw none. I looked carefully for any indication of special use the house might have but could not find any. After several minutes I walked back to the taxi, and Patwant Singh drove us back to Maiden's Cottage in Agra.

Next morning I had a leisurely breakfast, having time to kill before catching the 11:30 train for Delhi. I was standing at the window of my room, idly watching the traffic in the street below, when my eyes suddenly fell on *him. Him*, the beautiful man I had seen in furtive conversation with Rupert Wellstone; *him*, the Krishna Puri look-alike—according to Patwant Singh—who had accompanied Wellstone in Singh's taxi to Firozabad. He was getting out of a taxi and coming into the front entrance of the hotel. I quickly put on my seersucker jacket and walked down to the lobby. The handsome one was signing the hotel register, a small suitcase and a briefcase on the floor beside his feet. I sat down in a musty armchair on the other side of the lobby, picked up a nearby copy of *The Times of India*, and watched around its edges. Shortly, the peon picked up his suitcase—the man insisted on carrying the accordion-style briefcase himself—and they went up the stairway.

I waited only a moment before going to the desk, a twenty rupee note in hand. The Hindu behind the counter had anticipated me and swung the register around for me to read. The signature was "Ramji Tilak, New Delhi." I immediately gave up any idea of going back to Delhi that day. I spent virtually all the rest of the morning and the afternoon sitting in that musty armchair in the lobby, ostensibly reading a newspaper but keeping an eye out for Ramji Tilak. I suppose Ralph Rowley would say I was conducting a surveillance operation against my target.

My handsome "target" made no appearance in the lobby all day long, apparently having had his lunch brought to his room on a tray. Thinking he might be planning to emerge in the evening I went outside just before six and secured the services of Patwant Singh and his battered taxi on a standby basis. At dinner time I managed to get a table in the dining room that gave me a view of the lobby and the front door but still the quarry did not show. After a highly forgettable dinner of mushy, overcooked fish and gluey rice I resumed my watch from the armchair.

About a quarter to eight Tilak came down the stairs carrying the leather, accordion style briefcase. He looked neither right or left and strode quickly through the doorway and out to the line of waiting taxis. I watched from beside the door while he tried futilely to obtain the services of Patwant Singh. Then he raised his right hand in a sharp upward swing in disgust and moved on to the next taxi in the line.

There he conducted a brief negotiation and shortly the taxi was pulling out into the roadway. I waited until it was well past and then hurried out to Singh. "Can you follow that taxi?" I asked.

Patwant Singh lifted his bearded chin in an expression of disdain. "Absolutely, Sah'ib. That driver is Amir Khan." He snorted through his large nose as he opened the car door for me. "He drives always twenty-five miles an hour. No cowardly Moslem can escape a Sikh!"

"Don't let him see we are following him."

"Certainly not, Sah'ib. We will track him like a tiger in the jungle."

We set off in pursuit of the dim tail-lights of the other taxi and, just as I hoped, the trail led us eastward out of Agra and on the road to Firozabad. As Singh had said, Amir Khan never exceeded twenty-five miles an hour so the journey was leisurely. I leaned back in the seat and gazed at the dim lights of houses as they swam by in the dark night. And I wondered, as I always do, about the lives of the human beings who lived in those houses here in the heart of the vast Indian plain. I wished I could somehow become a disembodied observer who could enter those dim rooms and penetrate the minds and lives of those who lived there. The countryside, those miserable houses, and their occupants were so utterly alien, so impenetrably exotic, to my life in midwestern Ohio. I longed to experience vicariously the goings and comings and the textures of those other lives.

About an hour and half after our departure from Maiden's Cottage we arrived at the lane on the eastern outskirts where Patwant Singh had taken me the night before. From some distance back we had watched the other taxi turn into the lane, and now we slowly followed. I stopped Singh just inside the entrance. "Turn off your lights, turn around, and wait here," I said. I got out and walked slowly down the lane toward the house. Ahead through the blackness I could see the taxi's tail-lights glimmering and then wink off. I heard a car door slam and then silence. I walked slowly on down the lane until I could see the lighted windows through the branches of the pungent *neem* trees. In a moment light burst out the front door as it opened and outlined the figure of Ramji Tilak, briefcase in hand. He stepped inside. Then the doorway went dark again and I tried to find a vantage point where I could see into the windows. I was moving quietly down the lane when suddenly a whiff of cigarette smoke drifted by, the nasty smell of cheap tobacco that identifies Indian cigarettes. It meant Amir Khan or some other Indian was very near, and I slid back into the bushes and froze. Then in a few moments I heard a man cough, seemingly fifty feet or so away, and I relaxed but did not move from the spot.

Through the window I could make out figures moving in the room but I could not tell what was taking place. By this time a half moon, orangey yellow in the evening haze, had lifted above the eastern horizon, and as I waited and watched it climbed the sky above the house. Suddenly, by its silver light I could make out some kind of structure on the roof, a curious shape of rods and bars. And then I saw occasional glints as the pale light struck something metallic on the structure, and I realized with a sudden rush I was looking at an aerial, a *big* aerial. It was clearly not merely a reception aerial. Given its size and its intricacy it had to be an aerial for the transmission of messages.

That was it! There was the answer. My quest was over. I hurried back to Patwant Singh and his Morris and soon we were churning along at the top speed of the ancient, well-worn machine—a respectable forty-five miles an hour. Back at Maiden's Cottage I went to bed quite content with my night's work. I felt that even Ralph Rowley would approve of my activities.

That night I had once again that warmly satisfying dream in which I assured the president of Maumee University I would be delighted to return to take over the editorship of *The Student Record* for the rest of the college year.

Sixteen

The bar in the Delhi Golf Club was filling fast as hot and thirsty golfers finished their rounds and came in out of oven heat. I watched across the table as Diana, a row of tiny sweat beads across her upper lip, wiped her forehead with a pale blue handkerchief and took another sip from her Pymm's Cup.

It had been a happy round of golf. Diana was hitting the ball off the tee long and straight in the light, dry air. I had had a satisfactory round, about as good as I ever managed, shooting an 81, and I was still revelling in that six iron shot I hit from about 130 yards out on the seventh hole. The ball had lifted nicely in a high trajectory, landed on the front apron of the green, bounced twice, and ran straight into the hole for an eagle three. But as I gazed happily at the lovely face before me, the green eyes cast down at the table, I realized she was unusually quiet and pensive.

"Something wrong, Di?" I asked.

She looked up quickly. "Oh, nothing serious. I'm just disappointed. Some plans I had for next weekend have fallen through."

"Plans?"

"Yes, you remember Peter Billington, the Navy lieutenant. I introduced you to him at Monty Gilpin's do."

"I think so."

"Peter is an aide on the Viceroy's personal staff. He was able to get spaces for four on a staff airplane flying up to Kashmir next weekend. He is taking his fiance, Pamela Knightbridge, and has offered me the other two places. I had invited that nice American Red Cross girl, Francie Wells, but she just got an invitation from the Maharajah of Mysore for a weekend party and she feels she simply must accept. I was looking forward so much to seeing Kashmir. Everyone says it is so lovely, and Peter has taken a houseboat on Dal Lake. It would have been scads of fun."

"I see." I gazed across the table at her as she took another sip from her Pymm's Cup, a slight frown creasing her forehead. "You can't just make it a threesome?"

"I don't think that would be fair. Peter has space for four, and I would be depriving someone of that chance."

"Well, what about—" I paused, summoning courage for the rest of the sentence. "Uh, what about asking a man instead of a woman? What about asking me, for instance?"

Her head came up quickly and she looked at me with an expression I could not read. There was a pause which lengthened and grew as she looked intently at me. Diana pursed her lips for a moment and then smiled softly. "Could you get away, Dana, if I asked you?"

"I'll know tomorrow," I said. I could not explain to Diana but that morning I had got a message from Kandy saying Ralph Rowley was arriving next day for consultation. "I can know for certain by tomorrow afternoon."

She looked thoughtfully across the table, the soft smile still on her face. "Then let's talk about it tomorrow."

I made a special effort to arrive at my office promptly the next morning, but Ralph Rowley had not yet arrived. I got my report on Wellstone and Tilak out of the safe and read it over again. I made a few corrections and retyped one page. There was a discreet knock, and when I turned around Ralph Rowley was in the doorway.

"Good morning, Brown. I assume you got my message. Anything to report?"

"Yes, indeed. I've got a written report here." I held up the yellow pages.

"Good enough. I'll take the written report now, and we'll go outside for an oral briefing." He put the papers in his briefcase and led me out onto the walkway. "Let's hear it."

I recounted the evening with Wellstone, the agitated conversation I had observed with Ramji Tilak, the slip over the word "Agra", my trip there, and the observations I had made at the house outside Firozabad.

"Good stuff," he said. "Not bad at all." He put his hands behind his back, head down, and walked slowly up the walkway. Then he grunted, "Umhuh." He turned to me. "What we'll do, Brown, is go back to Kandy and lay out a plan to be coordinated with the Indian Bureau."

"I was planning to go out of town this weekend."

He looked surprised. "Oh, no, no. I didn't mean *you* would go to Kandy. By 'we' I meant *I* will go back and work out a plan with the operations people. Matter of fact, I seriously doubt that you'll be involved in the future at all."

"Then it's okay for the weekend."

"I guess so. When will you be back?"

"Probably Monday."

"All right. We'll proceed on that basis." He gave a perfunctory shake of my hand and stalked away.

When Diana had said we would be staying on a houseboat on Dal Lake, I had no real idea what to expect. I guess I vaguely expected to find one of those square boats powered by an outboard motor such as I had seen on the Ohio River near Cincinnati. I also imagined we would cruise somewhere on the lake and anchor offshore.

When we got out of the taxi after a ten minute ride from Srinagar, I saw before us a long gray structure with rectangular, multi-paned, un-boatlike windows, looking more like a cottage than a vessel. But the cottage-boat clearly was riding on the water, secured to the bank by heavy lines. To compound the confusion between cottage and boat, a permanent set of wooden steps and a platform with railings gave onto what was presumably the bow.

Peter Billington led us up the steps and through the doorway. Inside we found one of the most elegant small sitting rooms I have ever seen. Flanking the windows were beige draperies adorned with intricate Kashmiri crewel work done in soft gray green, pale pink, and wine. A sofa along one wall and three easy chairs were similarly embellished with complex designs inscribed in crewel. The floor—I could not even think "deck"—glowed with ornate Kashmiri oriental rugs woven in soft white and indigo. I was still admiring the handsome room when Diana took me by the hand and said, "Dana, look!" She pointed out the window and there, in a single view, was comprised the glorious beauty of Kashmir. Dal Lake lay before us mirror-calm. On its broad surface floated two elegantly-shaped boats, slim and narrow with long overhanging bow and stern lifting high off the water, their lines resembling floating curved leaves. As a triumphal backdrop, snow-topped mountains lifted steeply into the sky on the shore across the lake. "Did you ever see anything so lovely?" Diana asked.

I looked down at her upturned face, radiant with delight. "Just one other thing."

She looked away quickly and snatched her hand from mine. She jabbed me in the ribs. "Nonsense," she said.

Peter took us on an inspection tour of the boat. Next

to the sitting room, we went through the dining room, furnished with gleaming maple table and chairs. A large square window looked out on the lake, and there, once again, that transcendent scene lay shimmering. Beyond the dining room a hallway led past two bedrooms. Momentarily, I had uneasy thoughts of sharing a bedroom with Peter, but then he opened a door at the end of the hall and we found a second boat, lashed firmly to the first. A tiny sitting room gave onto a hallway and two more bedrooms.

"No kitchen," said Diana.

"No," answered Peter. "The food is cooked onshore, brought aboard, and served by the bearers."

"Good show," said Diana. "You'd all starve on my cooking."

"Mine, too," said Pamela. These were almost the first words she had spoken since leaving Delhi. Whenever I had looked at her on the trip she was gazing longingly into Peter's eyes.

"You and Dana can have the two front bedrooms," said Peter. "Pammy and I will take these two."

"Good," said Diana. I could see from the delighted, expectant look on Pamela's face that it was absolutely grand with her.

At lunch, Peter produced a bottle of champagne he had previously given to the bearer, Mamdoo, to chill. Conversation sparkled like the wine—Diana, Peter, and Pamela all chattering in that clipped, staccato chip-chip-chip of the English. Suddenly, my mind took leave of the conversation, leaving this almost unimaginably exotic setting—a houseboat lying on this jewel of a lake in fabled Kashmir—and stood apart in wonder. Wonder that I, son of a blue collar worker in an Ohio rubber factory, former coal passer and deckhand on Great Lakes ore freighters, college student who had labored and sweated at menial jobs to fund his education, should find himself here of all places on the planet, surrounded by these

English aristocrats. And the greater wonder, it seemed to me, was that these gilded people whose upper class backgrounds were so unlike mine, did not seem to regard my presence there as at all remarkable—which it most assuredly was.

My wandering, wondering mind was suddenly yanked back to the present when Diana turned to me, eyes crinkling with merriment, "You agree with that, don't you, Dana?"

Without the slightest notion of what there was to agree with, I said, "You know, dear Diana, I agree with everything you say. Especially when it is true."

"There, you see!" she said triumphantly to the others. "I knew I was right."

As lunch drew to a close, Peter stifled a yawn and said he thought he might take a nap. "The Old Man has had me working all hours this past week." Sleepiness seemed suddenly to overtake Pamela too, and with no more discussion they left for the bedrooms—or bedroom.

Diana looked out the window at the trunk of a huge tree on the bank beside the houseboat. "I would like to stroll around in that lovely garden out there. Look how the sun shines on the leaves of that enormous *chinar* tree."

We walked out on the little dock at the bow of the boat. "*Chinar* tree? I asked, looking up at the spreading branches of the tree whose massive trunk was at least six feet thick.

"Yes. It looks to be a sort of plane tree, doesn't it? It's very old. It might have been planted by the magnificent king, Akbar, in the 16th century. This is a Mughal garden, you know." She lifted her face and took a deep breath. "And smell that sharp, clean air. Mountain air, really. You know the altitude here is 4000 feet."

"You've been reading the guide book again." I said.

"Righto. Come, let's walk!" She took my hand and led me down the steps. We strolled around under the gigantic trees where the grass at our feet was lavishly sprinkled with small pink and white flowers, some with pink centers, some with yellow.

"Does the guide book tell you what these flowers are," I asked.

"Only an ignorant Yank would not know that. Those are daisies, English daisies."

"Ours are only white," I said humbly.

"Sah'ib," a voice behind me said. I looked back to see a Kashmiri who touched his brow and asked, "Would the sah'ib and memsah'ib wish for ride in *shikara*?" He pointed to a gondola-like boat tied to the dock of our houseboat.

"Wonderful!" exclaimed Diana. "Wouldn't that be fun, Dana? Yes, let's."

The Kashmiri boatman escorted us to his craft, a long narrow vessel with a single broad seat in the middle, lavishly cushioned. A canopy sheltered the seat while the boatman stood on a small platform at the stern and propelled the boat with a long staff pushing against the shallow bottom of the lake. Having seated us with gracious ceremony, he loosed the bow and stern lines and we glided away, silently and smoothly. A soft wind gently wrinkled the lake's broad surface, and the movement of the boat was silkily smooth. Diana dipped one hand in the water beside her. "Isn't this lovely, Dana?" she asked. "Isn't this perfectly grand?"

I took a long, deep breath of the crisp air and put my left arm around Diana's shoulders. "Couldn't be better," I said.

A long silence followed while we savored the scene—the snow-mantled mountains rising high in the sky above the emerald blue lake—and the luxuriously quiet motion of the boat through the water. After a time, Diana said, "You know, Dana. We have been friends now for several months, but all I know about you is that you come from a place called "Ohio," which I gather is out toward the Mississippi River west of Manhattan, and you were a newspaper man before the war. You never mention your family."

"Well, neither do you. My family are ordinary people, working people."

"And you grew up in a log cabin on the Ohio prairie."

"Yep. And walked five miles to school through waist-deep snow dodging hostile Indians all the way."

"Just a typical Yank. Any brothers or sisters?"

"One odious sister."

"I can match you there. I have *two* odious sisters and one lovely brother."

"Where is your home in England?"

"Actually, we have two, a town-house just off Berkley Square in town and a country place in Sussex."

"And *your* family?"

She sighed and said, "My grandfather was the Earl of Dunster. My father was a second son so he went into the army, fought in World War I, and went into Parliament afterward. He's still an M.P."

Diana went on talking about her family for several minutes while an image of her life in England formed in my mind: governesses and private tutors until her teens; then as a debutante, garden parties, masked balls, riding to hounds, tennis at great estates, trips to France and Italy, and all the pleasures of twentieth century English upper class life. "Looking back," she said, "I just sort of staggered along from day to day without thinking. At the time I thought I was having fun. Now, it just seems rather dull."

"Doesn't sound dull to me."

Diana suddenly turned away and pointed off to the left side of the boat. "Oh look, Dana, an island!" She was pointing to a grassy, brushy strip four or five feet wide and fifteen feet long, out some two hundred yards from shore.

"An island?" I turned back to the Kashmiri. "What is that?" I asked, pointing to the grassy strip.

"Float piece, Sah'ib. Float-ting."

"It's a *floating* island!" I said to Diana.

"A floating island! How romantic! I want to claim it as my own. Diana's island."

"We'll need Akbar's permission," I said.

By then the sun was well along in its long slide down the western sky, and the boatman headed his craft back toward the houseboat. We were silent most of the way but just before we docked, Diana said, "This has been such a lovely afternoon, Dana. I *do* enjoy being with you." She looked at the Kashmiri and then back at me. "Do you suppose we could go out again after dinner? In the moonlight?"

"Why not?" After we docked, I made arrangements with the boatman whose only comment was, "Tikay, Sah'ib. But much cold."

Dinner conversation was sustained largely by Diana and me. Both Peter and Pamela seemed remarkably languorous. Not even a pre-dinner drink of an excellent scotch Peter had brought along seemed to stimulate them much. After dinner, we sat briefly over coffee in the sitting room, and then Diana announced we were going out again in the boat. I looked back through the window as we left and saw our companions walking hand in hand back toward the bedrooms.

As the Kashmiri had said, it was "much cold," the keen air draining down the snow-topped mountainsides and spreading across the lake. But overhead the black sky was alive with glittering stars and a yellow moon was gliding upward through the star-fields. Diana snuggled close beside me. "Isn't this simply magnificent, Dana?" I answered with a squeeze of my arm across her shoulders. She was silent for a moment as the graceful boat slid quietly through the still water. Then she said, "I must tell you, I haven't enjoyed the company of any man so much since Phillip died."

I hugged her gently. "Tell me about Phillip."

She was silent again for a moment. "He was a nice man, my husband. We had pretty much grown up together since we were eight or nine. He was some sort of distant cousin. We were great friends, good companions. He was the man I liked more than any other one I knew so we got married. We had three nice years, and then the war came and he was killed in action in France."

"I'm sorry."

"Yes, so am I. It was a terrible blow." She sighed a deep sigh. "But then life goes on."

By the time we reached the middle of the lake the chill was invading my bones, and shortly later Diana said, "I'm getting really cold. Let's go back."

Inside the houseboat sitting room, snug with a fire Mamdoo had made in the small iron stove, I found Peter's bottle of scotch and made us both nightcaps. Sipping her drink, Diana looked at me and then smiled a soft, sweet smile. "You are a dear man," she said. "You've brought me back to life."

"I didn't know you had been deceased."

"Not dead, *deadened*. But no more." She got to her feet. "I'm going to bed, my dear." I walked her to the door of the first bedroom. She turned to me and I kissed her gently, lovingly, "Goodnight, darling," she said.

I went to the second bedroom and undressed, that "darling" still sweet in my ears. I lay in bed, re-living the day, hands cradling my head on the pillow, when suddenly the door softly opened. Diana's white nightgown loomed through the darkness as she approached and then slipped into bed. "I hope I am not being presumptuous," she said.

"Clairvoyant," I said. I took her in my arms, her small body soft and smooth under my touch. I kissed her, again gently and lovingly, but her response was passionate and intense. As my hands caressed her breasts and down her belly and her thighs I found that she was already deeply aroused. Her ardor ignited mine and soon I was as aroused as she.

"Don't wait, Dana darling, don't wait," she whispered. "Now! *Now!*"

I responded and then, joined together, her supple body surging and rippling beneath mine we moved swiftly up to peaks of ecstasy, prolonged and tumultuous ecstasy. Her intensity had startled me at first but then lifted me higher and higher until I passed into a transcendent oblivion. After several suspended moments of supreme bliss, I descended slowly and lay back, panting slightly. I could hear Diana breathing deeply beside me, the breath warm against my cheek.

After a moment or two, I turned to her, "I have a question I would like to ask, my dear Diana."

"After that, sir, you may ask anything you like."

"It's just this. Whatever happened to English reserve?"

She chuckled and put her arms around me. She kissed me on the nose. "*That*," she said, "we take off with our clothes."

Seventeen

About a week after our return from Kashmir a cryptic message arrived from Special Services Headquarters Kandy: IMPLEMENTATION OPERATION TRANSFERRED MI-5. LOCAL REP WILL CONTACT. The only MI-5 officer I knew in Delhi was Ian Ainsley, but I assumed some more senior officer would approach me. I was surprised then later that week as I was walking with Ian down the third fairway of the Delhi Golf Club, during a match he had suggested, when he moved close beside me and said in low voice, "I say, old chap, our masters say we should put heads together on this Wellstone affair. Come to my place afterward and we'll chat." I nodded; he moved away and proceeded to lay an elegant 3-iron shot dead to the pin.

Ian had a one bedroom apartment in the official compound, and it was furnished, as I expected it to be, in ornate, almost rococo style. The draperies were a flowered print, flowers upon flowers in the extravagant Indian style and done in one of those startling Indian mixtures of colors—purple, green, and pink, while the lamps on the carved fruitwood tables were brass with cut-out designs of crescents and exotic geometric shapes. The floor was flush with carpets of intricate and vivid oriental patterns.

"What may I offer you to drink, old son? A squash or a lager? It's too early for a dram of whiskey." It was indeed too early. My Bulova read 9:15. We had teed off at 6 in order to beat the heat of the day which now, in June, soared daily to 110.

"A cold lager, if you have it, Ian," I said. "When does this heat break?"

"Two lagers, Lahti," he told the bearer standing at the kitchen doorway. "Next month, probably. When the rains come the mercury drops 15 degrees. Still beastly hot, you know, and dripping with humidity."

"Still, 15 degrees would help."

"Right you are." The lager beers arrived, frothing at the brim, and Ian said, "Confusion to our enemies!" After he had swallowed he said, "Diana tells me you had a lovely time in Kashmir."

"Couldn't have been better."

"Splendid. She's a grand girl. Deserves happiness."

We both sipped our beer and sat quietly for a moment. Then I said, "Speaking of the ladies, Ian, what has happened to that gorgeous Indian woman you were squiring about, Kirin Rajiv?"

"Still gorgeous. But you know, my dear chap, these upper class Indian women are so bloody puritanical." He simpered briefly. "You know what I mean."

I knew indeed what he meant. Diana and I had encountered him at a restaurant a couple of nights previously with a large-mouthed, broad-hipped English girl, one of those girls whose figure, dress, make-up, and movements of her body causes every male over 15 to take one look and think, "Easy lay."

"But see here, old son, we've got to talk some business about this Wellstone blighter. I gather you have done some capital surveillance work."

"I made a couple discoveries,"

"Good show." He took a sip of beer. "Next step is to nab the bastard. That ought to be quite straight forward."

"Yes?"

"Next time either Wellstone or Tilak makes the trip to Firozabad, we'll stake out the place with the help of the Agra Region Chief Inspector and grab him red-handed."

"We?"

"Yes, certainly. We'll need your help, old boy, in locating the house."

"But how will you know when Wellstone or Tilak is going down?"

"DIB, Intelligence Bureau Delhi, has an informer in his staff of servants. Well-tested, solid source."

I sipped reflectively at my beer. Ian sounded competent, efficient, and I remembered Diana's warning not to underrate him. Later, as I got up to go, Ian said, "We'll need to stay in touch. We'll have to rocket down to Agra on short notice."

Another week went by as the heat mounted daily and dust storms darkened the sky. Some days the dust so saturated the air that the sun at noon looked like the full moon, a round, milky-white ball. Diana remained in remarkably good spirits despite the frightful heat though both of us were somewhat frustrated by circumstance. Acknowledged lovers now, opportunities for seclusion and privacy were few. One weekend, a friend of Diana loaned us her apartment and, under a swishing overhead fan, our bodies laved with sweat, we made love to the very edge of exhaustion. "Ah, Dana," said Diana afterward, as she lay back with golden beads of sweat trickling down between her breasts, "you are a lovely man! A lovely, *lovely* man."

"Dearest, dearest Diana," I said. "I do so love you!"

The following Monday Ian appeared at my door about nine at night. "We must fly," he said. "Wellstone is going down tomorrow. I have a staff car ready. Grab some things quickly."

In ten minutes we were moving swiftly through the darkness on the Agra road in a black Humber sedan driven by a tan-uniformed Sikh. "The Chief Inspector has arranged to put us up," said Ian. "Wouldn't do to be seen in a hotel."

Shortly after midnight we pulled up at a square, white house just on the edge of the commercial section of Agra. A white-uniformed Hindu opened the car door and led us into the house. "Ah, Ainsley," said a heavy-set Englishman. "Come you in."

"Dana Brown here," said Ian. "Chief Inspector Bramley."

"Welcome, Mr. Brown. The bearer will take your bags to your rooms. Come have a wet one to wash the dust from your throats." He led us into a sitting room off the center hallway. "Whiskey *pani*," he said to the bearer while making a circular gesture indicating the three of us. "Sit down, sit down, gentlemen." He turned and nodded at me. "I gather, Mr. Brown, that the house in question is on the eastern outskirts of Firozabad?"

"That's right."

"I think I know the place but of course we will need your guidance to make certain. My tentative plan, Ainsley, unless you have objection, is to drive with Brown over to Firozabad tomorrow morning to survey the situation, and then go back at nightfall to stake out. The local Intelligence Bureau chap will come along."

"Your show, Chief Inspector."

"Jolly good, Ah, the libations. Gentlemen, your health."

"Success," said Ian.

Next morning I sat beside Ian Ainsley in the back seat of the Humber gazing at the thick neck of the Chief Inspector and thinking to myself he was too perfect for the role. He was very nearly a facsimile of the actor who had played the part of Chief Inspector in an Agatha Christie film I had recently seen starring Margaret Rutherford.

Blunt-headed, full-bodied, jovial, and not stupid. He regaled us with stories of crime in Agra including a case of *suttee* in which he had succeeded three times in thwarting the widow's attempts to immolate herself only to fail on the fourth, arriving just in time to see the woman writhing in final agony amidst the flames. "Bloody persistent the buggers are about their ancient customs."

When the lane leading to the house came in sight I tapped Chief Inspector Bramley on the shoulder. "It's there on the left."

"Right you are. Pull up here, Singh." He opened the door beside him and as he got out he said, "If you gentlemen would please wait here." I heard him open the trunk of the car and then I saw him and the driver walk down the lane, the Sikh carrying a surveyor's transit.

"Good cover," said Ian. "Just doing some official surveying."

We sat in silence for at least twenty minutes, watching the entrance to the lane for the men to return. At last the broad figure of the policeman came trudging into view with the Sikh a few steps behind, the transit over his shoulder. "Right," said Bramley. "Looks pretty straightforward."

Ian and I passed that afternoon playing gin rummy in the sitting room while the Chief Inspector attended to official duties. We had an early supper, and then at dusk boarded the Humber and headed back to Firozabad. "Singh will drop us at the entrance to the lane," Bramley said over his shoulder as the car ran swiftly through the gathering darkness, "and then go a quarter mile beyond and park. I've got a four man detail coming along"—he looked back through the rear window—"ah yes, I see they are following close behind."

"If Wellstone is coming down here," I asked Ian, "what are you doing about Ramji Tilak?"

"Special Branch Delhi is picking him up at 8:30 sharp." He looked at his wristwatch. "Forty-five minutes."

The car stopped opposite the lane, and the three of us got out. "Hold just a moment, gentlemen," said Bramley in a low voice, "while I just have a word with these chaps." In a moment he was back. "Right. Now let's proceed quietly up to the house. I will deploy the detail so that the entrances are covered, and I want you two chaps to wait well concealed in the bushes until I signal that the capture has been made."

We moved on as stealthily as we could manage in the deep darkness. The track we were following was sand so there was no gravel to crunch, and a soft, hot breeze rustling the leaves overhead covered the sounds of our movement. The moon was still down and scudding clouds masked the stars. I led Ian to the spot in the bushes I had found the last time I was there, and we settled down for a long wait for the arrival of Wellstone. Now and then we could glimpse, through the lighted windows, figures moving in the room, and occasionally we could hear a brief murmur of conversation. But mostly the only sound was the gentle rustle of the *neem* leaves in the tense, expectant night. Time dragged on, then on and on. My legs began to ache from standing stiffly in one spot, so I knelt down on one knee.

A disagreeable thought passed through my mind. I stood up and pulled Ian close beside me. "Suppose he doesn't come," I whispered in his ear.

He pulled my head over to his. "He'll come. He has a delivery to make."

That gave me something to ponder over. How could Ainsley have got the information to make him certain that Wellstone was making a delivery of some sort? I thought of several possibilities and thereby managed, perhaps, to kill another five minutes of waiting. But then it was back to standing dead quiet and waiting—waiting for an unknown length of time with only uncertainty to sustain us.

Finally, after what seemed half a night-time but was

probably about an hour, we heard the hum of an approaching car on the road from Agra. Ian nudged my ribs and I nodded uselessly in the blackness. The car drew nearer, slowed at the entrance to the lane, and then rolled down the sandy track to the house. By the light glowing from the house I thought I could make out Patwant Singh's battered Morris. The taxi stopped and a burly figure got out and walked quickly up the front steps. The front door opened and closed, and then the only sounds in the hot night were the rustling leaves and a ticking from the nearby car as it cooled.

Five minutes passed as we waited, my mouth dry with expectation. Then suddenly there was a wild outburst of shouting and commotion. I could hear Chief Inspector Bramley bellowing, "You are under arrest! The house is surrounded!" We waited for Bramley's signal that the capture had been made, but instead we heard only more shouting and thrashing about. Then suddenly terribly loud crashes and banging and immediately three pistol shots rang out.

"Bloody hell!" said Ainsley. He broke out of the bushes and ran for the house. I followed behind. Bounding up the steps he opened the front door and stopped. Inside we saw incredible confusion—several men struggling in the hallway amidst the wreckage of broken chairs and shattered glass. Suddenly, out of this jumble emerged Rupert Wellstone running down the hall toward us.

"Out of my way, you bloody bastards!" he yelled. He raised his right arm as he came toward us and I saw the gleam of a knife blade in his hand. I began to back away but Ainsley took a step forward and spread his feet widely. "You son of a bitch!" shouted Wellstone and lunged forward bringing his knife hand sharply down. Then too swiftly for me to see clearly, the two men clashed with a heavy thump, Wellstone came flying through the air toward me over Ainsley's shoulder, and as I flinched and back away, one of Wellstone's flying feet struck my outstretched hand. He landed on his back with a fearful crash, and immediately Ian sprang on him like a cat and pinned him, but it was quite unnecessary. Wellstone was out stone cold, his large eyes staring widely at the ceiling.

Bramley came lumbering down the hallway with dangling hand-cuffs in hand. He knelt down over the prostrate body and snapped them in place. "Well done, lad," he said as he straightened. "Well done."

"Anybody hurt?" I asked. "We heard shots."

"Warning shots only," he answered. "The silly bugger didn't want to give up. And maybe," he looked back down the hallway, "a broken head or two." He walked back to the rear of the house and then returned. "You chaps go on back," he said. "I'll secure the place here with a detail before I return."

Ian and I walked down the lane and found the Humber. My knees were still shaky and my hands were trembling from the surge of adrenalin the violence in the house had triggered. Ainsley's quiet handling of the situation, his strength and agility and his raw courage in confronting a far stronger, heavier man, had left me speechless with admiration. We rode silently along for a time but then I could not hold back any longer. "How in the world could you handle Wellstone like that, Ian? A man fifty pounds heavier than you and armed with a knife."

"Jiu jitsu, old chap. When I was in school at Harrow, a couple of chaps used to bully me a good bit. I was slight, only seven stone, you know, and I got beat about pretty rough. My pater arranged for me to have jiu jitsu lessons during the Long Vacation, and I had no more trouble with those chaps after that." Sitting silently beside this thin-wristed, delicate-mannered, languid Englishman, I remembered Diana's warning not to take him lightly. "He's very brave," she had said. Now I did not need to ask her how she knew.

"I'm not certain I understand how this operation of Wellstone's worked," I said as the big Humber ran smoothly along, its headlights stabbing ahead through the blackness. "I assume Wellstone was getting hold of classified official papers somehow and bringing them down here to be transmitted by radio to the Japanese or the Germans."

"Japanese. He has major business interests in Japan and other ties there."

"But what was Ramji Tilak's role?"

"He procured the papers. He seduced one of our female clerks in the code room."

"With that pretty face."

"I suppose so, along with certain other charms he undoubtedly has." Ian giggled briefly.

I clung momentarily to the door handle while the Sikh driver swerved the Humber sharply to miss an unlighted bullock cart plodding down the middle of the road. "What do you suppose will happen to Wellstone now?"

"I imagine he will be tried for high treason by a military tribunal, convicted, and shot." Ian's tone was as laconic as a railway terminal announcer's.

"And Tilak?"

"Ah, that's different. Indian citizen, you see. The Viceroy will have to make some kind of a ruling, I suspect."

As the big Humber bored through the black night of the Indian countryside, I reflected that perhaps I had, by discovering the site of Rupert Wellstone's wireless transmitter, made a solid contribution to the Allied war effort. The intelligence in the coded messages to and from London that Wellstone and Tilak had obtained by seducing a code clerk was timely and significant and undoubtedly highly useful to Japanese army operations in Burma. Score one for my maiden—and only—counter-intelligence operation.

Eighteen

As Ian Ainsley had predicted, the rains came in July, the great heavy drops plunging through the thick layers of dust and striking the ground as viscous mud. Later, as the monsoon grew in intensity and huge black clouds raced across the sky and the wind blustered and lashed against trees and buildings, the rain fell sweet and clear and the dry earth, after first repelling the rain, softened and received the clear drops gratefully. After two months so hot and dry that nasal membranes cracked and bled, the moisture-laden air was soothing and one could almost forgive the 100-degree temperature. Still, as Ainsley had suggested, the 15-degree drop from 115 degrees only slightly lessened the discomfort, replacing skin-cracking with sweat-soaked days.

The change in the weather did nothing to relieve the daily frustration Diana and I were experiencing from enforced separation as lovers. One weekend we tried taking a room in a modest hotel in Old Delhi. Although it momentarily relieved the aching desire, we found it mostly demoralizing and depressing. After a night in the damp, lumpy bed with the unending bustle of street traffic outside the open windows and the stomp of walking feet in the hallway outside our flimsy bedroom door,

Diana said, "Dana darling, I want you terribly. You know I do—but not like this. This place makes me feel sullied, degraded—like a whore."

I took her moist hand in mine and kissed it gently. "You're right, darling. It's not worthy of us." We dressed, and left. After that fiasco we slogged through what was left of July and then suffered August. By mid-September, however, the rains fell less and less frequently and with steadily weakening intensity. Then they stopped altogether. The sun came back to India once more and set itself to draining the humidity from the air and drying the earth. Golf was possible again after many days when the course had been closed because the fairways were spotted with ponds and the greens puddled.

Along with the sun, fortune smiled on Diana and me. One day, as I met her at the Red Cross office, she came bounding down the steps with a broad sunny smile. "Can you believe it, Dana? Peter Billington has got four places on the Viceregal staff plane flying up to Kashmir next month and has invited us to join him and Pam!" We hugged each other joyfully in sweet anticipation.

With that glorious prospect before us we took care of the rest of September with lazy days of golf on the lush, grassy fairways and quiet evenings strolling hand in hand along New Delhi's fragrant flowered boulevards. Then at last the awaited day arrived and we boarded the airplane for Srinagar. On the trip north it seemed to me, when I glanced over at her, that Diana's gaze meeting mine was no less expectantly longing than Pamela's with Peter.

Kashmir's dominant colors in April had been pink, blue, and white—the pink of peach blossoms on the laden trees, the blue of the sapphire sky, the dazzling white of the snow-crested mountains. Now in October the dominant colors were *gold*, blue, and white—the bronzey gold of the *chinar* trees in autumn foliage, the unchanging blue of the crystalline sky, and the eye-piercing white of the mountain snow. But in the garden beside our houseboat the color that prevailed was gold, the gold of thousands of leaves adorning the magnificent trees of Akbar, their massive trunks lofting branches high into the sky and spreading them broadly in a golden embrace of the garden below.

For Diana and me the days were as golden as the leaves of the *chinars*. On the days we did not take long walks along the lanes outside the houseboat compound, we spent gliding across Dal Lake in the *shikara* with the boatman standing on his platform on the stern poling us through the water, while Diana and I lolled in cushioned comfort. And always on our passage across the lake we encountered the elegantly shaped boats of the Kashmiri, floating on the water like leaves curled up at either end and resting on a mirror. Sometimes the exquisite craft were off in the distance, black silhouetted shapes on the water, and sometimes we passed them close by, the boatman poling his vessel carrying some unidentified cargo bound for an unknown destination. "Isn't it romantic?" said Diana. "Isn't it too perfect?"

One day the boatman proposed to take us to the Shalimar Gardens across Dal Lake from the houseboat and in the lee of the snow-topped mountains. Part way across we passed the floating island Diana had once proclaimed was hers, Diana's Island. "Ask him to stop so I can set foot on my island," she said. But the boatman showed no inclination to stop and as we glided past Diana said, "Oh well, another time."

We spent an hour walking around the Shalimar Gardens with their massive flower beds beside terraced pools. Down the center of each pool ran a row of fountainheads, now turned off for the winter. "Can you imagine how glorious this must have been for Akbar and his court, sitting in state in that gilded pavilion between the pools, with the fountains playing on every side, cooling and misting the air?" asked Diana, her lovely face glowing with pleasure.

"Magical." I answered. "And all the while those white-peaked mountains as backdrop."

On the way back Diana rested her golden head on my shoulder and murmured, "Oh Dana, I've never been so happy. Let's not let it ever end."

"Never."

After dinner that night with Peter and Pamela, the two affianced lovers who had emerged from their end of the houseboat with flushed faces and had made excuses shortly after finishing their coffee for returning there, Diana and I sat on the sofa in the beautiful little sitting room and talked at length about ourselves and our futures. "What will you do after the war is over?" she asked.

"Go back to newspaper work I guess. What about you?"

"Oh, I'll go back to England and try to find something useful to do—volunteer social work perhaps or maybe find a job of some sort. You know, this Red Cross work is the first useful thing I've ever done in my life."

"Except brighten every corner where you were."

She poked my ribs with a stiff finger. "Stop it! I'm being serious."

"So am I." I leaned over and kissed her. I had meant it to be a gentle kiss but somehow it developed into something a bit more involved than that.

Diana pushed me away. "You're being serious, my lad, but in the wrong way. Just at the moment I mean. We're *talking,* talking seriously."

I straightened up "All right, Diana Ainsley. You want serious. I'll give you serious." I took her left hand in mine. "Diana dearest, I love you very much and I want you to marry me."

Her green eyes widened and then moistened slightly. She pulled me to her and kissed me softly. "Dana, I love you too but I can't marry you."

"And why not?"

"Dozens of reasons. You are American and I am English, just for starters."

"Are you suggesting that that would be miscegenation?"

She chuckled. "No, silly. It's just not feasible. Where would we live, out on the Ohio prairie?"

"Probably. You could feed the chickens and milk the cows while I fought off the Indians."

"Just as I thought."

"Look here, you witty little Limey. You're the one who wanted to be serious."

"You're right. Bang on right. I'm sorry."

"That's better. Now, listen my sweet. To me the important thing is that we love each other. Therefore we should get married. Where we live we can deal with later."

"How?"

"Unstoppable, aren't you? Well, for example, I could find a job in England as correspondent for an American newspaper. Or I could work in London for one of the wire services, AP or UPI."

She looked at me earnestly. "You *are* serious, aren't you?" She held my hand and raised it and kissed each fingertip separately. Then she looked up. "You know, darling, the difficulties look enormous to me now but one thing is clear. I don't want to lose you after the war is over."

"Then we have two alternatives, get married or go on living in rapturous sin."

"That's all right for now but it won't do for a lifetime." She put her hand up to my cheek. "Darling, we both know what we want. We just don't know how to get it. Let's put our decision aside until the war is over."

"All right, but only if you'll agree it's a decision that's really been made."

"I'll agree on one condition."

"Which is?"

"That you'll kiss me now and take me to bed."

So we went to bed and made love. And what love we made! Finer than passion, it was the pure, incandescent love of two people who seek immersion into the other self, lovers who are expressing transcendent admiration and transcendent affection. But then it was passion too, hot-blooded, clasping, panting, surging, driving passion. To me it was incredible that so small a body as Diana's could be both a receptacle and a bestower of such intense sensual ecstasy. Afterward, we lay holding each other close, joined and silent, while our bodies went on speaking—speaking love.

The next day was another golden one. We walked down the orchard lanes through the crisp, bright air in the morning and sailed in the *shikara* in the afternoon. The boatman suggested we cross Dal Lake to an ancient Mughal bridge over a small mountain stream on the other side. It was a flawless afternoon with the brilliant sun slicing through the keen air and glinting off the mirrored lake. We could see the Mughal bridge ahead, a classically curved shape, part of the arc of a circle, and it stood firm and serene after three centuries. Beyond, lifting high into the blue, were the glistening snow peaks, glorious harbingers of the majestic Himalayas rising not far beyond.

Dinner that evening was more lively than usual. Diana was gay as a lark, and soon had the other two chittering away with her in that high-pitched, staccato manner only the English can manage. I lay back against the sofa cushions, a glass of Peter's fine scotch in hand, and watched the play of expressions of Diana's lovely face. I have never been more content.

After dinner Peter and Pamela made their usual rather prompt retreat to their room. Diana suggested we go outside and look at the night. The air was sharp and chill as we walked out on the little dock beside the houseboat. There was a slight ripple on the lake and the *shikara* lying beside the dock chuckled and slapped gently in the little waves. Overhead, the black sky was ablaze with myriad stars and Orion, the great hunter with his broad shoulders and glowing blue dagger, was looming up in the eastern sky. "Dana!" cried Diana. "Doesn't it simply take your breath away?"

I squeezed her hand by way of answer.

Then she looked down at the *shikara* and turned back quickly to me. "Darling, let's go out in the boat! It's such a glorious night."

"But the boatman isn't here."

"You can make the boat go, can't you? An old Great Lakes sailor like you?"

"I suppose I could. He just poles it along."

"Then we'll do it! Let's go put on warm clothes."

In a few minutes we were back. I handed Diana aboard and loosed the lines both fore and aft. The pole had been lashed to the canopy over the seat, but I undid the fastenings and pushed her away from the dock. It took a couple of shoves with the pole against the bottom to get the knack of it but soon we were gliding along with a slight hiss of the water at the bow and stern.

"Darling," said Diana. "I can't see the stars under this canopy. I'm coming back with you." She climbed over the seat and stood just in front of me on the platform. In the blackness we could see nothing close by but far out on the lake there were flares blazing aboard a native houseboat. Their dancing flames shimmered in long streaks across the glassy surface of the lake, making bright lanes through the sparkles of the reflected stars. After a couple of hundred yards out from the dock, as I judged it to be, I turned the boat to starboard and set a course more or less parallel to the shore.

Several minutes later, while Diana sighed and exclaimed over the dramatic beauty of the night, the boat bumped softly against something. "What is it, Dana?" Diana asked. "I can't see." She peered over the port side. "Oh yes I can. It's my floating island! It's Diana's Island.

Hold the boat still, darling, I'm going to get off on my island."

"Diana! I'm not sure—"

But I was too late. She had already stepped over the gunwale onto the grassy, bushy surface. "Oh, Dana, this is wonderful! I'm walking on my own island!"

I could barely make out her dim figure in the darkness as she stood on the floating surface and took several short steps. Suddenly, there was a surprised "Oh!" followed by quick rustling sounds and Diana was gone. My first thought was she had gone through a soft spot in the floating island and would soon surface on one side or the other. I pushed away a little so she would not come up under the boat and then waited. Seconds passed and Diana did not come up but I could hear a kind of boiling in the water. More seconds passed and panic began to mount. "Diana!" I yelled. "Diana!" But there was no sound in the darkness except the water whispering against the boat.

I knew there was nothing else to do. I had to go down and find her. I ripped off my heavy jacket and dove off the side into the icy black water. I am no great swimmer but desperation is a powerful stimulant, and I got down several feet below the surface and groped around under the floating sod. What I found with my flailing hands was a thicket of roots dropping down from the floating sod, extending farther down than I could reach. I surfaced, gasping for air, and dove again. And again and again and again. Once when I came up I grabbed the side of the boat and yelled, "Help! Help!" I took a deep breath and screamed as loudly as I could, "Help! Help!" But seconds were passing and I went down again. I tried to force my way through the thicket of tightly bunched roots, and once when I reached in and groped around I thought I might have touched Diana's hand but it may have been only a smooth root. I kept on diving, sobbing now and swallowing water and gasping for breath until suddenly blackness closed swiftly and engulfed me.

I have only shards of memory of that night after that until one day I found myself back at my desk in Delhi. I dimly recall a spotlight blasting into my eyes and Peter Billington pulling me up over the side of a boat, and I sometimes have a shattering image of Diana's white, dead face, hair plastered tightly to her head and mud oozing from the side of her mouth. But that is all.

Nineteen

I had become a mechanical man. I sat at my desk day after day, and I attended meetings and read reports and wrote reports, but all the while I was as numb as a stone. Something else was going on inside my head, something I find hard to describe. I seemed to be aware only of those things or thoughts I was focusing on directly. That small circle of focus was surrounded by darkness. It was almost at though my mind had lost its peripheral vision. Sights, sounds, or smells outside the flashlight beam of my attention did not seem to exist.

Once, Ian Ainsley—who was kinder to me than I had thought that effete Englishman could be—asked me to play golf with him. I fought back the pain of playing on that familiar course without Diana, but the round was a disaster. All my judgment skills seemed to have vanished. I sometimes hit the ball thirty yards over the green and sometimes fifty yards short. My putts strayed widely to one side or the other of the cup. After the round, I turned down Ian's offer of a lager and went back to my room. "Thanks, Ian," I said as I left the Club.

"Don't mention it, old chap."

The days dragged by one by one, and then one day I noticed something very strange. As I started to turn the page of my little desk calendar, I noticed it was reading October 31. But yesterday, when I had attended the weekly Council meeting, was Thursday the 27th. Then how could today be the 31st? Had I turned too many pages? I picked up the nearby copy of *The Times of India*. The dateline was *October 31*! Time had jumped forward four days!

That was beyond explaining but I decided to put it aside for the time being. Then it happened again. I had spent Sunday alone, reading and walking in the afternoon. When I went into my office the next day the desk calendar read Thursday, November 4. Baffled, I turned to the day's newspaper. The dateline read unmistakably, November 4! It was clear to me that something strange was happening to the flow of time in India. Of course, it could be a world-wide phenomenon, I told myself, but I had tangible evidence that it was occurring here in Delhi. I decided to talk with Ainsley about it, so I dropped by his place that afternoon. He offered me a lager or a squash but I said no, I couldn't stay. "I came to ask whether you've noticed anything odd about the passage of time lately."

"Passage of time?"

"Yes, you know. Time suddenly speeding up."

"Oh, you mean, sometimes time seems to pass slowly and sometimes quickly?"

"Well, sort of. But this is different. Big chunks of time, like three or four days, zip by just over-night."

I thought Ian looked at me a little strangely so I tried to explain. "Well, you know, this *is* India," I said reasonably, "and very strange things sometimes take place here, things for which it is hard to find a scientific explanation."

Ian nodded. "That's true. Tell me, old son, how have you noticed this speed-up in time?"

"Well," I said, happy for a chance to lay out the evidence, "after a Sunday at home I go in the office next morning and my calendar says Thursday. The newspaper says Thursday too, so you see it's not just a mistake in my calendar. Time *has* speeded up." To me, the evidence seemed irrefutable.

"Yes, I see. Hmmm. You know, old boy, I've been frightfully busy of late, and I may not have been paying close attention. I'll watch carefully from now on and let you know. Umm, sure you won't have a lager?"

"No, thanks. I've got to get on back." I walked home happy to have another observer joining me in keeping track of this extraordinary behavior of time.

Next morning I hurried to the desk in my office and checked the calendar. It said Friday, November 5 just as it should. After checking the dateline on *The Times*—it also read November 5—I sat down to read the morning news. In a moment two men appeared in my doorway, Ainsley and a stranger whom Ian introduced as Dr. Morrow. "I was telling Dr. Morrow about your observations regarding jumps in time," he said, "and he would like to hear more about it."

"Yes, it's very interesting," Dr. Morrow said. "An unusual phenomenon."

Pleased to have a professional man inquiring into the evidence I had gathered, I laid it out for him just as I had for Ainsley.

"And this has happened several times?" Morrow asked.

"Twice I can be certain of. Maybe more times when I was not particularly paying attention."

"I see."

The three of us went on discussing the matter for several minutes. Now and then Ainsley and Dr. Morrow exchanged glances, and I assumed they were making certain that the other was also convinced by the evidence I had presented. To me, the fact that the date on the calendar was *the same each time* as the dateline of the day's newspaper was conclusive. Time *had* jumped.

Finally, Dr. Morrow said, "You've certainly made a

fascinating discovery, Mr. Brown. I would like to confer with my colleagues about it and come back to you this afternoon."

"Fine. I'll be here."

That afternoon, Dr. Morrow appeared by himself. He sat down in the chair beside my desk and smiled at me in a most friendly way. "My colleagues in Kandy and I—"

"Kandy! Then you're with—"

"Yes, I'm on the staff of Special Services. We have decided that we want to send you to London for further consultation on this matter."

"London! But what about my work here?"

"An officer is coming to take your place while you're gone."

I was puzzled by the suddenness of this decision and appalled by the thought of the long journey to England, but I decided it did make sense. People in London needed to be informed about this phenomenon too, and I was the best person to present the evidence. I was telling Dr. Morrow I agreed with the decision when Ian Ainsley appeared. "Oh, Ian," I said, "Dr. Morrow thinks we ought to take this matter up with London."

"Yes, so he's told me."

Dr. Morrow took me gently by the arm. "There's a P and O freighter in Calcutta making ready to sail for England in a day or two," he said, "We need to get you down there tonight or tomorrow."

"Come along, old son," said Ian. "I'll help you pack up."

While Ian and I were gathering clothes and books and shoving them in my suitcase, a thought suddenly came into my mind. It brought with it a sudden sharp pain so I pushed it back, but then it came again and after weighing it against the pain for a moment or two I turned to Ian. "You know, I was just wondering, Ian, whether—" I stopped. I was right at the point where the pain grew sharpest.

Ian straightened from the packing. "Yes, old boy, wondering what?"

"Well, I was wondering whether I could—" I stopped short again because I realized that a sob was rising in my throat and about to burst out.

He put his hand on my shoulder. "I'm certain I can help whatever it is."

"Well, it's just—" Then I decided to plunge ahead, sob or no sob. "I wondered whether it would be all right for me to visit Diana's family in England." Then I did break down and sobbed into my hands for several moments.

"Dana"—Ian had never before called me by my first name—"I feel certain they would like to see you. I'll get word to Lady Bixley that you're coming."

The voyage from Calcutta to Southampton was uneventful but long. With my background in ships and my fascination with foreign places the trip through the Red Sea and the Suez Canal should have been memorable, but I was immersed in thick, gray dullness, pierced only by that narrow beam of my attention. From Cairo on we travelled in convoy which meant we could sail no faster than the slowest freighter. We had a couple of submarine or bomber alerts but nothing happened. Since I had no calendar with me I was unable to observe any anomalies in the flow of time and one day seemed to succeed another in orderly fashion aboard the ship. I was beginning to wonder whether the time-jumps were exclusively confined to India.

There was one episode during the voyage that in retrospect I found embarrassing. I woke up with a start in the dark and fumbled around to get my left hand free from the covers so I could read my radium-dialed Bulova. To my horror it said 6:15, and I realized I was late for standing my 6 to 10 watch. Don would be furious and rightly so. I threw on a shirt and pants and hurried up on deck. Nothing seemed familiar, and I had trouble locating the hatchway leading down to the firehold. At last I found a doorway, and as I opened it I could hear the familiar sound of the ship's engine turning. I had gone only a little way when a ship's officer stopped me. "Where are you going, sir?"

"Down to the firehold. I'm late for my watch."

He looked at me strangely. "You're mistaken, sir. You're not a member of this crew."

Not a member of the crew! Who had been standing the 6 to 10 coal passer's watch all this time? But then I looked over the officer's shoulder, and I suddenly realized that the companionway we were standing in bore no resemblance to anything aboard either the *Morse* or *Maunaloa*. I was confused by this and stunned for a moment. Then I realized the officer was right: I was aboard the P and O *East Wind*, and I was a passenger not a crew member. I hardly knew what to say, but I finally stammered, "I must have had a bad dream, officer. Sorry."

The office in London I had been directed to was located just below The Strand, I walked there from the Armed Services Club off Albemarle Street where I was billeted. The destruction I saw as I walked that fairly short distance was appalling. Whole blocks of buildings in the heart of London were mere piles of rubble. There were stacks of charred timber and rubbish everywhere and great gaping holes both in the pavement and where buildings had stood. I realized then as I had not before that World War II as seen from New Delhi had nothing to do with reality. Here it was tangible and hurtful, even to someone as benumbed as I.

My appointment had been made with Dr. Andrew MacDougal who turned out to be a stocky man of medium height with a quiet smile. He had a dark mole on his left cheek that reminded me incongruously of the beauty spot on the cheek of the silent movie star, Pola Negri. We sat opposite each other in arm-chairs in the sterilely plain office. Until he spoke I could not be certain of his nationality but just a few words disclosed his American heritage, probably New England.

"I understand you've had some interesting experiences in India," he said. "I've never been in India. Must be a fascinating country. I wish you would tell me about your experiences there if you feel so inclined."

I was not merely inclined; I was eager. So I told him about the instances when time had leaped forward three or four days over-night. To make certain he understood that this had really occurred I put heavy emphasis upon the coincidence of the date on my desk calendar and the dateline of the newspaper.

Dr. MacDougal nodded calmly when I finished. "You must feel as I do," he said, "that *anything* can happen in India. We both know of cases which are comparable in some ways to this."

"Yes, indeed," I said, pleased by his response and the way the conversation was moving.

"You must have had other interesting or possibly disturbing experiences there," he said.

"Ye-s-s." I hesitated, wondering whether the incident with Rupert Wellstone would be appropriate to mention. I decided not. "But I can't think of any in particular."

"I understood from someone that there may have been a boating accident of some sort."

"Well, yes, that's true." I pushed back an oncoming rush of pain. "Unfortunately, I don't remember anything much about it. I blacked out apparently."

I wanted to get Dr. MacDougal back to the time business but before I could speak again, he said, "I would like to help you remember."

A violent surge of anger jumped up in my throat. I was furious. "God damn it, I don't *want* to remember!

It's very painful. Besides, I came here to tell you about those jumps in time I observed in India."

He smiled gently and the mole on his cheek rose slightly. "Do you suppose the two things might be related somehow?"

"I'm damned if I see how. Do you think I *imagined* it? Are you forgetting that the date on my desk calendar and the newspaper dateline coincided exactly?"

"No. No, indeed. I'm sure it happened exactly as you describe it."

"Then how in hell can you think there is any connection?"

"There may not be. But from what I've been told it was a very unusual accident, and I am interested in hearing more about it. I've been around boats all my life and anything to do with them fascinates me. Bear with me for a few minutes and try to remember what you can. We can come back to the time business later."

I pondered this for a minute. After all the man's interest seemed sympathetic, not mere curiosity. "Well, all right. I'll try as best I can."

He smiled warmly. Then he asked softly. "How did you happen to go out in the boat at night?"

"Oh, Diana"—I gulped—"Diana wanted to go out."

"Yes, I see. Go on."

And for the next three quarters of an hour, I painfully dredged out one recollection after another. But then my memory went blank again and I broke down sobbing. Dr. MacDougal brought me a glass of water. "You did fine, Mr. Brown. That will be all for the day. Come back tomorrow at the same time."

As I walked back to the Armed Services Club, picking my way around and through the terrible piles of rubble and gaping craters, I thought about the session with Dr. MacDougal. In the first place, I realized now he was clearly a medical man, not a scientist. And his probing deeper and deeper into the accident on Dal Lake must mean he thought there was a connection between it and my observations of the time discontinuities. Was it possible that during those four day periods I had blacked out, in a sense, even though I had apparently carried out my normal duties?

I accosted him next time we met. "You think I'm delusional, don't you, and that that stuff about time jumps is all imaginary."

He smiled warmly. "Not imaginary. I'm certain you experienced just what you've described. But suppose for a moment it was some kind of delusion. Would that be so terrible? You have suffered a severe shock. Sometimes our minds take extraordinary measures to protect themselves."

"But it doesn't make sense." And I reminded him again about the identical dates on the desk calendar and the newspaper.

He smiled again, "Let's go on reviving your memories of the boating accident. When we get that all laid out maybe we can make sense of the time phenomenon."

I agreed reluctantly, and we proceeded to rehearse the progression of events I had remembered in the previous session. Then we pushed on a little further until suddenly I hit a black wall. I could remember hearing Diana exclaim over the beauty of the night and I could recall the soft lurch as the *shikara* bumped something in the dark. The next thing I could remember was Peter Billington's flashlight blazing into my eyes. And that is where the situation remained throughout the next four sessions with Dr. MacDougal. Try as I might—and I could try to remember now without breaking down—I could not fill in that interval. I could see that MacDougal was frustrated, but it was simply impossible for me to break through that black barrier. And though I could now talk freely about what I could remember, I still felt numb as a stone and I still saw the world through a knothole, so to speak.

By this time we were coming into the third week of

December, and I still had not got in touch with Diana's family. I broached the matter with Dr. MacDougal. He brightened instantly, the mole on his cheek moving upward with his smile. "I think that would be a good thing for you to do," he said.

The following Friday I took the train down to Winchester. The sun was smiling on England and her tidy fields and woods as the train rolled through Surrey and Hampshire. I got off at Winchester station, and as I walked into the waiting room a man in a black uniform approached me. "Mr. Brown?"

"Yes."

"I am Lady Bixley's chauffeur. Her Ladyship is expecting you. I'll take your bag, sir." He led me through the waiting room to a black Bentley outside. "It's a short journey, sir," he said as he handed me inside the sedan with its high seats and beige upholstery.

It took about twenty minutes as we drove east out of Winchester until we came to a lane with a sign reading "Winterbourne House." At the end of the lane was a circular gravel driveway before a large, square, pink-bricked building set in the middle of a wide expanse of green lawn. Off one corner an enormous cedar tree spread thick branches over a circle of flower beds.

The front door opened as I got out of the Bentley, and a tall, blonde version of Diana stood in the doorway. She held out her hand as I approached. "Hello! I am Penelope, Diana's sister. We are so pleased you came. Mummy is in the drawing room, expecting you."

She led me down a broad hallway with a winding staircase off one side and a door to the drawing room on the other. Lady Bixley sat in the center of a white sofa and as I approached she held out her hand to me. "Welcome, Mr. Brown. Come sit down and have tea. I'm delighted you wished to come see us."

I sat in a chair placed diagonally to the sofa and after accepting a cup of tea from a black-uniformed maid, I gazed admiringly at Lady Bixley. She was small, about Diana's size, with remarkably bright blue eyes and a shapely head crowned with soft white hair. There was a patient sweetness about her and a gentle kindliness. I could almost feel her reaching out to me, seeking to put me at ease.

"You know, Mr. Brown, I feel I already know you. Diana's letters always spoke of you and the things you did together. To tell you the truth, I began to think I might have an American son-in-law someday."

I looked quickly away from her sweet face and down into my cup of tea while tears welled up.

"Oh dear," she said. "I'm afraid I've upset you. Forgive me for being so impulsive. Please don't mind. We'll talk about something else. Tell me about your home. Is it in Iowa? I'm frightfully bad about geography."

"Ohio," I said and told her a little about Denton.

We chatted a while longer over our tea and then Lady Bixley said. "You must be tired after your journey. Penelope will show you to your room, but please feel free to walk about as you like. We will all meet here at seven for a glass before dinner."

The room Penelope led me to was at one corner of the house. It looked out one way over a meadow running up a gentle hillside and out the other over large stables with brick foreyards. A fireplace with white mantel and side panels stood on one wall beside the canopied bed, while the wall behind the bed was decorated with dark blue and white patterned wall-paper. I sat down in a corner chair and admired the room. It had a grace and a charm that was like Diana. Indeed, I told myself, Diana had walked about in this room, perhaps had slept in it. Diana's presence was here. I could feel it for the first time since that tragic night. Somehow I found the thought comforting, not painful.

We were four at dinner. Penelope's husband, Michael Leigh, hobbled toward me supporting himself with a cane in his right hand. He shifted the cane to his left hand in order to shake hands with me. "Forgive my awkwardness with this damned leg," he said. "I took a hit during the landing last June in Normandy."

"Sorry."

"Damned nuisance." He smiled at me below a crisp black moustache. "Decent trip down?"

"Very pleasant."

"Good show." He turned then to Lady Bixley sitting on the white sofa holding a glass of sherry. "And how are you this evening, Mother dear?"

"Splendid, thank you, darling."

Conversation at dinner was mostly about the war with Captain Leigh doing most of the talking. "It looks to me," he said, turning in my direction, "as though it can't last much longer in Europe the way your chaps are tearing across the Continent. That fellow, Patton, is a real demon, isn't he?"

I could only agree that General Patton was indeed something of a demon.

After we had coffee in the drawing room, Penelope and Captain Leigh said their good-nights, leaving Lady Bixley alone with me. We sat silently for a few moments and then I tried to express to this gracious lady what I was feeling while in her presence. "I must tell you, Lady Bixley, how very much it means to me to be here with you. In Diana's house, with Diana's family."

She held out her hand to me, and I got up and took it. Then I sat down beside her on the sofa. "It means a very great deal to me as well. To meet you and have you here with us. My dear"—she paused and looked directly at me with her sapphire eyes—"would you mind very much if I called you 'Dana'?"

"It would please me a great deal."

"Thank you." She patted my hand once or twice. "My dear Dana, you must know as I do that Diana loved you very much. Her letters went into raptures about you in a way I had never known her to do before. As I said, I fully expected you two to be married after this hideous war is over."

"We planned to be. And then we had that godawful accident!" I paused, collecting myself again. "I loved Diana so deeply that I will never be able to love anyone else."

"Oh no, Dana, you must never say that! That's not being fair to yourself, and Diana would not have wanted that." She stopped, smiling softly as though recalling a secret thought. "Let me tell you in confidence about myself. When I was twenty I was deeply, deeply in love with a man I met at a weekend house party. He was a *lovely* young man. To me, he was absolute perfection! We went together to other house parties and London balls for the next two years—actually twenty-six months. And then he was killed one day in a motor car accident on the road to Bath. I was devastated. I could think of nothing else for the next year or more, and it really took me three years to get over it. And I have never stopped loving him. Then I met Sir Harold, and we have been very happy together for thirty-two years."

"I see." We sat quietly then, each thinking his own thoughts.

Lady Bixley spoke again. "I have been wondering, Dana—and please don't answer if you had rather not—just how the accident happened. Diana was such a strong swimmer. Did the boat capsize?"

"Oh, no. Diana stepped off the boat onto a floating island out on the lake. There were several of them on Dal Lake. She walked about a bit and then stepped onto a soft spot which gave way beneath her. She fell down into a mass of tangled roots under the surface which trapped her and held her until she drowned."

"How extraordinary!"

I went on then describing in detail all the incidents of that dreadful night. It was unbelievable. This gentle lady, patient and understanding, the mother of my dearest love, had succeeded through kind sympathy where the professional skills of Dr. MacDougal had failed. She had enabled me to breach that implacable black wall in my memory. For the first time since Dal Lake had closed over Diana I could speak freely of what had happened. We talked quietly for another half hour. Then I gave my arm to Lady Bixley and we climbed the winding stairway to her room where I gently kissed her offered cheek and we said affectionate good nights.

Later, as I stood at the window of my room looking at the hillside meadow glooming dimly in the night, I realized that the visual knothole through which I had been peering was now gone. My peripheral vision, both mental and visual, had been restored. The world, or at least this dear and special part of Hampshire, lay before me, whole and complete.

That night, as I lay in bed in Diana's house, I dreamt again that wonderfully satisfying dream. I had again been summoned to take over the editor's job on *The Student Record*. I awoke and rolled over, smiling.

Twenty

I had plenty of time on the troopship bound for New York to reminisce about my weekend with the Bixley family and the subsequent days in England before my departure. My session with Dr. MacDougal had been short and decisive. He nodded understandingly when I told him about my conversation with Lady Bixley and my sudden ability to recall all the details of the accident.

"Being Diana's mother and kind and sympathetic, she offered release from your guilt, your latent doubts about whether you should have stopped Diana from stepping off the boat or whether you should have somehow managed to rescue her. She gave you unspoken forgiveness."

"Yes, I see." I went on remembering that conversation and Lady Bixley's kind eyes until MacDougal spoke again.

"So, with that behind you, I think this should terminate our sessions. You don't need to go back over those time jumps now, do you?"

"I guess not. What happened probably is that my memory just shut down for several days at a time. Is that right?"

"That's it. To forestall any recollection of events which were exceedingly painful to recall."

I shook my head. "It certainly was a persuasive experience."

"I'm sure it was." He looked at me thoughtfully for a moment. "Well, now, Brown. We have two choices. I can pronounce you fit to return to duty in Delhi or I can give you a medical discharge and send you home. I can do either one with a clear conscience. What's your choice?"

That choice was easy. To return to Delhi for the duration would have been torture. I would have met remembrances of Diana wherever I turned. Besides, I did not feel my work there was of much significance. The Allies were capable of winning the war without the help I had been providing. So I applied for passage home at the transportation office, and a week later I was boarding a troop transport at Southampton.

It is no news, I am certain, to say that January is not the month to cross the North Atlantic. Especially not going westward, beating into northwest winds and twenty foot seas. Or even more especially, not with a boatload of sick and convalescent warriors returning home from war. From the time we cleared the Isle of Wight until The Battery came in sight, the ship never ceased to wallow and roll and pitch and plunge. The mess room, the sleeping quarters, the corridors, and every nook and cranny of the ship all reeked of vomit from day one to the end of the voyage. As one Army sergeant, hobbling on one leg and a crutch—the other leg a stump ending at the knee—said to me one day. "There's no need to worry now about goin' to Hell 'cause Hell sure's hell can't be worse than this!"

It took two hours of standing in long lines in the dockside shed after berthing at seven a.m. to complete arrival formalities but then I was free to go my own way. An Army bus took me to midtown Manhattan, and I walked two blocks to Grand Central Station to investigate train schedules. I decided on the Twentieth Century Limited, departing at four p.m., which would take me to Cleveland where I would transfer to Denton. A four o'clock departure left most of the day to kill in New York.

Out of idle curiosity I went to a nearby telephone booth and leafed through the Manhattan pages of the directory, running my fingers down the long columns of names beginning with G: Grant, Grauer, Gravely, Graver. Ah, Graver—James, John, Julius, Justin. No Judson, *no* Judson Graver. I tried turning to the O's. O'Hara, O'Keefe, O'Reilly, O'Shaugnessy. O'Shaugnessy—Arthur, Patrick, Ruth, S., Samuel. "S."? Could this be Sally? There was one way to find out. I argued with myself for a moment and then dialed the number. After three rings a woman's voice answered. "Yes?" It was a throaty voice, slightly querulous, not recognizably Sally's.

"Sally?"

"Who's this?" Now the tone was irritable.

"Dana Brown. I'm trying to reach Sally O'Shaugnessy."

There was a gasp as sudden as an explosion. Then in a voice that was almost a croak, "Dana! Where *are* you?"

"Grand Central. I just got off a ship and I'm catching a train to Ohio this afternoon."

"This afternoon? So soon? Well, will you, have you time—Can you come see me?"

I hesitated. The warmest sentiment I could arouse for Sally was a mildly friendly nostalgia. There were so many bad memories lying between us. True, beyond them in the more distant past there were good ones too. But more than anything, I guess, I was curious. What was Sally like now?

"I believe I can. For a little while. Where are you?"

"East Seventy-third. Come now and I'll put on my best new dress, your favorite color, blue."

Sally's apartment was a third floor walk-up, and when the door opened to my knock a gust of stale tobacco-laden air swept out. A short, fat woman stood in the doorway, no one I knew. She *was* wearing a blue dress, one that ballooned down from the shoulders with no waist. "Dana!" she said and her pulpy-skinned face broke into a smile, making her eyes crinkle in the old Sally way. It *was* Sally. She held out her arms to me and we hugged, her full belly bumping against my thighs. I tried to kiss her cheek but she managed to hit my mouth with her tobacco-flavored lips. "I'm delirious, darling, seeing you again. I thought I'd lost you forever. Where have you been?"

"India."

"India! My God, not really!" She led me into the small living room. Two doors led off it. Through one I could see a double bed, through the other a refrigerator. She sat on a couch against the wall. I sat opposite her in a wooden-armed chair. "What took you to India?"

I told her about joining Special Services and being assigned to a liaison job in Delhi. After a few minutes I could see her attention was waning. "But what about you, Sally? Still working on magazines?"

"Yes, free lance." She took a deep drag on her cigarette, her round cheeks hollowing slightly around her mouth. She shook her head and then blew out a long stream of blue smoke. "I've had a rotten time, Dana. Simply rotten. Two years ago I married a man I knew in the magazine trade, Barry Martin. We were together less than a year but in that time he managed to get his hands on what little money I had and then one morning he simply walked out. Without a word. I heard later he was living with a colored girl, a model. It knocked me for a cock-eyed loop. He absolutely destroyed all my confidence and messed up my self-esteem. That's why I've gotten so goddamned fat."

I could think of nothing worthwhile to say just then so I sat silently looking at Sally, trying to reconstruct the blithe, slender young woman I had known. I had no success.

After a moment she dabbed her eyes with a kleenex.

"Well, hell," she said. "Can I offer you something to drink? Join me in a martini?"

"Do you have a lager?"

"Lager?"

"A beer."

"Will Budweiser do you?"

"If that's what you have."

I watched her get heavily off the studio couch and walk with short, fat-lady steps to the kitchen. When she came back she handed me the long-necked brown beer bottle and a glass. "You're headed for Denton. Are your family still there?"

"No. My father and mother have moved to California. Long Beach. He's managing a bowling alley."

"What about your sister?"

"Irene. She married an insurance agent. They're living in Akron."

Sally sipped her martini from a tall, 8-ounce glass. "Then you have no family in Denton, so why are you going back? What are you going to do there?"

"Try to get my old job back at the *News*."

She shook her head almost angrily. "Oh, Dana, that's so tiresome! So stodgy. You ought to get out of that old rut. You used to talk about being a foreign correspondent."

"No more. I think India more than satisfied my desire for life abroad."

"But Dana, not Denton! Why don't you stay in New York? I've always felt you belonged here, here in the major leagues. For that matter, stay in New York and you can move in here with me."

"No. Thanks, Sally, but no thanks. New York to me is as bad as India. I want to get back to Ohio. Somehow, Ohio feels right to me now and the rest of the world feels wrong."

"You baffle me," she said. She sipped heavily at her martini which was now half gone. I watched as her face passed from thoughtful to pensive to sad. "You know,

Dana, that son of a bitch Barry never loved me. Never did." She shook her head angrily. "And Judson never loved me either. He just wanted to screw me. Told me I was a great lay. The bastard!" She looked across at me, her expression a mixture of sorrow and betrayal. "Do you know what I've come to realize, Dana? I realize now that you were the only one who ever really loved me. Absolutely the only one."

Once again I could think of nothing worth saying, and I did not want even to think about those long ago years when I did indeed love Sally. I sipped slowly from my glass and stared down at the golden liquid with the ring of tiny bubbles circling the edge.

When I looked up, Sally was gazing at me with a soft smile. "Do you know what I regret most, Dana? What I really regret is that you and I never really made love together. We always had a fiasco of one kind of another. It's so ironic! Never to have been to bed with my only true love!" She took a long swallow from her glass. "Don't you agree it's ironic?"

"Ironic" was not the word that came to *my* mind, but groping for something to say, I said, inanely, "Life has its peculiar quirks."

"Well, *I* think it's ironic. When I think of those other guys who didn't love me, not a bit!" She sat brooding a moment, gazing down into her martini. She shook her head angrily. "No, it's worse than that. It's lousy!"

I could hear that the martini was beginning to smooth the edges off her consonants, and her smile when she looked up was slightly blurry.

"You know what I think, Dana?" she asked, her wobbly gaze exaggeratedly inviting, almost a leer. "I think we ought to do something about it right now."

I looked across the room at this misshapen, life-battered relic of my youth and quailed at the thought.

But Sally was not deflected by my lack of response. She got heavily to her feet and held her pudgy hand out toward me. "Dana, it's not too late for us. Let's make love now. At last." Again, she smiled that grotesquely inviting smile. "Come, Dana. Come, darling, let's do this for us, for our lost love."

The time had clearly come for me to leave. I set my beer down on the side table. I walked over and took her round face between my hands. I kissed her forehead. "I'm leaving, Sally. I'm sorry, but it *is* too late. For me, that time has passed. *Long* passed." I stepped back. "I must go."

"Dana!"

"Goodbye," I said.

Twenty-One

My old editor, Walt Murphy, was his same gristly, gritty self. "Christ, yes, I want you back! All I've got working for me now are draft-dodging 4-F's with fallen arches and hernias. And they all write like fifteen year old girls. You know, words like 'muchly' and 'thusly.' Crap like that." He looked at me wearing his version of a friendly smile, a little like a wounded chimpanzee's . "You all settled? Get your old apartment back?"

"One in the same building. First floor, corner rooms."

He nodded jerkily. "When can you start work?"

"Tomorrow."

"Fine. Eight-thirty. And for Christ's sake don't be late!"

On the following day I rejoined the newsroom with its clicking typewriters, ringing telephones, and disorganized bustle. Murphy put me back on foreign news which meant I handled all the stories about the war which by this time was going great for the Allies. The Russian and Anglo-American forces were applying a giant squeeze on the reeling Wehrmacht, the Russians plowing through Poland headed for Berlin and the Americans and British vaulting the Rhine and driving eastward across Germany. In the Pacific, MacArthur was recapturing the Philippines and preparing to move north toward Japan. Besides the war I also handled prime local news from time to time, such things as election campaigns for mayor, school board, or sheriff, and now and then I got a murder, such as the famous one involving the Ohio State University professor and his reportedly lecherous female assistant.

Shortly after I got settled I called my old friend, Saul Zollerman, at the Cosmopolitan men's clothing store. Saul and I had dinner that evening at the Van Steed. The place was only sparsely patronized and the piano in one corner stood silent. "Last time we were together here," Saul said, "was the night before Pearl Harbor."

"I remember," I said and went on remembering a great deal more.

"A lot has happened since then."

"More than I can tell you, Saul."

"I didn't mean to *us*," he said his sorrowing Jewish eyes smiling at me. "I suppose *you've* seen and done a lot but I've been going to the store every day and selling all over again what I sold the day before."

I smiled across the table at Saul, my comfortable old friend. Good company. A few laughs now and then, pretty mundane conversation for the most part, but a lot of silent, sharing companionship. Saul and I played golf now and then on Sundays and had dinner together at least once a week. He was an easy chair in the furniture of my life.

Then there was Dotty Alton. Dotty was the company cashier at *The News*. She worked in a small office at the front of the building and passed my pay check to me through a metal grillwork each Friday afternoon. She was a plump little body with a pixie face, and the fragrance of her perfume as it wafted through the grillwork was mind-numbing. She was always cheerful, always smiling, often giggling. And her fingertips when they touched mine as she passed the check across the wooden counter were smooth as wet suede and caressing.

As I was leaving work one raw March evening with the rain pelting and slashing against the sidewalk I found Dotty standing on the front steps, huddling against the side of the doorway. "Dotty," I said, "are you waiting for someone?"

"Oh, Mr. Brown, no. I'm waiting for the rain to let up so I can get to the bus stop."

I looked out at the glistening walk, pocked and dotted with wind-driven rain. "Doesn't look as though it will stop very soon."

"Well, it will just have to," she said determinedly. "I can't get these brand new shoes soaked."

I glanced down at her gleaming black pumps with outrageously high heels. "Let me give you a ride."

She offered mild, polite resistance but then agreed. "You're being awfully nice," she said. When we arrived at her bus stop the rain was beating down even harder, so I insisted then on driving her home. She directed me down a side street off North Main Street and told me to stop before a small white bungalow with a broad front porch. "Here we are!" she said in her chirpy voice. "How can I thank you enough? I would have been soaked right down to my satin undies." She giggled and leaned toward me quickly and kissed me. It was a brief thank-you kiss but her wide mouth was soft and plushy on mine, quite impressively so. I suddenly became aware that I had been celibate since leaving India.

About a week later Denton was suddenly taken with one of those late March wet, slushy snowfalls. Again, I found Dotty on the front steps, and soon had her in my car headed for North Main Street. But before we got far down Main Street in the late afternoon traffic I had a sudden impulse. "Dotty," I said as I braked for a red light, "how about having supper with me? Are you expected at home?"

"Supper? You mean eat out at a restaurant somewhere? Gee, that would be swell!" She giggled. "I mean, is it okay with you? I can telephone home."

Shortly later we walked into the Van Steed dining room. The headwaiter led us over to a small side table and lighted the candle in the little glass lamp between us. Dotty glanced around, her eyes dancing. "Gee, this is swell!"

"Will you have a cocktail?" I asked.

"Gosh, I don't know. What are you going to have?"

"I guess a manhattan."

"Then, me too."

Throughout dinner Dotty prattled happily, chewing her food in rapid chipmunk bites between words, her conversation dwelling most on gossip about other office girls. Occasionally, there was a startling revelation about a liaison I had not suspected between one of the girls and an executive at *The News*. Before we left the dining room I had come to the conclusion that male and female relationships were preeminent in Dotty's universe.

The snow had stopped by the time we left the Van Steed. We stood indecisively for a moment on the sidewalk. "What now?" I asked. "It's still early. Would you like to go to a movie?"

"No, I don't think so." She looked up at me, her wide, furiously red mouth pursed and her eyes narrowed. "I'd ask you to come to my place but my folks will still be up."

I did not need to be a mind-reader to get that message. "Well, then, how about coming to my place?"

"Okay." She smiled guilelessly and took my arm. "Let's go!"

Once inside my apartment things moved very fast. Dotty took off her coat, threw it on the nearest chair, turned to me with arms held out, stood on tiptoes, and fastened her wide, soft mouth on mine. Her hands started at the back of my head and moved down my shoulders and my back to below my waist and pulled hard. When we released, she said, "Ummm, I *knew* you'd kiss like that. I could tell by your eyes. You're passionate. Like me." Then she pulled my head down and we kissed again, her soft plump body pressing hard against mine. This time when we let go she asked, "Where's your bedroom?"

What I discovered about Dotty during the next two hours was that from head to toe she was one sizzling erogenous zone. She responded to my touch, no matter where or when, like a struck match—instant flame. And she was as knowing and as adept in her love-making as Aphrodite.

During one lull in the tempest she turned to me and said conversationally, "You were in the war, weren't you?"

"Yes, I guess you could call it that."

"My Jimmy's in the war, too."

"Jimmy?"

"My boy friend. My fiance. He's a supply sergeant at Fort Bragg."

"Fiance? You're engaged to be married?"

"Soon's the war's over."

"But, Dotty—" I paused, baffled. How was I to ask what I wanted to ask?

"What?" She looked across the bed at me with her guileless eyes, puzzled. Then she smiled her perky smile. "Oh, you mean—*this*?"

"Yes, *this*."

"Oh, Jimmy don't mind. He knows me too well to expect me to be a good girl all the time. Anyway, I know for darn sure he's getting his nooky regular too. He's like the both of *us*, passionate as hell."

I lay back and stared at the ceiling, trying to absorb this insight into the mores and folkways of a society newly revealed to me. But Dotty had no time for sociological reflection. "Hey!" she said, swinging a soft, silky thigh over mine, "don't go to sleep. Time's passing." And she slowly eased her luxuriously plump body, with its luscious slopes and vales, over atop me and glued her deliciously soft mouth on mine.

The experience I had that night with Dotty is one any man with a full complement of hormones would want to repeat. And I did. *We* did. It never occurred to me as the weeks passed to think of Dotty as a mistress. She was simply a playmate, a blithe as May, guilt-free playmate who found the eternal transaction between the sexes life's greatest treasure. Dotty had never held a truly serious thought in her head for an instant, but she was as merry and carefree as a young puppy, finding joy in each passing hour, and she was fun to be with, both in and out of bed. And eventually she helped me get the goods on Paul Bragdon.

The spring of 1945 was frantic in the newsroom. First there was the death of our great war leader and president, Franklin Delano Roosevelt, and then the collapse of German resistance and VE-Day. And just as in 1941, Walt Murphy kept me at my typewriter until my fingers were sore. Then spring moved into summer and August brought Hiroshima, the Japanese surrender, and VJ-Day. The war, the most cataclysmic event of my lifetime, was over. Tension in the newsroom eased substantially, and for me the foreign affairs portion of my workload lessened considerably. Murphy then put me on coverage of the campaign for US Congress of a local politician, Paul Bragdon.

By this time it was October and the leaves outside my apartment window were bronzing slowly. One Friday as I stopped by her cashier's window to pick up my pay check, Dotty held onto the check as I tried to take it. She was grinning mischievously. "Not to be personal," she said in a low voice, "but are you busy tonight?"

"I don't think so, Dotty. Why?"

"Oh, I was just wondering—Jimmy's coming home tomorrow."

I was dumbstruck. "Tomorrow?" I looked again at her dancing eyes. You mean you—we?"

"If you'd like to. May be our last chance. For a while at least."

Whether or not it was "our last chance" Dotty treated that night in my bedroom as though sex was certain to be outlawed at dawn next day. She was ravenous, exuberantly athletic, and, finally, exhausting. As we lay back side by side on the bed, both panting, Dotty said, "You know something, honey? I bet this was *not* our last chance. Jimmy's likely to go out of town sometimes after we get married."

"Well, *I* think this was our last chance. The last time. I wouldn't feel right about it after you're married."

"Oh, honey! What a stick in the mud you are! Why should that make any difference if we are just having fun together? Nothing serious. Just having fun?" And as I turned my head on the pillow and gazed into her guileless, amoral, blue eyes I found I had no good answer handy.

Twenty-Two

Paul Bragdon was the golden boy of politics in southwestern Ohio. He had seemed to come from nowhere, bursting upon the scene five or six years earlier as town councillor in Elmwood, the Denton upper crust suburb and independent village. Bragdon's curly blonde-headed good looks, his flashing smile, and his all-encompassing charm swept all opposition before him. His proposals for improving municipal administration in Elmwood, not radical but pragmatic and effective, won him state-wide attention in the press. He moved on from there to the Ohio state assembly where his programs for improving highway safety caught the eyes of the national media. Now he had announced his candidacy for a seat in the House of Representatives of the United States Congress.

Walt Murphy called me into his office one day. "Brown," he said, "I want to do a series on this Bragdon guy. He's a local boy heading for the top, and I want *The News* to be in his corner right from the start. I'm gonna turn you loose on the series, no other assignments until you wind it up. So give it your best shot."

I called next day and without difficulty got an appointment with Paul Bragdon that afternoon. Seemingly, he resembled most politicians in an unceasing willingness to talk with the press. I had spent the morning reading everything I could find on him in the files which was remarkably little, considering the acclaim he had received. He had said on one occasion that he was "an Ohio boy all the way, Ohio born, Ohio bred, and Ohio educated." So the first question I asked him after several courtly flourishes on his part was about his birthplace.

"Birthplace? Oh, well, I was born on a farm up in northeastern Ohio."

"Near Akron?"

"Well, no. There wasn't any big town near us. Just itty bitty places."

"What county?"

He hesitated. "Well, it was called Holmes County, I believe. You see I left there when I was five years old."

"Where did you go to school?"

Bragdon laughed as though I had cracked a rare joke. "Lots of places." he chortled. "You see my daddy was in the construction business, and he kept moving us around."

I paused for a moment, trying to measure the man before me who seemed as elusive as Red Grange, the fabulous Illinois halfback of my boyhood days.

Bragdon smiled his 10,000-watt smile at me. "Forgive me, Mr. Brown, if I seem to be telling you how to do your business, but I doubt the good people who read your fine newspaper are interested in where I was born and so on. I think they would rather read about my ideas on how to improve the daily lives of the citizens of this great state after I'm elected to the United States Congress."

"Sure," I said. "I meant to get to that later after we've filled in some background. But go ahead. Let's hear what you want to say."

"Good," he beamed. "Well, now, here's the way the future looks to me." And he proceeded for the next twenty minutes to lay out a typical political campaign speech. But it was pretty good, pretty persuasive, not too laden with cliches, and had a few original ideas. When he came to a close, he smiled earnestly and said, "Now that's my idea of what your readers want to know."

"Got it all down in my notes," I said. "But I may want to come back to you later." Then as I got up to leave I asked, "Where did you go to college?"

"Ohio."

"State or Ohio U.?"

"Oh, State. But I never graduated," he added quickly. "Ran out of money and had to go to work."

Back in my office I found an Ohio map and located Holmes County. Bragdon was right; there was only one town larger than 1500 in the whole county with Millersburg, the county seat, leading the pack with 2500. I got the long distance operator on the telephone. "I want to talk to the County Clerk in Millersburg, Ohio."

After several minutes while the Denton operator conferred with a trunk line operator, I could hear reedy ringing and then a wispy voice answering. The operator asked the wispy voice, "Is this the County Clerk?"

"Well, no. He's out front talking to some folks. You want to speak with him?"

"I have a long distance call for him from Denton, Ohio."

"Oh, my sakes. Let me go get him."

"Your party is coming on," said the operator.

In a moment a thin tenor voice said, "Hello, what can I do for ya?"

I identified myself and said I wanted to check on the birth record of one Paul Bragdon.

"Bragdon." Pause. "Well now, they's some Bragdons down Glenmont way but I don't know's we got any birth records on them." He paused again. "What year would this be?"

"1910, 1911."

"Oh, now mister, we got a problem. We had a bad fire here last month. Chimney took fire and burned half the roof off afore the volunteer fellas got it stopped. A lot of them records got soaked with water, you know, puttin' the fire out, and we ain't got 'em back in order yet."

I hesitated for a moment. "If I came up there, could I look through those records myself?"

"Sure could. If you want to go to that trouble. They're sure in a mess."

"I understand. I'll be along sometime tomorrow."

"Okay, that's fine. 'Bye now."

At seven o'clock next morning I cranked up my Plymouth coupe and headed up Route 4 for Columbus. Millersburg was a little over 150 miles, and after the first 70 miles to Columbus the roads looked on the map to be distinctly secondary. As the Plymouth droned along at a solid 50 miles per hour I asked myself again whether the trip was necessary. Did I need to establish Paul Bragdon's exact date and place of birth? For writing the series I knew the answer was no. It was not essential. But it *was* essential for putting to rest some doubts Bragdon's answers had created. My newsman's nose had sensed a slightly strange odor. Bragdon had seemed surprisingly hesitant in answering some rudimentary questions. Was there something for him to hide, possibly an unsavory family background or even an illegitimate birth? Those were the questions that made the trip necessary, and their answers *could* become the material for an extremely interesting story.

Millersburg was somewhat more than a wide place in the road, possessing a Main Street with a grocery, a drug store, a Chevrolet dealership, a post office, and a feed and grain store. The red brick courthouse, two proud stories high, stood in the middle of the town and dominated the scene. Standing guard before it was a Union soldier, with the dates 1861-1865 engraved below his bronze feet.

The County Clerk, Owen Rister, was turkey-necked with sandy hair running thin strands across his narrow head. "Oh, yeah," he said. "Talked to you yesterday on the long distance. C'mon back to the records office." He led me down the hallway where the oak flooring was hollowed in the center from generations of passing feet. "You know," he said over his shoulder, "I got to thinkin' after your call, and I don't believe we've got any Bragdons in them birth records. Leastways, not around 19 and 10."

"I'd still like to have a look."

"Oh, sure, and I'll give you a hand."

Owen Rister and I searched the water-soaked pages for two hours, prying the pages gently apart, but we found no Bragdons. For good measure, we tried 1909 and 1912, in case Paul Bragdon's assertion that he was 35 years old was incorrect. But still no Bragdons.

"Looks like you've come on a wild goose chase," said Rister.

"Looks like it," I said, but I thought to myself that I might have caught the wild goose by one leg.

I thanked Owen Rister for his help and turned the Plymouth back toward Columbus. A thought came to me as I moved across the flat plain of the countryside where the roads ran at right angles to form a giant plaid on the landscape. Bragdon had said he attended Ohio State for a time, a statement I could stop and check at the University campus as I passed through Columbus.

About an hour later I turned in through a stone block gate where a bronze plaque announced "The Ohio State University". I found the Administration Building with the aid of a passing coed student. Inside I was passed from one office to another until I found the door with "Registrar" embossed on the frosted glass. A gentle-voiced woman in her middle 40s came to the counter. I stated my business and said I could not be certain of the likely year but suggested it might be 1928.

"There should be no difficulty," she said with a soft smile. "Our records are alphabetized, and we'll look at that year and others either side." She went to one side of the office and selected a large red ledger bound in black leather along the spine. "Now, let's see." she said. "You said the name was Bragdon."

"Paul Bragdon," I offered.

"Yes." She ran her finger down the page. "Beeley, Blankenborn, Blanton, Buechner—. No. No Bragdon that class. Let's try another." She got out another ledger. And then another and another. She looked up from the page, her blues eyes smiling sweetly through her gold-rimmed glasses. "No luck," she said. "I'm very sorry to disappoint you but we don't seem to have had a Bragdon in any of those classes."

I thanked her warmly and did not try to explain that it was not exactly disappointment I was feeling. By this time, I had the scent of the hunt in my nose and excitement, not disappointment, was mounting.

The next problem, I told myself, as I drove down Broad Street on the way back to Denton, was what to tell Walt Murphy. Assuming I might have caught Paul Bragdon in something strongly resembling lies about his past, what would Murphy's reaction be if I told him? It was unpredictable. He had been expecting the series on Bragdon to be a puff, an endorsement of the local hero. Would he pull me off the story if he knew it was taking a contrary direction? Or would his newsman's sense override his previous expectations and urge me to proceed? Should I ask him what to do now? It was then, as I was driving down that concrete highway between Columbus and Springfield, that I formulated a rule I have ever since been guided by: Never ask a question of a superior when one of the possible answers is one you do not want. So when I met Murphy next day I answered his question about how the series was coming with "Okay, so far."

He nodded briskly and said, "Stay on it."

The next question was where to go from here. Surely not back to confront Bragdon with what I had found. Or not found. But then very shortly my old playmate, Dotty Alton, unwittingly gave me a new scent to follow. I ran into Dotty as I was hurrying out the door for lunch. "Hey, Mr. Brown—" she looked behind me slyly—" honey. Long time no see."

"Hi, Dotty. Come have lunch with me at Stouffer's Cafeteria."

"Love to."

After we off-loaded our lunch from the aluminum trays we sat munching on hash with poached egg and across from me Dotty prattled away, offering a mix of earthy revelations on married life with Jimmy and some new tidbits of office gossip. Then she looked up, her bright eyes questioning, "Say, you didn't come to work yesterday. I noticed and wondered whether you were sick."

"No, I had to go out of town. I'm working on a story about Paul Bragdon, the politician. Sort of a biography."

"Oh, yeah. I see." She was silent then, chewing her food with quick chipmunk bites. Then she looked up, her eyes narrowed. "You know, that's a funny thing."

"What's a funny thing?"

"Oh, a coincidence about that Paul Bragdon." She took a sip of her coffee. "You know I've got an older sister. She's married and lives in Illinois. Down toward the south, sort of. Little town called Sparta. Well, Elly—her name's Eleanor—likes to keep in touch with what's going on here so I send her clippings from the paper sometimes. Well—" Dotty took another fork-load of hash and chewed it quickly—"one of the clippings I sent her—about the divorce of Esther Cook—she's one of Elly's old chums—had a picture of that Mr. Bragdon on the back. And Elly wrote back that he's the exact spittin' image of a guy who disappeared overnight from Sparta six or seven years ago. She said they look identical. Isn't that some funny coincidence?"

I looked at Dotty across the table while the scent of the hunt quickly overpowered the smell of roast beef hash. "She said six or seven years ago? Just disappeared? Did she mention his name?"

"Yes, she did. Let's see if I can remember it. It was kinda like Paul Bragdon's name. It was—let's see—Paul—Paul—Paul *Blanton*." She smiled triumphantly across the table. "That's sort of like Paul Bragdon, isn't it?"

"Quite a bit. Did Elly know any reason for his disappearing?"

"Some sort of scandal, I think. I don't remember exactly. May have been money embezzled. Something like that. Left a wife and two little kids though."

"Hmmm." I could hardly keep from bolting away from the table and back to the office but fortunately Dotty's quick little jaws disposed of her lunch shortly and we soon headed back to *The News* building. In my office I went straight to my Rand McNally atlas and leafed to Illinois. Sparta, I found, was in the southwest part of the state, about 45 miles southeast of St. Louis. That, I decided, was where the trail would lead me next.

Next morning I boarded a train at Union Station. In my Gladstone bag, the same one I carried in India, I had packed a folder with pictures of Paul Bragdon. Most were the original glossies from which the cuts were engraved, and they were sharp and clear. After transferring at Cincinnati, I arrived in St. Louis at dusk. I located a small hotel near the station and next morning found a car rental place and pointed the Chevrolet coupe I had acquired toward Sparta, Illinois.

Part way down Main Street as I entered Sparta I spotted the office of *The Sparta Ledger*. I parked the Chevy in a diagonal space in front of the building. Inside I soon found myself in conversation with a bright-faced man about my age who said he was Bill Newsom and the *Ledger's* editor. I explained I was doing a story on an Ohio politician and was tracking down his background. Newsom's response when I showed him the glossies of Paul Bragdon was explosive. "Jesus Christ! That's Paul Blanton, sure as shit!" He looked up at me, eyes snapping with excitement. "Hey, man, we've got to run these pix right over to the sheriff's office. They've been looking for this son of a bitch for six years!"

It took me several minutes of talking and reminding him of journalistic considerations to calm him down. It also helped that I offered to arrange for simultaneous publication of the story in his paper and mine and that he could alert the sheriff just prior to publication.

"Okay, okay," he said, "you've got yourself a deal. Now, where do we go from here?"

"First, fill me in on what happened before he vamoosed."

"Oh, I'll make copies for you of the stories we did at the time. But the kernel of it is that he arranged the transaction in the sale of the Pritchard farm just south of town. Paul was in real estate. Old man Pritchard had a real big spread but when he and his wife died within a month of each other they left no immediate kin. All there was was a gaggle of nephews, nieces, and first and second cousins. Over twenty in all. Paul worked out a sort of group receivership and then sold the property to a big Centralia outfit for $175,000. The next thing we knew Paul had disappeared into thin air and so had the 175 thou."

"And left behind a wife and two kids?"

"That's right."

"Are they still here?"

"No. They moved back to Wisconsin with her folks." Newsom pursed his lips. "How soon you going to be ready to go to press on this?"

"Couple of days. But, you know, we ought to be absolutely positive about this guy's identification or we could run into a hell of a libel suit."

"Oh, well. I don't have a doubt in the world that those are pictures of Paul Blanton. Paul used to run around with my older brother and he hung around our house a lot." His eyes narrowed, remembering. "He was always a smart ass. Always trying to put something over on you." He picked up one of the pictures of Paul Blanton. "No, that's the guy all right."

"I'd still like some positive identification."

Newsom looked up from the picture, "I'll give you positive identification. My brother Dick and Paul went to the 1933 Chicago World's Fair together. One night after five or six beers they got tattooed, a small rosette on the back of the left hand with a girl's initials underneath. Paul's was 'KEM'. He was running around with Katie Miller at the time. If this guy's got a tattoo on his hand, he's your boy. And *mine*!"

It took me a day to get back to Denton but the next day I was back in Paul Bragdon's office. "I wondered if you would expand a bit more on your plan for education programs," I explained.

"Most happy to," he said. "It's something dear to my heart." He launched into a discussion and as he talked I kept my eyes glued on his hands. Much of the time he held his left hand with his right covering the back. Now and then he gestured with both hands but always it seemed with the palm up. Then he said, "You know, I made a speech on this subject at Rotary Club last week. Let me give you a copy." He began sorting through papers on his desk while I stood up as though ready to take it from him. I watched his hands as they moved among the papers and then suddenly in a flash I saw the little blue rosette with red initials beneath.

BINGO!

It took pretty much all the next day for me to put the story together. The lead paragraph ran: "Paul Bragdon, the meteoric hero of Ohio politics, can he be a fraud, a man who abandoned his wife and babies and absconded with thousands of dollars of other people's money? The citizens of Sparta, Illinois believe so. They say that Paul Bragdon's true name is Paul Blanton."

When I finished I took the five page piece into Walt

Murphy's office. "Is that the Bragdon story?" he asked. "Turned out to be quite a fellow, didn't he?"

"Beyond your imagination, Walt," I answered.

He grunted and began to read while I watched his face. The transition in expressions was beyond description. After about thirty seconds he put the page down and glared at me. "You son of a bitch, Brown! Is this some kind of joke?"

"Every word is gospel truth." I went on then to recount my visit to Sparta and to lay out the simultaneous publication arrangement I had made with *The Sparta Ledger* and for their notifying the law authorities.

Murphy sat for several minutes shaking his head like a man who had been pole-axed. "I'll be God damned!" he kept repeating. But in the end he agreed to go ahead with the story and to carry out the arrangements I had made with Bill Newsom.

Paul (Bragdon) Blanton was presented with a warrant for his arrest at dawn of the day my story ran on the front page of *The Denton Daily News*. After Walt Murphy got over the shock he began congratulating me several times a day. "Hell of story," he said. "But I can't figure out how you got the lead to Sparta, Illinois."

"Just a lucky break," I said.

But Dotty Alton knew the answer to Murphy's question. The next time I went for my pay check she held on to the other end as I reached for it, her eyes dancing mischief. "Hey, honey," she said softly. "You owe me a dinner and a little something at your place afterward."

That and a runner-up finish as a Pulitzer Prize contestant were my rewards for running Paul Blanton to earth.

Twenty-Three

For a couple of months after my great success with the Bragdon-Blanton exposé I sailed serenely along on the kindly breezes of applause and acclaim. Then like a balloon slowly losing its lifting helium I began a gradual descent to the routine, everyday level of the newspaper world. A story like Bragdon's flaming plunge from glory comes along once or twice in a newsman's career and a crime like the murder of the Ohio State professor by his lust-crazed assistant even more rarely. So I trudged along through 1946 and into 1947 with a succession of mundane assignments—a municipal election or courthouse scandal here, a spectacular truck accident or three alarm fire there—and nearly every day I found it less and less satisfying. I was not quite in the situation of Saul Zollerman who said he sold each day the clothes he had sold the day before, but the resemblance was uncomfortably close.

One September Sunday Saul and I played golf at the Community Golf Club and afterward went back to my place for a few beers. The Carling's Black label was cold and delicious, and we sat in my two easy chairs with our golf-worn legs stretched out comfortably before us. We each had had a reasonably good day on the golf course.

Saul, who only occasionally broke 100, had shot 94, and I had managed with several one-putt greens to garner an 82. We took turns recalling our best shots. Saul harked back to the 140-yard five iron on the fifth hole that struck the flag on the first bounce and ended up six feet away, while I dwelt with pleasure on a sand wedge from the bunker on the twelfth that trickled into the cup.

After a while the talk turned to work. Paul said he had to be at the store an hour earlier the next day to set up a men's shirt sale. "These sales are a damned nuisance," he said.

I murmured understandingly and then fell to wondering how Saul, this sensitive, intelligent man, could spend a lifetime selling men's shirts. Or, if not shirts, shorts. I took a sip of the cold, golden liquid. "Saul," I said, "how do you do it?"

"Do what?"

"Get yourself out of bed each morning and go back to the Cosmopolitan to do the same thing day after day. I remember once you said you sold the same clothes today you sold yesterday. I don't see how you do it."

Saul sighed with a resigned smile. "Yeah, I did say that." He sipped his beer and set it down on the side table beside him. "But, you know, there's a slight exaggeration there. In the first place, I really do enjoy selling. I get satisfaction from getting the customer to buy more than he intended."

"But day after day for twenty years?"

He sighed again and this time his smile was rueful. "Sounds deadly dull, doesn't it?" He looked off to one side into space. "I faced up to this whole question some years back. How could I keep up this same old routine the rest of my life? And after going round and round, alternating between anger and depression, I came to the conclusion that what I did eight hours or so a day was just a job. But whether I liked it or not , a job was essential. So all right, I said, I would do my work faithfully each day but the rest of the twenty-four hours would be mine, and that's when I would do my real living."

"Doing what?"

"Doing this. Drinking beer with a friend. Playing golf. But also feeding my mind and spirit"—he looked over at me, his expression asking forgiveness for such exalted language—"with reading and listening to good music."

"I do that too, but it doesn't seem enough."

Saul shrugged. "Different strokes—"

As I sat thinking about what Saul had said, it occurred to me that he and I seldom discussed the things we read, "What do you usually read, Saul? Fiction, history?"

"Philosophy, mostly. Plato, Epicurus, Democritus, Erasmus. Right now I'm re-reading Plato for the third time. What a lovely, serene universe he envisioned!"

I was slightly staggered. I wondered how many Cosmopolitan customers suspected they were buying their underwear from a student of Plato!

"My main interest right now," Saul went on, "is Bach. I met a woman at the concert the other night—woman in her fifties—and we were talking about the Bach suite we had just heard. I told her I much preferred Mozart, and she said she had not really appreciated Bach until she reached forty and now she thinks there is no other composer even close. She said, 'Just wait until you're forty.' Well, I've got a few years to go before I reach forty but I'm giving it a try now. So far, I like the slow, stately passages but I'm still having trouble with the diddley-diddley-dees up and down the scale."

We chatted a while more about music and then, after Saul had finished his beer he got to his feet and left, saying he had to get up early in the morning for "the goddamned sale". I saw him to the door and then went to the refrigerator and cracked another beer. On the way back I turned on the radio and the voice of Jack Benny emerged amidst studio laughter. After the talk about

Plato and Bach, Jack Benny seemed a bit off-key. I turned him off and went back to my easy chair and thought about Saul. His solution for dealing with an unfulfilling job, I realized, was essentially the characteristic American way to relieve what Thoreau called "lives of quiet desperation." That accounted for the universal reverence for The Weekend which of course most of my countrymen celebrate with more earthy pleasures than reading Plato. And I supposed I could deal with the problem the same way, by making my reading and music listening more programmed and directed.

But, it seemed to me, there was more than the everyday sameness of my job that lay beneath my discontent. Since my return to Denton from India I had never really felt settled. It was an ill-defined feeling, one I found difficult to isolate and describe even to myself. I felt dislocated somehow, without mooring or anchor, in a state of suspension—I really do not know quite how to say it. But, why was I unsettled? I had lived in Denton most of my life, excepting only the years at college and the war years. The place ought therefore to feel like home territory. It was true that my parents and my family home were gone from Denton, but the city whose streets and buildings were as familiar as my own face in the mirror was still solidly and reassuringly there. Then why, I wondered, did I have this vague feeling of impermanence? Was it that after two years in India I had a vague sense that India, or any place away from Denton, was where I really belonged? Well, hardly. India had been a horizon-widening experience but it had never seemed like a place to live and the experience had not created a yen to live abroad any where else. All along, I had yearned to get back to Ohio. But if that was not it, might it be the soul-searing tragedy I had experienced with Diana? Well, perhaps, but I doubted it. I had loved Diana so deeply that I felt disqualified from love ever again, and it *had* been a totally disorienting catastrophe, but it did not really have anything to do with *place*. I had known Diana only in India. Her memory still resided there for me, and also perhaps in a shadowy way in England. But I had accepted the finality of Diana's death, and I had no desire to go back to the scene of that unthinkable tragedy. That being so, then what? Would I never feel moored or anchored again?

Stumped, I decided no amount of Carling's Black Label would produce an answer that night. So I took my glass to the kitchen and rinsed it. Then I picked through my small record collection, located the Bach Third Suite and set it on the turntable. On my way back to my easy chair I picked up the Columbia Encyclopedia. I had just settled back with the article on Plato before me when the first brisk strains of Bach sounded from the speaker.

September drifted into October and October dwindled into November while I droned away each day at *The News*. Saul and I decided golf was no fun when hitting a two- or three-iron off the stone-hard fairway made your hands sting. I persuaded Saul then to go to a couple of high school night football games with me but the Stowell High team, which had held the city championship for two years while we were there, was sloppy and lost both games. So we gave that up.

I was about to go away somewhere, anywhere, on a vacation when I got a letter from Professor Howard Nicholas, my old Maumee University professor whom I had last seen in Washington before departing for India. The prim envelope read "Department of History, Maumee University" on the top left corner. "Dear Brown," the short note read, "I am inviting a number of former students to participate in a discussion with my modern history class regarding the changes in American life brought about by World War II. I hope you can come sometime the first week of December. I cannot pay your expenses but I can offer a good dinner at the Faculty Club."

Next day I got Walt Murphy's permission to take a

few days off, and one brisk December morning I drove down to Bedford. It was an easy drive of about 50 miles, and I reached the village shortly before lunch. As I approached, the Maumee campus greeted me like an old friend. Under the bright crystalline sky the brick of the pre-Civil War buildings glowed a rosy pink. The venerable oaks and elms stood proudly at wide intervals on the spacious campus and lifted their bare arms high in the sky. A rush of nostalgia and affection swept over me for the old place, a place where I had spent happy and fruitful years of self-discovery. I was surprised how keenly I felt it.

I went directly to Professor Nicholas' office in Irving Hall, the building where I had attended his modern history class almost a decade earlier and where, also, I had an office as editor of *The Student Record*. The long-forgotten smell of the schoolroom—oiled wooden floors, chalk, erasers, and slate blackboards, varnished student desks—met me as I entered the building, and I remembered my joy on first smelling that academic aroma after leaving steel-bound *Maunaloa* to return to the University.

The rest of the day was unalloyed pleasure. Professor Nicholas took me to lunch at the Faculty Club where I recognized several of my old professors who greeted me kindly and convinced me they remembered me. The seminar at two o'clock was a rousing success. Nicholas had also invited two of my classmates and old friends, Phil Cronsky and Dick Blaisner. We three had shared a table at the University dining hall where we had engaged in daily verbal joustings, often disagreeing for the mere pleasure of disagreeing. We carried on that tradition in Professor Nicholas' discussion group as though no years of widely varying experience had intervened. Whether the undergraduates acquired any understanding of the changes World War II had wrought in American society I cannot say, but Phil and Dick and I had a hell of a good time and Professor Nicholas seemed pleased. As for me,

I felt like an undergraduate once again and found it exhilarating.

After dinner at the Faculty Club that evening, Phil and Dick went back to their rooms at the Maumee Lodge while Howard Nicholas took me back to his house where, as he explained to the others, he had just one guest room. After we had hung up our overcoats, Nicholas said, "How about joining me in a glass of cognac? My wife gave me a bottle for my birthday last month."

"I would love it."

"Good. Then you can tell me about your newspaper career. You made quite a splash a year or so back with that Bragdon exposé."

Over our small snifters of the rich, amber liquor I talked for a while about Phil Blanton and one or two lesser exploits. "Must be a different challenge every day," Professor Nicholas said.

I shook my head. "Actually not." I went on to describe how one political campaign strongly resembles another, one fire is much the same as the next, and every crime of passion is like all the rest except for the odd bloody detail. "In fact," I concluded, "I've got very stale on the newspaper racket. I'm beginning to think I've used it up as a career."

He nodded understandingly. "I'm surprised because you seem to be highly successful. Have you any idea what else you'd like to do?"

"Not really. I've pumped gas in a filling station, thrown coal on a steamboat, and performed something called liaison during the war, but I can't see any one of them as an alternative. About all I'm certain of is that I don't want to bang a typewriter in a newsroom the rest of my life."

"You know, Dana," he said kindly, "There are few things any one of us would wish to do the rest of his life."

We sat silently sipping our cognac for several minutes. A large grandfather clock in the nearby hallway ticked contentedly, and after the stimulating two hours in the seminar, the bright intellectual conversation during dinner at the Faculty Club, and the soul-warming cognac and conviviality of my host, I could feel my inner clock ticking contentedly too. After a while Harry Nicholas said, "I wish there was some way I could help you. A good mind is too precious to waste in a non-satisfying career. Does the academic life have any appeal for you?"

"Earlier I would have thought not but I found today exciting." I paused. "But I suppose it's too late for me to think of that."

"Never too late, really. But it would take some sacrifice. You'd need to get an advanced degree. At least a master's.

I sighed. "Yeah. And live on bread and water meanwhile."

Nicholas smiled over the top of his cognac snifter. "Or maybe just give up eating." He put down his glass. "Well, I think it's time for bed." He got up and gestured toward the stairway. "I think you'll find everything you need in your room."

We said goodnight, and in a few minutes I was snuggled down in the soft bed. Just before dropping off I heard the chimes in the library clock tower ring eleven o'clock, the sound of the bells floating over the serenely dreaming campus. Later, I dreamed my old familiar fulfillment dream: being called by the University president and asked to take over the student newspaper for the remainder of the college year. I had not dreamed that dream in three or four years. Apparently, returning to my old college campus had reawakened it.

The Denton Daily News newsroom had not gained anything in allure during my brief absence, and I went back to droning away day by day. When Christmas came I asked Saul to have Christmas dinner with me.

"Christmas is not really my kind of thing," he said with a gentle reproachful smile.

"Oh, hell, I know, Saul. But Christmas, or a celebration very much like it, was a pagan festival for centuries before Jesus was born."

"That's true."

"Well, let's be pagans together for one day. I'll order a bottle of champagne and we'll raise rousing toasts to pantheism."

During dinner on Christmas Day, as the bottle of champagne began to reach low tide, I said, "Well, this has been a roaring success. What will we do to top it on New Year's Eve?"

"I've thought about it," said Saul, keeping his long face deliberately expressionless. "I'm going to get a bottle of Virginia Dare wine and we'll listen to the one Bach composition I have found I like all the way through, 'The Musical Offering.'"

"I'll have to check with my doctor," I said. "This aging heart can stand only so much excitement."

Twenty-Four

Outside the newsroom window on a dark February afternoon I could see the sleet beating down in a steady, determined way. Bored and having finished all my assigned stories and sent them on to the copy desk, I still had to stick around in the waning afternoon in case something turned up. I wandered over to the AP ticker and scanned the yellow sheets as they rolled a story about ice jamming the Ohio river and causing flooding at Marietta. Next I watched the ticker print out the name Ralph McGinley. That was the name of the Maumee faculty adviser for *The Student Record*, and it had been Mac's compliments—mixed now and then with spiky criticism—that had encouraged me to think of newspapering as an occupation. "Ralph McGinley, 52, director of public relations at Maumee University, died today of heart attack," the story began. I tore off the sheet and took most of it back to my desk. The details of Mac's life were mostly already known to me. "Graduate of Maumee in 1917, *Stars and Stripes* correspondent in France during World War I, later reporter for *The Columbus Dispatch*, widower since the death of his wife, Mary Porter, in 1939."

I sat at my desk thinking fondly back to those weekly *Student Record* staff meetings when Mac would do a critique of the recent issue. Once he said one of my editorials was "worthy of *The New York Times*," undeserved hyperbole but no less pleasing. Most of the time he was acerbic, sounding to us fledgling journalists, just as we felt he ought, like a tough, hard-boiled professional. Those sessions were fun and instructive.

My musings were broken by a shout from Walt Murphy. "Brown! Look here. Are you sure of your facts in this medical fraud story?"

"Sure I am. Checked them out with the prosecuting attorney."

Murphy growled, "Well, okay." He looked through a sheaf of yellow copy paper he had in his hand. "You might as well go on home then. No use your sitting around here waiting for the sun to go down."

Next day I was writing a follow-up on the medical fraud story—a pharmaceutical supplier had apparently bilked the Maumee Valley Hospital out of $145,000—when the phone on my desk jangled. "'You have a person-to-person call from Bedford," the switchboard operator said.

"I'll take it," I said. "Hello."

"Dana Brown?" asked a somewhat orotund voice. "This is President Downham at Maumee University."

I had recognized that voice without his identification because I had attended a year's worth of obligatory weekly meetings with President Downham when I had been editor of the student newspaper. He was a kindly but somewhat over-stuffed man, almost always just at the nigh edge of pomposity. "Yes, sir."

"Brown—er, uh, Dana. Have you heard about the untimely and tragic death of Ralph MacGinley?"

"Yes, sir, I have. I was terribly sorry to hear it. Mac was one of my heroes."

"A fine man." President Downham coughed a hollow cough. "His departure leaves the University with a severe problem. As you know, this year is the 150th anniversary of our founding, and Mac was handling the public relations aspect of our ceremonies in June. Left us in what you might call a—well, a hole." He chuckled briefly over this colloquialism. "Well, to get right to the point. Howard Nicholas came to me and said he thought you might be willing to take a leave of absence from your newspaper and take over Mac's work for the rest of the college year." There was a weighty pause. "Is there any possibility you might wish to do that?"

I nearly laughed in the good man's ear. It was too pat. Too perfect. Talk about *deus ex machina* in real life! If I had seen such a staggering coincidence in a movie or read it in a book I would not have believed it. Here was my familiar midnight dream, spawned over the years by a momentary sense of well-being, now being played out in the real daylight world. Surely, the gods were joking! I managed to push the laughter back and said with what I hoped might be taken as thoughtful restraint. "I believe I would be interested, President Downham. But of course I will have to see whether I can make arrangements here."

"Yes, of course."

I thought a moment. "How long would you want me to stay, sir?"

"Why, Dana, I should think until after Commencement and the Anniversary celebrations. Say, June 15th?"

"I see. Well, let me look into it. Can I call you back tomorrow?"

"Certainly, and I hope your answer is affirmative."

I decided not to say anything to Walt Murphy that day. I wanted time to mull it over and sleep on it. But sleep, hell! I rolled and tossed and constructed all kinds of scenarios about the future and slept maybe two hours, or three. But in the morning I knew without question I wanted to accept President Downham's offer. The pull to go back to Maumee was powerful, like a great magnet. So strong an urge, I told myself, must be a response to that fine day at Maumee in December.

I did not expect Walt Murphy to respond well to my suggestion and he certainly did not. "Leave of absence until June 15? Christ, no! What the hell do you think I'm running here, a goddamned boarding school?"

"Well, Walt," I said calmly. It was important to keep calm while dealing with Walt. "If you don't like that idea I can give you another option. Would you prefer my resignation?"

He glared at me with hot, angry eyes. "Tough son of a bitch, aren't you? You damned smart ass." He turned away, picked a pencil off his desk, and threw it down again. "No, you stubborn jackass, you know I don't want your resignation. You know goddamned well you're the best newshawk I got here." He sighed heavily and shook his head in exasperation. "Leave of absence until June 15th. Is that it?"

"That's it."

He sighed again. "Well, all right, you spoiled bastard. But if it's one day longer than June 15th I'll come down to Bedford and drag you back with my bare hands."

That night I went home and started packing. Next day I cleaned out and closed up my desk in the newsroom and went by Dotty Alton's cashier window to pick up my check. "I'm going to miss seeing you, honey," she whispered as her soft fingertips rested on the back of my hand, "but if ever you come into town let me know and I'll tell Jimmy I have to stay late to do an audit."

Next morning I loaded up the Plymouth and set out for Bedford. If I said I had a song in my heart it would be to use a tired cliche to express something deep, fundamental and joyous. Inside me was a sense of release and happy expectation such as I had not felt since I climbed down the ship's ladder onto the dock at South Chicago and headed toward the train station to make the journey back to college. It was like being a freshman all over again, and suddenly a popular song from that year popped into my head. "Margie," I sang as the faithful Plymouth hummed along at a steady 50, "I'm always thinking of you, Margie. I'll tell the world I love you"—forgot the words—"dum dum dum da da di da. *Margie*."

Like many times in the past, I had to wait outside President Downham's office before he received me. But then he was all warmth and bumbling graciousness. "I am delighted you could come and help us out. You are a real friend in need. Please sit down while we go over some details."

The details first of all had to do with my living arrangements. "We're putting you up in the Maumee Lodge for the present while we redecorate Ralph MacGinley's quarters in the Faculty Apartments. Will that be satisfactory?"

"Yes, indeed."

"Splendid. Now, I did not mention on the telephone that Mac taught a remedial English course twice a week and a journalism course, also twice weekly. I would like to ask you to take those over, if you thought you could."

I hesitated. Remedial English, I supposed, could not be too much different from copy desk editing: make certain subject and verbs agree; watch out for dangling participles; and so on. As for journalism, I had never regarded it as a matter for serious study. You just observed a few traditional rules: lead paragraphs must contain who, what, when, where and sometimes why; paragraphs must be short and snappy; and you put most important details first followed by less to least important ones through the paragraphs—certainly the worst possible way to narrate a story but one designed for cutting it from the bottom up. "Well, President Downham," I said after a moment, "I don't know how well I can do but I will be happy to try."

"I feel certain you will do well. And you may grow to like it. Teaching is pleasurable—well, fun." He smiled rather roguishly.

With these few words of guidance I left to get myself

established. After unloading the car at the Lodge I went to the Office of Public Relations and introduced myself to the small staff. They were a bright-faced, cheerful group, almost unnaturally wholesome in contrast to the harried newspaper types I had worked with in Denton. My new secretary, Betty Dillon, was a tall, dark-haired handsome woman of 30 who wore, I noticed, a small wedding ring on her left hand. She led me to my desk, and said, "All of us are delighted you would come. You knew Mr. MacGinley in your student days, didn't you?"

"Yes, I did."

"We all miss him terribly but we know you will carry on his work for him."

I thanked Betty and took my seat at the desk. My first move was to make my number, as the British say, with people at various newspapers around the state: the *Cincinatti Enquirer*, the *Columbus Dispatch*, the *Cleveland Plain Dealer*, the *Toledo Blade*. Most of them were surprised by my move, but only Robert Deringer at the *Blade* wanted to chat at length. After making those calls I reviewed with Mac's deputy, Harry Belieu, the public relations program for the rest of the year. Harry was a short, intense man whose Gallic name and quick nervous motions reminded me of Shorty, my randy wheelsman friend on *Maunaloa*. He soon had me convinced that Mac had left a well designed program which was proceeding nicely according to plan. We finished just before the office was due to close at four o'clock. Each staff member paused at my door to wish me goodnight on leaving.

I closed my desk and walked out into the late February afternoon. The air was damp and cool but the sun was a fiery red ball hanging over the rooftops of the campus buildings. I moved down the walkway under the bare elms to Spring Street, and strolled slowly along, savoring the sensations of renewed acquaintance. I walked slowly past Buster's place where I had taken many a date for coffee and toasted roll, past the Phi Delta

Theta house with its innumerable memories, past the Delta Kappa Epsilon and Sigma Chi houses, arch rivals in my student days, and then on to the Lodge at the east edge of the campus. Though I was alone and out of the element recently familiar to me, I was more contented and at ease than I had been in years. I spent the evening unpacking while listening to a broadcast of Ted Fiorito's dance band playing at the Netherlands Plaza in Cincinnati. Finished, I went to bed and was just falling asleep as the library clock chimes rang out 10 o'clock in the night air.

The teaching part of my new job was a revelation and a pleasant surprise. I had looked over the textbook for the journalism course and found, as I expected, only systemized common sense. With some trepidation and uncertainty I walked into the classroom where twenty-two students awaited me. I introduced myself and opened the textbook to the chapter titled "How to Develop the Story." I was groping for something to say when a trim, red-haired girl in the second row raised her hand. "Mr. Brown," she said, "I'm Dorothy Mitchell. I've read this chapter on story development but I don't get much out of it. It's too abstract. Could you give an example from your own experience on how to go about it?"

Delight and salvation burst through the opening that question created. "I believe I can, Miss Mitchell," I said and proceeded to detail how I had taken the report of a murder off a police docket and through questioning neighbors and tracing relatives had put the slaying into a perspective which revealed that the husband, the killer of his wife, was driven by compassion not passion. I could tell by their keen attention and the probing questions of the students that I had managed a teaching success. It was very satisfying. I decided to adopt that technique for all future sessions.

The next day was the class on remedial English which Mac had taught through group critiques of bad sentences. I floundered along for twenty minutes or so on that line, but then, as had happened the day before, I was rescued by a student. "Sir," a spiky-haired, long-necked boy at the back of the room said, "can I make a suggestion?"

"Certainly. Go ahead."

"Well, I don't know about the rest, but I don't get much help out of fixing up these bad sentences. I wouldn't have written them that way in the first place."

"Oh, sure, Barnet," another student said. "You're Shakespeare."

Barnet ignored the jibe. "*My* problem is I never know how to start. How to get going. What word to pick."

"What kind of writing are we talking about? Exposition?"

"Yes, I guess so. Science. I plan to be a physicist."

"Then start with the subject of the sentence. Umm, let's see, give you an example. Here's one: 'The pulse moved the meter.' Subject of the sentence, 'pulse' followed by the verb, 'moved,' followed by the object 'meter.' Subject, verb, object—the best possible sentence for exposition. Works every time."

"But wouldn't that be repetitious?"

"Who cares? You're not writing a suspense story." Snickers from the back of the room. "You are trying to state the facts as directly as possible. So just knock out subject, verb, object—sentence by sentence."

"Okay. Thank you."

After class, as I walked up the Angle Walk from Irving Hall to my office in the Administration Building I decided that although I may not have scored a pedagogical triumph with Barnet, I *had* found a technique I liked for teaching remedial English. Henceforth I would have individual sessions with each student and get him to tell me what part of writing he found most difficult.

After a week at the Lodge I moved into Mac MacGinley's old apartment, a snug, first floor, one bedroom, kitchenette, and sizable sitting room set-up. The Faculty Apartments were on the west edge of the campus, around the corner from Beta Theta Phi. The first afternoon I moved in I heard a knock at the door and found a stocky, round-faced man about my own age smiling there. "Welcome, neighbor," he said. "I'm Bill Dickson. I live across the hall, and I've come to invite you to join me in a martini as soon as I can get the ice out."

"Bill," I said, "thank you. You've got a customer."

It took less than ten minutes and the first sips of my second martini to discover that Bill Dickson was a delightful, life-loving companion. When I asked what sort of things he liked to do, he replied, "Teach, drink, and screw—though not necessarily in that order." He laughed joyously and infectiously. "Oh, and also, play golf. I hope to hell you like golf," he said. "Mac was a great guy but he didn't play golf. He preferred to watch the varsity baseball or football practices."

"I love golf."

"Great. We've got a good little course here. Tight, hilly, and great greens."

As we talked I learned Bill was an associate professor of English. "I had fun today in my sophomore survey course," he said as we sat in his book-lined sitting room sipping our ice cold martinis. "That old canard that Shakespeare was really Edward DeVere or Bacon or Little Boy Blue came up, and, man, I hit it out of the park!"

"You get it often?"

"Every year. I've got the spiel down pat by now."

"What do you say?"

"Oh, I start out by telling them how tiny the literary and theater scene was in 16th century London. Less than a hundred people, and they all knew each other and gossiped like mad. There was a guy named Robin Greene who was a sort of Walter Winchell who put out gossipy broadsides. He knew Shakespeare and called him 'Shake-scene'. Ben Jonson also knew Shakespeare and referred to him as a writer. For the secret to be kept that some nobleman, like DeVere, was writing these plays and using the name of one of the players in the company, Will Shakespeare, and was attending the rehearsals to make necessary fixes—and there are plenty of examples in the text where changes have been made—well, to have kept that secret in Elizabethan London would have required that someone establish and maintain a water-tight conspiracy among some of the most roaring individualists the world has ever known. Robin Greene would have given his eye teeth to blow that secret all over London." Dickson shook his head seemingly in sorrow. "Sweet Jesus! You have to be totally ignorant about the Elizabethan literary scene to believe that crap."

That drinking session with Bill Dickson was the first of many we had that spring in Bedford. Some evenings we went uptown to dinner and then attended a concert by a visiting symphony orchestra or string quartet. Sometimes we caught a movie and tried to make out the dialogue amidst the whistles and catcalls from irreverent undergraduates. Later, when the tulips and daffodils flowered beside the campus walkways and the redbuds and dogwoods blossomed along the green fairways, Bill and I played golf on the University course. We discovered to our delight that we were very evenly matched. "Thought I had you," said Bill as we sat drinking beer at my place one afternoon after a round, "until you sank that monstrous putt on 18."

"Luck, my friend. Just luck."

He shook his head. "Hey Dana," he said raising his glass to me, "it sure has been great having you here. I'm not looking forward to June 15th."

"You know, I don't think I am either."

"Why don't you stay on? You like your job don't you?"

"The public relations job is okay, but what I am really enjoying is the teaching. I get a charge out of helping straighten the kids out. But there are certain limitations in just teaching journalism and remedial English."

"Well, hey!" said Bill. "Come join me in the English Department. We can work out a part-time program to get you an M.A. in a couple of years, and then you can help me beat kids over the head for thinking Shakespeare was Edward DeVere."

The next day I broached the idea to President Downham. He smiled an unctuous smile. "Well, Dana, forgive me if I'm not entirely surprised. Howard Nicholas has been telling me how much you were enjoying teaching. I had some hope things might take this turn so I have made no effort to find a permanent replacement for MacGinley. And now I believe I have found one." He smiled broadly and held out a large hand. "Welcome to the faculty of Maumee University!"

I wrote to Walt Murphy that night and wondered, half amusedly and half regretfully, what precise form the explosive reaction of that admirably rough-hewn man would take.

Twenty-Five

It was late in April before it occurred to me one day that along with the 150th anniversary of the University's founding, 1948 was also the 10th reunion of my graduating class. I do not regard myself as a college reunion type—Bill Dickson said, "only the worst ones come back"—but I was still mildly curious as to which of my classmates I would see again. Perhaps some of my Phi Delt brothers like Harry Baker, Jeff Letvold, or Larry Whittaker. But maybe also some of the girls I had once dated such as Mit Daley. I found that quite a happy thought. It would be fun to see Mit again and see what changes ten years had wrought. Remembering Mit for the mature girl she was in college I doubted that time had altered her much. But then the passing years and probably a marriage, happy or unhappy, ought to have had some effect.

I could have checked with the Alumni Office to learn which of my friends were coming to the reunion, but the pace of work at my office increased steadily as June drew nearer. I had to go over each of the press releases before they went out, and I also had to write a number of them myself. So, right up to the first day of the three-day reunion I had no idea which friends, if any, I would be seeing.

The Friday afternoon of the reunion weekend I walked over to the tent where returning alumni registered and received their room assignments. On the second page of the register I found "Millicent Daley Roberts." Her room assignment was 212 Hankins Hall. I left the tent and strolled across to Hankins Hall, one of the new dormitories built since my time. The early June sun cast deep shadows from the full-leafed trees and lustered the walls of the brick building. The air held the soft promise of blossoming spring.

The door to room 212 was open but the room was empty. Next to it, room 214, the door was also open and peals of female shouts and laughter came ringing from it. Hesitantly, I stuck my head inside. "Is Mit Daley here?" I asked. A tall, smartly clothed woman leaped to her feet and ran toward me. "I'm just going to have to do it," she said. It was Mit, and she grabbed me with a big hug and kissed me robustly on the cheek. I took her by the shoulders and held her off at arms length. She was indeed good to look at, not quite as well-upholstered as she had been at 20 but the slight loss of weight gave sharper definition to her figure. She had acquired an elegance to replace the-big-wholesome-girl look of before. Her high firm cheekbones lent her face a distinctive, womanly character and her gray eyes brimmed with warmth.

"Dana! How wonderful to see you!" she said. "You know all these Tri Delt girls, don't you?" She waved her hand at the three women behind her.

I recognized Peg Dawson, Betty Ann Page, and Mary Lou Peters and said hello to each. I turned back to Mit. "I was hoping to take you somewhere for a drink before dinner," I said while the rest of the group sat silently.

"I'd love to, Dana. But we were just leaving to go to the reception before the dinner." She smiled appealingly. "Perhaps after dinner?"

"Fine. I'll meet you at the Alumni Center."

I had already decided to skip the dinner so I went

back to my apartment and fluffed the pillows on the sofa, straightened the pile of magazines on the side table, and put away several books lying on the floor beside my easy chair. Later, I walked over to the Alumni Center and waited for the dinner to be over. It was ten minutes past nine when I heard the chattering of the alumni crowd as they left the dining hall. I soon spotted Mit and led her out into the night. The soft air of the afternoon had taken on a slight edge but the sky was clear and one glowing planet, Saturn or Jupiter, bejeweled the field of stars.

"Oh, look, Dana! How lovely!" Mit said. "Doesn't being here on a night like this make you feel twenty all over again?"

"Yes, especially being here with you."

She turned and gave me an enigmatic look. "Where are you taking me for this drink?"

"To my place."

"Your place? Do you have a place here?"

"Yes I do. In the Faculty Apartments. I'm now a member of the Maumee faculty."

She stopped quickly and stared at me. "You *are*? I thought you were a star newspaper reporter in Denton. Tell me, how in the world did this happen?"

Over glasses of Dewar's scotch and soda I recounted the events that had led to my appointment as Maumee director of public relations. Mit sat on the sofa across from me listening. The lamp beside her cast a radiant sheen across her dark brown hair. She was wearing a simple black dress highlighted by a double strand of pearls, her long legs crossed at the ankles. She seemed to me just then as completely attractive as a woman could well be.

"Are you happy now with the change?" she asked.

"So far, very happy. I start summer school next week. Two courses, Chaucer and 17th century literature."

She smiled. "I'm envious." Then her smile faded.

"But what about you, Mit? You live in Cincinnati and you're married?"

"No longer married. James died three years ago." Her voice as she said this was sober and matter of fact. She went on to tell me about James Roberts, a Cincinnatian whom she had married a year after graduation. He had inherited his father's highly successful construction business, had made it even more successful, and then had died suddenly of cancer of the liver. "We had a good six years," she said. "It was a quiet marriage, not many excitements." She smiled confidentially across the room at me. "I can say that to an old friend." She went on, "No children, a couple of trips abroad, but mostly James worked from dawn to dark and fell into bed exhausted each night." She looked up from her lap then and her smile was both slightly confessional and mysterious.

We talked until midnight, filling in the ten-year space in our lives. I told her about India and Diana and about the waning of my enthusiasm for newspaper work. She listened attentively, murmuring understandingly now and then but asked no questions, letting my story unfold. I told her about my meeting with Sally in New York and she smiled wryly and said nothing. Then I walked her back to Hankins Hall and arranged to take her to the reunion picnic the next day. At her door she turned and kissed me gently. "Goodnight, dear," she said.

Rain began to fall steadily out of the sky about four o'clock next afternoon, and an announcement was made that the picnic was cancelled and supper would be served at the University dining hall. I drove around to Hankins Hall in the Plymouth and picked up Mit. "I suggest we skip the supper," I said as we drove down McGuffey street, "and have a quiet dinner at Foster's."

"Fine with me," she said. "I've been talking all day with my Tri Delt sisters. I am exhaustively informed now about the birthing of five children, their teething and toilet training problems, and some details about marital relations women do not talk about with men. I am ready for a change."

After a fine dinner in Foster's with its small tables and white tablecloths lighted with tiny brass lamps, we went back to my apartment. We ran into Bill Dickson at the entrance. "Mrs. Roberts, Professor Bill Dickson," I said. They smiled briefly at one another as I opened my door for Mit. Over scotch and water we took up where we had left off the night before. Mit was wearing a soft blue sweater, a gray skirt with large pleats, and flat oxfords. Somehow, glowing with quiet beauty, she combined youthful nonchalance with mature assurance.

"It's so wonderful being here, Dana," she said. Then she smiled meekly and said, "I guess I'd better say it more honestly—being here with *you*."

I still felt too inhibited for a number of reasons to be as honest as Mit about my feelings just then. Instead, I must confess, I was feeling a little confused. Being with Mit had reawakened feelings I had thought asleep forever: warm affection and its handmaiden, loving desire. But I was uncertain whether this was not merely a state of mind created by the college reunion atmosphere, the momentary and false sense of being twenty again and falling prey to the short-lived impulses of twenty and experiencing something alien to the real world—like a shipboard romance. Still I managed to say, "It *is* wonderful, Mit."

Several hours of intimate conversation had worn the edges off our initial strangeness. We were talking with one another now with the easy companionable directness of our college years. "Tell me, Mit," I said. "How do you spend your days?"

"Much as I did before James died. Good works with a couple of charities, meeting of the League of Women Voters, afternoon bridge once or twice a week."

"Sounds like a full schedule."

"I keep busy but—" she cocked her head and smiled that mysterious smile—"I could use a little more excitement."

I nodded and sat reflecting about my own daily life.

"You know, Mit," I said, wanting to share my contentment with her, "I really have not felt so entirely at peace before in my life. I almost can't describe it. Besides my job and the kick I get out of teaching, I also feel *centered* in a strange way, almost as though I have been drawn back here to Maumee and held in place by a magnetic force. I honestly feel I want to spend the rest of my life here. Here, where I somehow seem to belong like no other place. But it's hard for me to understand why I feel that way. I don't see why it should be so."

Across the room, her legs curled up beside her on the sofa, Mit shook her head and smiled maternally. "You know, Dana, for a man so intelligent as you are and so sensitive, you can be remarkably dumb sometimes. I suppose it just comes with being a man, being a male."

I bridled a bit. "Oh? Being a woman, you think you can explain it to me?"

"Of course, dummy. Think back to your college days, remember what finally getting to college meant to you. You told me once about your life at home where you said family affection was expressed in constant nagging, bickering and grudging approval. You told me coming to Maumee was like dying and going to heaven."

"That's true."

"And then remember how you found success here. After mediocre grades in high school you became an excellent student, you succeeded in winning the editorship of the college newspaper, and you won the respect of your peers who made you president of your fraternity. I don't remember your saying it quite this way, but I think you feel you discovered here at Maumee who you really were, what your capabilities were."

"That's true too."

"So why shouldn't you feel drawn to come back here? Why shouldn't you feel you belong here as nowhere else? Maumee is the magnetic center of your life—your *lodestone*."

"Yes-s-s." I sipped my scotch thinking about it. "But to tell the truth, Mit, I feel a little as though settling down here means I am sort of giving up. Withdrawing."

"Nuts!" she said with her old bluntness. "You haven't gone into a monastery. Your public relations work keeps you involved with the world, and you find great satisfaction in teaching. You're a lucky man. Frankly, I envy you."

"What you say is—"

"Don't interrupt! Besides, why shouldn't you turn to the slower pace of the academic world? Look at all you've done up to now: stoker on Great Lakes freighters, successful newspaper reporter, served your country overseas in India during the war, had a splendid love affair with a lovely English aristocrat, and suffered a terrible, horrible tragedy. Most people would find that enough for one lifetime but now here you are, happy as a rabbit, just over 30, with a whole new career lying ahead of you. What you need to do my dear Dana is *enjoy* it. Not ask dumb questions about it. I wish I had the future you have."

I got to my feet and held out my hand. "Mit, my sweet, after that long speech you must need a drink. Your throat must be dry."

She stood up also. "No, I don't. I just looked at my watch and it's midnight again. I've got to go to bed." She reached up, pulled my head down, and kissed me sweetly. I held here close for a moment until she pushed away, "I'm very fond of you, you dumb lug." She turned and picked up her purse.

"Will I see you tomorrow?" I asked.

"I'm leaving in the morning."

"Don't leave. Stay another day."

"I must leave my room in the dorm. Where would I stay?"

"I'll get you a room at the Lodge. Or," I cocked my head questioningly, "you could stay here and I'll sleep on the sofa."

She smiled that mysterious smile again. "The Lodge will do just fine."

That night I lay awake a long time thinking about my talks with Mit. I marveled over her subtle understanding. As I thought about Mit, about her elegance of person and character, and the deep sense of companionship I felt with her, I began to feel for the first time since Diana's death that a deep commitment might be possible with another woman. I realized that with Mit I might be able to possess what I had never really had, what I had hoped to have with Diana, and then lost: a deep-down sharing of life day after day with another person—with Mit, sharing it with a strong, handsome woman. But, I told myself, Mit and I had never really got beyond the good friend, good companion stage. There was a vast distance between that status and marriage, and I knew no reason to think or to hope that Mit had any interest in closing that gap. And yet perhaps in time, in time, if we could go on seeing each other. I rolled over then and sought sleep. I heard the tower chimes mark two o'clock, then the quarter hour, but then no more.

Next morning I met Bill Dickson as I was going out the door. "Hey, Dana," he said. "Who was that stunning woman you introduced me to last night?"

"Classmate."

"My God! She is glorious. She 'doth teach the torches to burn bright!' Is she married?"

"A widow."

"Grab her, boy! Grab her. They don't come like that often. She would adorn any living room, any bed, or any breakfast table."

"I'll tell her she has won your blue ribbon."

"Do. And if you don't want her, tell her I am irresistibly charming, gallant, and hell on wheels in bed."

"I'll tell her every word."

I had driven over in the Plymouth but Mit said as she came out to meet me, "Let's walk." It was one of those ravishing spring mornings that southern Ohio serves up with regularity. The air caressed our skins like butterfly wings and the trees overhead, still wearing the young greens of spring, resounded with the calls and melodic whistles of songbirds. Walking with Mit, walking with Mit in Bedford, I was happy beyond expression.

We first walked out to the edge of the village to the place by the winding stream where Mit and I had picnicked with my fraternity brothers in our senior year. Then we walked back into the village under the spreading trees. Quiet, white-faced houses stood on either side of the street with flowering spirea and lilacs adorning their front yards. "I had forgotten how lovely Bedford is," Mit said.

Mit and I walked and walked, sometimes hand in hand, always chatting companionably, and then we had dinner again at Foster's and ended up once more in my apartment, scotches in hand. Mit kicked her shoes off and leaned back on the sofa, her long legs stretched out straight before her. "Ah, Dana," she sighed, "I don't know when I've been so happy, so totally and completely happy. I don't want this weekend ever to end."

I gazed fondly across the room at this splendid female. "I wish it did not have to end either."

"But I guess it does," she said. She said. She sighed and smiled fondly at me. "The best part of this reunion has been that you and I have got back that wonderful companionship we had when we were in college. Don't you agree? It seems just the same to me."

"You mean before we had that, uh, misunderstanding over Sally."

"We're not talking about that—but, well, yes." She was quiet for a moment. Then she raised her head off the sofa cushion, her mouth pursed in a quirky smile. "Well, maybe there is *one* small difference now. I seem to remember we used to do a lot of kissing back then." She smiled archly. "Not so much of that now."

"Come to think of it, I remember that too," I said and slid over next to her on the sofa.

Mit put her hand up to my chest to stop me. "Just one question first," she said, her expression again mysterious. "Do you still have that deplorable tendency to *maul* the ladies you kiss?"

"Will you accept a lie?"

Her gray eyes, smiling at the edges, measured me. "If it's an answer I like."

"Well, then, I must confess I still have that tendency. May even have got worse, more exploratory."

"I see. Well, I'm not sure that we have the basis for an understanding. However,—" She let her head fall back on the sofa cushion and I leaned over and kissed her, gently and tenderly and then more and more thoroughly. She came with me all the way, and as my hand slid down and cupped her breast she put her hand on the back of my head and pulled me closer. In a fairly short time the sofa seemed unnecessarily confining, so I gently released Mit and got up, taking her by the hand. She came with me as we crossed the sitting room and reached the door of my bedroom. There she stopped.

"There is something I think you ought to know," she said, "before I go through that doorway."

I stopped and turned to her, baffled, my face a question mark.

"And that is," she said, "that I go to bed and make love only with a man I've already married or intend to marry."

I stood speechless, trying to absorb the meaning of those words "intend to marry." Had I just heard from this wonderful woman a proposal for marriage? Had she just said, bless her forthright heart, what I had been hoping to find opportunity and words to say someday? Could this really be true? "Mit," I croaked, "do you mean—I mean, did you mean to say?—My God, I really ought to be the one to ask the question. Mit, you darling, will you marry me?"

She smiled serenely and put her hand gently on my face. "Of course I will, dummy. I have been trying to tell you that since I first saw you standing in the doorway Friday afternoon." She smiled and kissed me gently. "Of course, I should have known I would have to make the first move just as I had to ask you to take me to the Senior Ball."

"Once a dumb lug, always a dumb lug," I said.

"A *sweet* lug," she said. She took my hand and led me into the bedroom, flipping the light switch off as she passed.